when the
caterpillar
thought the world
was over...

...it became a

butterfly

A PUBLIC ENEMY STANDALONE
CAMBRIA HEBERT

ISBN: 978-1-946836-09-0

BUTTERFLY Copyright © 2017 CAMBRIA HEBERT
Published by: Cambria Hebert
http://www.cambriahebert.com

This is a work of fiction. Names, characters, places, and incidents either
are the product of the author's imagination or are used fictitiously, and
any resemblance to actual persons, living or dead, business
establishments, events, or locales, is entirely coincidental.

Interior design by Cover Me Darling
Cover design by Cover Me Darling
Edited by Cassie McCown
Interior Illustrations by The Illustrated Author Design Services
Typesetting by Athena Interior Book Design

Drunken brawls. One-night stands.
No-show interviews. Toilet-papering my hoity-toity
neighbor's house.
Insulting my fans. Trashing hotel rooms.
What's it take to become public enemy number one?
I just told you.
I've done all that and more.
My poor conduct got me on the Celebs Behaving Badly list
and ultimately ruined my career.
From the world's number-one pop star to world's most
hated.
That's me. Ten Stark.
Go underground, they said. Stay out of the spotlight.
Most importantly, stay out of trouble.
Everyone loves a good comeback story.
For once, I listened.
I met someone who didn't know my name,
my face, or the bad behavior that defined me.
She taught me I wasn't who everyone thought I was—
everyone including me.
Then someone whispered my name and things got messy,
as they always do.
Now I want her back.
I'm not a caterpillar, but a butterfly.
My wings are in full color, not just black and white.
But first, I have to shed my cocoon and fly.

For anyone who's ever felt like a caterpillar.
Spread your wings and fly.

butterfly

prologue

Ten

Five countries. Thirteen cities. Four weeks.

A show in each city, interviews, press... people. Masses of people.

This was my life. A never-ending cycle of shows and appearances and, as of late, an ever-growing list of bad behavior.

I lifted the silver flask up to my lips, then screwed my face into a snarl when my lips and tongue stayed dry. "Why is this empty?" I said to everyone and anyone.

"Because you drank it all?" someone to my left offered.

I gave them a withering look. "You don't get paid for sarcasm. Fill it." Thrusting the flask toward the minion, I dismissed him and gazed out the window. My knee bounced rapidly. The nervous energy coiling in my system was never satiated. Not even when my veins had more alcohol in them than blood.

Seconds later, the flask appeared under my nose, and I swiped it up and tipped it back. The familiar burn of vodka slid down my throat. After two long draws, I pulled it back, tucking it into my chest to sigh.

"Where are we again?" I asked as the limo slid to a stop. Even through the heavily tinted windows, the flashbulbs from all the press and fans were blinding. I slid the Versace sunglasses down off my head, over my eyes.

"It's nighttime," the person sitting beside me intoned.

I glanced over, not bothering to remove the glasses. "Do you value your job?"

People were banging on the windows, trying to peer in. Their hot breath left clouds on the outside of the glass, and security shouted at everyone to get back.

My assistant shrank. "Well, yes."

"Then shut up." I turned away, back to the window and the chaos that reigned beyond it. I took another long swig of the top-shelf vodka.

"We're in Amsterdam," my manager said from across the limo.

Beside her, my bodyguard pressed a finger to the black piece in his ear. "All clear," he told me.

As the door opened, I stuffed the flask into my tailored, leather designer jacket. It wasn't available to the public yet, not for anyone who wasn't me.

Screams and shrill cries cut through the night, drowning out all my own thoughts, making me feel numb.

The second my foot stretched out of the ride, the noise level went up about twenty notches. Unfolding from the backseat, I felt the familiar weight of the flask in my pocket.

The second the car door slammed behind me, I threw up my arms and grinned. "What's up, Amsterdam?"

Everyone went crazy. Women were crying, even some dudes. A plethora of hands and arms reached out over the guardrails, straining to touch me, as everyone screamed my name.

I gave a couple high-fives as flashbulbs burst around me, making my eyes strain.

"C'mon," my bodyguard said, ushering me toward the entrance.

As we went, I would pause for a couple photos and stop to sign a few posters featuring my face.

"Please, Ten!" Girls were begging, trying to get my attention.

Just before the entrance to the venue, I stopped and went to the rail again, posing to take a selfie with a few fans.

"Oh my God, I love you!" someone screamed.

"You and everybody else," I muttered.

I moved toward the door, but a dark shape darted out in front of us. I blinked.

A man with a camera and a bag of white shit clutched in his hands jumped in front of us. "You suck!" he spat and lifted the bag, no doubt to bomb me with whatever that shit was.

"Whoa!" My bodyguards pushed me out of the way as the powder disbursed all over the ground instead of all over me, as was intended.

The asshole lunged to the side, managing to get out of the clutches of my guard. He sprang toward me. I didn't think. I just reacted and threw out my fist, nailing him right in the face.

He went down, falling right in the center of the mess he created. His body writhed as he screamed and yelled. "My nose!" he wailed. "You broke my nose."

Men ushered me away, stepping in front of the spectacle, and whisked me into the building.

"I'm going to sue you!" the man roared. "I'll see you in court!"

That was the last thing I heard before the doors cut off the circus.

"You shouldn't have done that."

I turned around, the flask clutched in my hand, to face the door my manager was filling.

"That asshole had it coming."

"Probably." She amended, no give in her voice. "But it doesn't matter. You know this is going to be yet another PR nightmare. One you can't afford."

I drained the contents of the flask and then dropped it on the table beside me. My assistant was nearby, and I motioned for him to fill it up again.

"You've had enough."

"You're my manager, not my mother."

"Seems to me you could use some mothering," she snapped. "You have a show to perform."

I spread out my arms. "I'm here, aren't I?"

"You can't perform if you can't stand up."

A stage tech stuck their head in my dressing room. "We need you backstage."

I moved across the room, swiping the flask out of the minion's hand to take a lengthy, healthy swig before thrusting it back. Wiping my mouth with the back of my hand, I belched.

"Let's do this."

On my way out the door, my manager, Becca, grabbed my wrist. "You know the deal."

"I know. Say nothing. Even when the fans act like entitled little assholes."

"Don't mention what happened outside either."

I laughed.

"You smell like a fucking brewery," she said, disgusted.

Snatching my arm back, I strode out and went down the long hallway toward the stage. People parted as I walked, making room for me.

The wail of the crowd could be heard even back here. The act who warmed them up must have done their job. I couldn't even remember who it was.

I didn't care.

"Suit up!" someone yelled, and I was gestured toward the back. A few minutes later, I was strapped into some kind of harness with cables, and the crowd began to chant my name.

Anger rose up inside me. Anger at everything and everyone. Energy from the crowd, the music, everything in this entire building pressed in, fighting for room inside my body, pushing out who I was as a person, and dominating.

I was just a guest here. A guest in my own skin.

The air was thick with heat, even the A/C pouring through the large vents was no match for the way it suffocated everything around me. The crush of bodies, the lights, equipment—all created a barrier. The heat would only grow more intense as the show went on.

"You good?" one of the stagehands asked beside me.

I nodded.

"Just like rehearsals." He reminded me.

I nodded again. I'd done this so much sometimes I dreamed about flying. Some nights it was a nightmare, falling into a dark, bottomless abyss. Just me falling, rapidly plummeting farther into nothing.

Other nights, it wasn't so scary. It was a tease. I started out here, backstage, hooked up and ready to fly high. Only when my feet finally left the stage, everyone and everything fell away. I flew off, suddenly unbound by a harness and able to go anywhere I pleased. Away from here. Away from it all.

Free.

Music started up. Lights dimmed. People went wild. Adrenaline flooded my veins, and my stomach tilted a little. I blinked back the woozy feeling and shook my head slightly. When I opened my eyes, the world wasn't tilted like my stomach and my feet were hovering over ground.

My voice filled the arena as it did every concert night. The fans couldn't see me yet, but my words were everywhere.

"Perfection can be found between the rhythm and the beat."

The familiar whooshing sound of fog machines pumping out mist filled the stage, and I stared down, watching it fill the space like fog on the set of a horror movie.

I kept going higher and higher above the thousands of people in attendance. Some had glow-sticks, waiving them around. Others had lighters. Some people just screamed.

The crush of bodies made me instantly tired. The anger I felt warred with the exhaustion. All these people claimed to love me... but I knew better.

Maybe some did, sure. But most? They were here to watch me fail. Hoping to see some bad behavior. Hoping I'd give them yet another reason to hate me.

I'd be front page news tomorrow, regardless of how well this concert went tonight. Regardless of how successful this entire tour had been.

I'd be the lead headline because I decked a "fan." Never mind he was trying to fucking flour-bomb me, then attack me when that was thwarted.

Fuckers.

All of them.

Up here above it all, I got some sudden clarity. Like I was finally blissfully alone in a crowded arena.

The familiar beat of a song written just for me obliterated all other sounds. Below me, the crowd roared and bounced around, looking like a giant mosh pit.

A spotlight clicked on, illuminating me.

I went through the motions, the carefully choreographed movements.

"Who's ready for the best night of your life?" I asked the crowd, and the harness swung me down closer.

Everyone seemed ready.

Everyone but me.

Maybe it was the vodka.

Maybe I was bat-shit crazy.

Maybe I just didn't fucking care anymore.

Or...

Maybe it was the catalyst that saved my life.

Right there as I soared overhead all the adoring fans, something snapped inside me.

Since I was basically tied up, flying high, my options for getting away, for getting the hell out of there, were limited.

I did the first thing that popped into my mind.

Nimbly, my fingers reached for the zipper on my jeans. As the crew swung me toward the stage, I opened up. I released all the vodka that had been filling up my bladder and making me uncomfortable as hell.

I let it rain.

People started shrieking.

I heard my manager screaming in my earpiece. I ripped it out and threw it into the crowd.

"He's pissing all over us!" someone shouted.

Complete chaos reigned.

I finished up and gave it a little shake. My feet hit the stage. The cords holding me snapped free. My band, everyone on stage with me, was gaping in shock.

I tucked myself back into my jeans, feeling much lighter than before. Everyone was still losing their minds. I held up my hands, and the place went silent.

Tomb silent.

I could have heard a freaking pin drop. Instead, I actually heard my own thoughts.

What the fuck are you doing? You just pissed on your fans. Literal piss.

Everyone waited for me to say something. Apologize. Claim I was sick.

Rotating my hands so my palms faced the crowd, I gave them the finger.

With both hands.

Now you know. The culmination of events.

How I became Public Enemy Number One.

one

Violet

Crowds of people were not my jam. Loud, large events and the stuff everyone deemed OMG-worthy was, to me, more cringe-worthy.

Did that make me boring?

My brother said so. In fact, my absolute refusal to be on campus tonight for even just a glimpse of the main attraction made me his least favorite person on the planet.

He'd get over it. He was a drama queen.

I wasn't boring. I was creative. How was a creative person such as myself supposed to hear her own creative thoughts when people were crying and fainting over someone they didn't even know?

I would be embarrassed if it were me.

Which is precisely why I was far away from campus this evening. Far away from the music department and the gaggle of people gathering outside the building. What a circus it must have been over there. For a split second, I almost felt regretful I wasn't present to witness it all, but I got over it just as fast as the thought came.

I loved my brother, probably more than anyone on this planet. However, there were some things I just wouldn't do.

Like stalking some used-to-be pop star with a history of heinous behavior.

Blaylock University was an artsy college. Filled with free spirits, dreamers, and what people who were not of the same mold deemed lazy and unmotivated. The students here weren't those things. Well, maybe some of them were. I didn't know everyone. I mean, hey, every crowd had its bums.

In general, though, I knew we artistic types weren't lazy. We just showed our motivation in different ways. We sought out success in less traditional environments and marched to the beat of our own drums. BU was here to cultivate that. To show the more creatively inclined how to succeed in a world that sometimes behaved rigidly.

Insert Ten. Not a number, but a person. The aforementioned washed-up star who went by only one name... a name that was sort of already a number.

Apparently, he was on campus tonight, invited by the head of the music department (and approved by the dean), to talk to all the rising music students enrolled here.

Ironic, isn't it?

The university known for showing artists how to succeed in a traditional world would bring in a man who failed epically.

Actually, I thought it was kind of genius.

Showing people what *not* to do was better than droning on about what *to* do. I mean let's get serious here. Everyone looks at a train wreck. There's an actual name for it: rubbernecking.

People were drawn to drama. To scandal.

Ten was all of those things. He was the poster child for how to ruin your career in music. Singlehandedly.

Not that I actually knew much about his downfall. I only knew what my brother told me, and most of that I tuned out. Vance was obsessed with Ten. Maybe obsessed was an overstatement. How about actively involved in finding out every detail about his favorite pop artist of all time?

Nope. That sounds like the definition of obsessive. Hey, I tried.

Add in the fact that Vance was holding on to dreams of someday meeting his idol and turning him gay so they could run off together and live on an island of sublime happiness. I supposed obsessed was the only way to describe him.

Now that I thought about it, I was going to have to grovel to get Vance to forgive me for not going.

The lecture was only open to students in the music department, something that caused quite the stir on campus. Apparently, Ten's ruined career wasn't as ruined as I thought. I mean, if everyone hated him so much, why were they all scrambling and camping outside the building to see him?

Rubberneckers. The whole lot of them.

I wasn't part of the music department, thankfully. I was an art major.

Yes—*gasp*! An art major. In the words of my mother, "Whatever will you do with an art degree?"

A lot. I was going to do a lot.

The crowd started gathering hours before the lecture. I could see them all walking across the campus in herds, so I grabbed my essentials and left. The walk would do me good anyway. Gotta get them steps in, you know.

The first thing I did was walk to a café near campus (but not on it) and order a venti almond milk latte with extra caramel and no whipped cream. I glanced longingly at the scones, but I resisted. The warmth of the hot drink seeped into my fingers. The sensation was enjoyable. As I walked, I imagined it penetrating my fingers, the heat loosening everything and making my hands more pliable.

It wasn't something many people had to think of or even hope for. But for me, it was a constant thought. Even when I didn't actively think about it, it was there. Being an artist only made it more important.

I walked a little over a mile. The air was crisp, and my cheeks tingled. It wasn't unpleasant, though. It was sort of refreshing.

When I arrived, light spilled out of the front windows, casting a yellow glow on the dim pavement. The sky was twilight; in just a matter of moments, it would be completely dark. I tried not to walk alone outside at night. I knew it wasn't the safest thing to do, especially for a girl, but everyone would be busy on campus tonight, so I hoped it wouldn't matter.

Besides, desperate times called for desperate measures.

Stepping up to the wide square window of the gallery, I peeked in at the new display. It was beautiful, as always. Before, there had been a sculpture, all white with such movement in the way it was created the eye never stopped moving around it.

Tonight, the sculpture was replaced with a large painting, unframed. The piece was hanging from the ceiling, suspended by cables that were so thin they were practically invisible. The painting appeared to be floating over the floor, hovering by sheer magic.

It was an abstract piece, and I could likely stand and stare at it for an hour and come up with several different versions of what it represented. I loved abstract art. I was terrible at it, but maybe that's why I appreciated it so much. It took a lot of talent to basically create an entire story out of what could arguably be called random placement of colors and shapes.

Every time I tried abstract, I ended up with a giant mess. In fact, I was pretty sure my finger-painting at the age of three produced better-looking results.

A spotlight shone down over the piece, creating more interest with shadow and light. Stepping closer to the window, I continued to gaze at the work until a gust of evening air blew, ruffling my hair and making it tickle the back of my neck.

There was no bell on the door or any kind of sound that went off when I entered. The sound would disturb the vibe here. Batiste Gallery was probably the artsiest place in this artsy college town.

It was owned and run by an alum of Blaylock University, a woman who was, at the time, a foreign transfer from France. Abella Batiste was not only an artist, but she also had the exquisite eye of one, which was why Batiste Gallery was well known and well respected in the art world.

Not only that, but I thought she was quite a puzzle. I mean, what woman who came from the beauty of France could possibly be so taken with a town in New York that would make her want to stay?

The main showroom was nearly empty. Aside from a few people milling about between the displays, I was alone. Soft classical music filtered overhead from the built-in surround sound, and I smiled ruefully to myself.

I smirked, wondering what all those stalkers—I mean *students*—over on campus tonight would think about me skipping out on the pop star to come here and listen to classical.

I hadn't visited since last week, so there were a few new things to study, which I did, taking my time as I finished off my latte.

By the time I was nearly done, the place had emptied out, and the stark, distinct sound of heels clapping on the spotless white tile floor (made to look like white-washed wood) brought me around.

"Darling," Abella purred when she saw me. "It's been too long." She extended her arms to me, and I leaned forward so she could kiss both my cheeks.

"I've missed this place," I replied. "The new displays are stunning," Pulling back, I smiled. "Anyone I know?"

"Perhaps," she allowed, and we talked shop for a while as she told me who did what.

I didn't have any thoughts or even aspirations of being featured here one day. I knew I wasn't considered a "serious" enough artist. That's the thing about the art world. Even the creatives can be rigid and haughty. As it turns out, some art is considered better than others, and unfortunately, the kind of work that bled out of me wasn't the legit kind.

Abella was still good to me, even though we both knew my art wasn't the displaying kind. She was still encouraging, and sometimes she scoffed about the rules in this world.

"Almost closing time," she said, glancing down at the silver watch wrapped around her fine-boned wrist. Her dark hair was cut super short into a pixie style that looked chic and feminine on her. It emphasized her high cheekbones and straight nose.

"Already?" I sighed. "Campus is still probably a madhouse."

"Ah, yes. The singer. Not someone you are interested in?"

"Uh, no," I said. "You know me. I usually have earbuds in with the classics going." I held up my stained finger. Using my finger to blend out pastels and even pencils was a terrible habit of mine.

There were tools for that. Easier methods. But nothing quite worked as good as the tools I was born with. Of course, some days I used the smudge sticks and other methods in my arsenal. But some days I didn't have a choice.

She chuckled. "Feeling in the mood to draw?"

I nodded. "This gallery always inspires me."

"That warms my heart to hear." She patted my hand. "Go on. Find somewhere to sit. I have work in my office to complete. Don't ever let anyone tell you that being an artist doesn't come with paperwork."

My smile was fast. "Thank you."

"Of course. You're always welcome here." Her heels made the same clapping sound going away as they did when she approached.

Pulling in a deep breath, I gazed around for a spot to sit in peace. I had my choice of the entire gallery. It was empty, almost still, but the soft jazz floating overhead kept it from being stiff.

I left the main room and went into one of the smaller ones off to the side. The floor here was the same, tile made to look like white-washed wood, and it stretched out through the rectangular space. The walls here were high, at least twenty feet. There were exposed pipes along the ceiling, large silver ones that were very industrial and unpolished compared to the rest of the room. The walls were flat, stark white. There was lighting everywhere, not all of it on right now.

I picked this room tonight because the display was very clean, almost bare. It was like a clean slate, and I was hoping it would rub off me, as I was starting a new design tonight.

The room was sort of like a bowling alley, long and narrow. Down the center was the display. Large, white orbs in various places, some of them so large I would have to climb them to get to the top. Each of them were smooth and shiny.

I would be the first to admit I didn't really get the artist's message. It was sort of like he started the project and then stopped, leaving it unfinished—a blank canvas he couldn't quite figure out.

Maybe that was the message.

Realizing I could get lost in my own musings, I pushed into the room, my sneakers silent as I went. Beside one of the large, round balls, I stopped, placed my palm flat on it, and shoved. As I did, I winced, praying to God the thing didn't roll away.

It didn't. It was sufficiently glued or something to the floor. For good measure, I gave it another shove just to be sure. When I was positive I likely couldn't damage what was probably a very expensive piece of art (that looked like a giant gumball), I walked around and sat down, leaning my back against it, and stretched my legs in front of me. I dug around in my messenger bag and pulled out my sketchpad and a few pencils. After a few moments of adjusting (this floor was hard), I settled back and thumbed through the already full pages of my book.

When I got to a blank one I folded it back and leaned my head against the ball. It was as hard as the floor. I wasn't really sure what to do. I was in some kind of funky mood. These moods weren't always the easiest to draw inspiration from.

It was sort of maddening.

I always felt like drawing. Like creating. I even dreamed in drawing sometimes—fine strokes of a pencil and fat smudges of color with pastels. I thought about drawing, about creating. About stories I wanted to tell or emotions I wanted to evoke almost every minute of every day.

Most people thought eating, sleeping, and breathing art would make it easy to create.

Most people were morons.

Truth was sometimes even when I saw the finished product in my head, felt as though I already experienced all the emotions of creating it, getting that to translate onto paper was much more difficult.

Today, I'd been preoccupied. Well, no. I was preoccupied every day. It was sort of the way my mind worked. In the clouds, lost in a fog, deep in another world. I managed to create, regardless.

My preoccupation was being preoccupied.

By someone I didn't know. By a pop star my brother was practically in love with and a guy I probably wouldn't recognize if I saw him.

He annoyed me. Just his very existence.

He waltzed—no, probably drove into town in his long stretch limo with his driver and security, having flown in on his private jet as though he owned this town, and he was probably sitting back, glorying in the fact he still had so much power to whip everyone into this frenzy.

Of course, that wasn't what his people would have us all believe. I'd heard it fifty times and read it just as much in texts from Vance, who was practically blackmailing me to go snag a pic of him.

What kind of brother blackmailed his own sister?

Not that it mattered because he was terrible at it. I called his bluff, and he switched to texting me fifty times. Maybe he thought he was more intimidating over text.

He wasn't.

Anyway, Ten's people were spinning this lecture at the music department as a penance for all his bad behavior. Apparently, he was going to various universities, etc., and giving talks about how to handle the pressures of success. And of course, the press were all invited so they could see just how deeply apologetic he was.

Aka: he was telling everyone how sorry he was because if he didn't, his trashed career would never rebound.

I don't know why or how, but I seemed to be the only person in this town that could smell a phony when it was stinking up the air.

I'd been stewing over this all day. Chewing on the fact that he was interrupting my day, my life. Everywhere I went on campus, there was his name. His songs were playing in the food hall. Vance was blowing up my phone. I didn't like the upheaval. It was rude.

With a little sniff, I glanced down at the blank paper. A grin pulled at my lips when an idea popped into my mind.

Perhaps I should use this little experience as a muse. Put pencil to paper to show the world that not everyone was so convinced this little apology tour was sincere.

Just like that, inspiration was mine. I picked up my pencil and let it fly over the paper.

two

Ten

"What the fuck is that?" I asked, staring at the offered item as if it were birthed from Mars and just arrived on a flying saucer.

"You're going to need it."

I said nothing, just continued to stare.

"I know you're rich and all, but surely you remember what a roll of duct tape looks like." He waved it at me as if he thought I needed a reminder it was there.

I snatched it and held it down at my side. "I asked to borrow your car, and you give me duct tape?"

"You asked to borrow *a* car that no one would expect you to drive." My uncle corrected. "That car requires that," he intoned, pointing to the roll of silver tape.

"I was talking about your Honda," I pointed out. "You mean to tell me you have something else around here that's in worse shape than that?"

He smacked me upside my head. "You're supposed to be working on your shit attitude, not embracing it."

I rubbed the back of my head and glared at him.

He went past me through the small kitchen to open up a wooden door that led out into a small attached two-car garage. When I didn't follow, he turned back, standing in the dark opening, and looked at me. "You coming?"

Sighing heavily, I went along, my designer shoe-clad feet shuffling over the linoleum floor. A dim light flickered on inside the garage, illuminating the old space. It looked like a wood shop in there. Or some kind of hobby den with a bunch of tools and shit lying everywhere. Some of it was practically antique.

Including the car Derek gestured to. "Here she is."

I felt my eyebrows fly up with so much surprise it nearly knocked the backward baseball cap off my head. "You've got to be kidding me."

Derek opened up the door (if you could call it that) and leaned in to snatch the keys out of the ignition. Where else did one keep the keys to a car no one would ever want to steal? Coming back out, he walked around the hood and jingled them in my face in the same way he'd offered the roll of tape.

"You want me to drive that?"

"Why not?" He grinned, his white teeth flashing. "Most kids your age would love this beast."

"Most *kids* my age aren't millionaires with recording contracts and sold-out concerts."

"Wasn't your next album put on hold and all concerts cancelled?" He crossed his arms over his flannel-covered chest. "I think someone needs to eat a heaping slice of humble pie."

"Whatever," I said, disgruntled he would bring that up.

"Do you want the Jeep or not?" Derek intoned. "I thought the whole idea was to get in and out of the lecture tonight with as little drama with the press as possible. No one is going to be expecting you to drive yourself, let alone drive up in an old Wrangler that's at least twenty years old."

I held out my hand, palm up, for the keys. The roll of tape dangled precariously from one finger.

"Good choice," he said, slapping me on the back.

Commotion in the doorway had us both looking around. "Oh, good, you're still here," Nate said, skidding to a halt just before he fell down the unstable-looking wooden steps into this antique barn. "I'm coming with you."

"No," Derek rebutted instantly.

"What the hell, Dad?" Nate screwed up his face. "I'm too old to be getting orders from you."

"But not too old to live here for free?"

I stifled a grin.

"I stay for you," he said solemnly, placing a hand over his heart. "I know how lonely you'd be without me."

"Tennison can clean up his own messes. You aren't getting dragged into that world."

The amusement I felt watching them interact evaporated. *That world* he spoke of was *my* world.

Nate was about to argue, but I'd heard enough. "I gotta go."

Nate came down the steps, but I held up a hand. "You won't be missing anything," I told him. "But keep your cell on. I wouldn't be surprised if this hunk of metal doesn't leave me stranded."

He frowned but nodded reluctantly.

"Tennison," Derek called out.

I looked over my shoulder. "Yeah?"

"She has a tendency to overheat. And uh, stuff comes loose... Keep that tape handy."

"Why don't you just get a new engine?" I muttered, going around to the door, which wasn't a solid door. It was made from the same material as the soft top. The material wobbled haphazardly when I yanked it open.

"What fun would that be?" my uncle called out.

I gave him the finger from the interior of his time machine and then searched around for the button to open the garage door.

There wasn't one. Instead, there was a remote in the cup holder, the kind with a silver clasp on the back and a big button on the front. I hit it, and the loud door began to rise.

Derek and Nate stood inside and watched me back the Wrangler out of the garage, down the short driveway, and then into the street. My uncle and cousin lived in a brick duplex, basically a giant house that had been split in half. One family on one side and mine on the other.

The gearshift made a heinous sound as I put the Jeep into first and spurred it down the road. As I picked up a little speed, the top, windows, and doors all vibrated in the wind. I glanced down at the dash to turn on the radio to drown it out, but there wasn't one.

No radio.

I swear, this Wrangler belonged in a museum. I was surprised the white paint wasn't flaking off as I drove. 'Course, it was dark... Maybe there was barely any paint on it to begin with.

Speaking of... Why was it so fucking dark?

I glanced over the hood, to the road, which was not illuminated at all.

Jesus! The lights weren't on! "Shit," I muttered as I glanced down at all the old-as-dirt controls. The headlights flicked on the second I hit the button.

I was used to automatic lights. All of my cars were practically brand new.

I spared another glance around before returning my attention to the road. Nothing in this vehicle was electronic or automatic. Hell, if I wanted to put the windows down, I had to unzip them.

The gears made another strangled sound, and the body of the Jeep lurched on the road. My hands tightened around the feeble wheel. Probably a good thing I brought the tape.

As I drove, the headlights illuminated the street before me. Everything was familiar even though I hadn't been here for a visit in almost ten years. I used to spend a lot of time here with Derek and my cousin Nate. Most of my summers had been here in upstate New York. My mother always said it was good for me to get out of the urban jungle.

But then I got discovered, and my life changed in the blink of an eye.

The thought caused me to actually blink. The streets were growing dark, and I knew a crowd was probably already gathered outside the music hall.

I might have been the number-one-most-hated celebrity right now, but I was still a celeb. People still wanted every glimpse they could get. It was fucked up, really, but it was my life. My career.

33

It nearly slipped through my fingers once. I couldn't let that happen again.

Okay. Truth be told, it didn't slip anywhere. I decimated it when I literally pissed all over it. Even though it had been over six months since that night, I still recalled it with a clarity I now realized would never go away. I'd been drunk as hell, yet I still remembered everything. My tolerance for alcohol was nearly unmatched.

The anger, frustration, and flat-out loneliness I felt as I was suspended above the stage was still there inside me. Know what else was also there? Drive to get it all back. The career I pissed on. Being hated was just as exhausting as being loved.

A flash of someone on the sidewalk brought me out of my thoughts. I barely had time to look or even understand why I wanted to before the Jeep rumbled past.

I glanced in the rearview mirror, but the "window" in the back being made of plastic was not very clear. It was cloudy, sort of like a dirty shower curtain.

Annoyance slapped me in the back of the neck, and my eyes moved to the rearview on the door. It was a girl. That was all I could tell as I drove down the darkening street.

I couldn't make out any of her details other than she was carrying something, a coffee cup. There was a bag slung around her, and since we were like a mile from campus, it was obvious she was a student.

There was nothing that stood out about her. She didn't wave or even look up at the Jeep. I didn't know anything about her. My eyes were drawn to her shrinking frame anyway.

She shouldn't be out alone on the street at night. I might be rich, but I wasn't stupid. The streets of a college town were no place for a lone girl to be out and about.

Why am I even thinking about this?

Who cared what the girl did?

I was jealous.

Jealous she was a nobody. Envious she had the freedom to walk down the street, sipping coffee, without a care in the world. No one knew her. She didn't have prying eyes staring at her every move. She had the kind of freedom I had once, long ago, at a time in my life I couldn't appreciate it. The kind of freedom I would never have again. Unless, of course, I moved to another country and stayed out of the spotlight completely. Still, that wasn't freedom. It more like hiding.

I wondered, not for the first time, not even for the hundredth time (perhaps the thousandth), what it was like to move around without thought. To go to and from liberally. To attend classes while trying to decide what to do with my life. To eat meals in a cafeteria surrounded by people who barely gave me a passing glance. To sleep in a dorm filled with other people and not under lock and key. What was it like to stroll down the street at dusk, with autumn air swirling around me, coffee in hand, without a bodyguard or camera shadowing my every step?

I didn't know.

I was jealous.

The outline of the girl disappeared when I turned off the street, and the music building hovered in the distance. The closer I got to campus, the more people and cars I saw. The curb parking was full, not a spot for blocks.

People were walking toward the building, dressed up and dressed down.

All of them coming to the show.

To my effort to gain back my career.

My phone went off in my pocket. I knew it was my manager. I was late. Becca had wanted to drive me, probably because she was worried I wouldn't show. I gently reminded her it would look better if I showed up on my own, without an entourage... You know, to appear humbler.

Truth was I didn't want to listen to her lecture me the entire way.

The Jeep started sputtering, and I glanced down at the dash. It was already overheating, and I'd only been driving it for like five minutes. What a piece of shit. Derek was probably laughing his ass off right now because he knew this thing was one bolt away from falling apart.

I parked in the staff parking behind the music building. The lot was fuller than I expected. I guess that meant a lot of the staff wanted to gawk at me, too. No, excuse me. They wanted to listen to my story of how I shot to fame then succumbed to alcohol, child stardom, and the pressures of being the most famous singer in the world.

Bitterness splashed up the back of my throat like vomit. Making a face, I swallowed it back. They would listen to me speak. Some might even try to understand... But most? Most just wanted to judge me.

Still sitting behind the wheel, I pocketed the keys and stared out over the dash. I knew the second I stepped around the corner of the building, I would be swallowed.

My phone went off again, and I answered it. "I'm here. Parked in the staff lot behind the building."

"Security is here. New guys. I'll introduce you when you get inside. Come to the back door. The front is way too mobbed to even try," Becca said, her voice all business.

All security and staff quit after the yellow rain incident.

Yellow rain incident = the night I whipped it out and peed on my fans.

The only person that stayed on staff was Becca. Becca was under contract, and she was a shark. She knew she could spin my naughty behavior into something for massive promo and organize the biggest comeback in music history (her words, not mine). I was a giant dollar sign when she looked at me. I had no illusions that she stayed because she genuinely liked me.

She didn't.

I didn't like her either, so I guess that made us even.

I had to admit my manager knew what she was doing, though. After the yellow rain, all hell broke loose. The media was a pack of wolves who smelled blood. I was a hot topic for weeks. I lost endorsement deals, appearance slots, concerts—hell, I even got kicked out of a charity event. My face was plastered all over the news and media.

"Public Enemy #1," they dubbed me. *"Perfect Ten to a Zero."*

I did a month in rehab. Something I had been dead set against. Becca pushed it because it would be good promo. Make it look like my addiction to alcohol made me do all the shit I'd been doing. It wasn't the alcohol. It was me wanting to do that shit. The alcohol just gave me the balls to do it.

I went to rehab, though. Not for Becca. Not for me. For my mother.

My fall from grace was harder on her than it was on me. She blamed herself. Nothing I did was her fault, but she was beside herself. So I went to rehab and stayed for twenty days. The media thought I stayed a whole thirty.

When I got out, I went dark for five months. All my social media was wiped clean. I disappeared from the public eye.

I learned something in all my time off.

I missed music. I missed losing myself in a beat and in the lyrics. I missed the recording studio, the large headphones that would hang around my neck, the sound booth with a single chair and a mic. I missed my passion.

A month ago, Becca announced it was time to start laying the groundwork for my comeback.

I agreed, reluctantly, because the promise of new music was too alluring to deny. And now I was here, serving my penance. Trying to earn back my right to sing.

Thing was I missed music. Desperately.

But everything else that came along with it?

Not so much.

Stabbing myself in the eye with a fork seemed like it might be a better time.

Yet here I was. That was the thing about passion. A true passion was nearly impossible to give up on. Music was a piece of my soul. Without it, part of me was dead.

"Ten," Becca said into my ear, reminding me she was still there.

"Yeah."

"They're at the back door. See them?"

I glanced up toward the building. Two men in black-and-white suits poked their heads out a brown-painted metal door. "I see them. I'll be right there."

The call cut off, and I ejected myself from the time machine. The white paint nearly glowed in the dark, and the brown ragtop nearly disappeared. It looked like half a car sitting here, even more ridiculous than it did in full light.

Realizing it was useless to even lock the doors (they could be ripped off), I didn't bother. Instead, I went ahead, my eyes darting around to make sure no one had spotted me yet.

I got about five steps when the shrieking started. "There he is!" someone screeched.

The hair on the back of my neck rose.

"Ten!" someone yelled, and then it was echoed by a hundred other voices.

I glanced up to see a herd of people (mostly girls) running around the building toward me.

My bodyguards stepped out of the building, glancing between me and the fans. One motioned for me, and I dashed toward them.

As I ran, as people ran after me, I thought about that girl on the street. How lucky she was.

But also that she wasn't here. It made me a little less jealous and slightly more curious. Somewhere in this town there was woman who wasn't interested in me or the fact that I was here.

And that made me *very* interested in her.

three

Violet

Time passed. How much, I couldn't tell you. When inspiration struck and pencil met paper time, no longer existed. Time was merely a construct created by man who needed to measure the hours and moments in a day because, without time, he might be lost.

The dial of a clock didn't matter to me. Nothing did really, except the strokes on the page.

Not even my own reality, which, to me, was the greatest reward of art.

Know what was the greatest consequence?

Coming back to reality—or rather, being summoned back before I was ready.

I didn't expect to be forced cruelly back as I sat against the giant gumball in the uninterrupted gallery, but interrupted is exactly what I was.

At first, it was more of a feeling. No longer being alone. I brushed it off, thinking Abella was just moving around, readying the rooms for the night.

But the familiar and audible clap of her heels never came.

I paused my drawing, pencil poised just above the sketchpad. My head didn't lift, though. I just listened to the silence around me and wondered what in the world was disturbing it.

When no voice or sound came, I lifted my head, tilting it to the side. I wasn't imaging this. There was a very distinct disturbance in the air. A disturbance that was beginning to creep me out.

For the first time ever, the constant emptiness of the gallery wasn't a peaceful feeling. I thought about calling out to Abella, but the thought of even my own voice echoing through this place gave me the willies.

Using the protection of the giant gumball, I sat forward and leaned around to peek into the rest of the room.

Ahh! The pencil in my hand fell onto the pad when my body jolted in surprise.

I wasn't alone! And it wasn't Abella in here with me.

I blinked, as if to make sure I wasn't just conjuring up this scenario with my sometimes overactive imagination.

Fine. Not sometimes. It was overactive *all* the time.

My lids squeezed shut, then sprang open. Nope. He was still here. His back was to me, his chest pressed close against the wall he faced. Both hands were up, palms flat against the smooth surface, as if he were being held up in a robbery. Or arrested for being a felon.

Oh Lord. Wasn't it just my luck that some art thief would break in here after closing to steal the art and sell it on the black market?

The universe hated me. This was proof. Well, additional proof to the already rather large pile I had.

His head was turned away, his face glancing toward the window that looked out onto the street. It was a narrow window in here, as opposed to the large ones out in the main room. He seemed primed, as if he were waiting for something. Or someone.

Was he hiding?

How did he even get in here?

I leaned out around the white orb just a little bit more. He thought he was alone in here. But he wasn't. My eyes swept over him, trying to pick out any identifying features so I could relay them to the cops.

Except there were no details to tell. He was exceptionally boring for a crook.

Nice jeans, slightly loose, the kind that draped over his lower half, molding to all the parts they should. Criminal or not, he had a nice butt. His sneakers were clean and pretty nice. Actually, *really* nice.

Stolen. He was wearing stolen shoes.

From behind, his shirt was all white. A plain T-shirt that clung to his shoulders and tapered in with his narrow waist. There was a baseball hat on his head, and from here it appeared to be all black.

Trying to conceal his features!

A muffled noise from out on the street filled the room, and the guy moved suddenly. He spun around, plastering his back against the wall as if he were trying to

42

make himself small. The movement was so sudden it scared the crap out of me.

I gasped and lurched back behind the protection of the ball. My heart was thundering in my chest, and I pressed my palm against it, trying to calm myself down.

The pencil that lay forgotten on the sketchpad in my lap rolled. I tried to catch it, but I needed to be quicker. The stupid pencil fell on the floor with an audible click. Instead of stopping where it landed, the traitorous instrument began to roll. It took its sweet time turning over on the floor right out into the open, totally giving me away.

Pressing my back and head against the ball, I glared at it, clutching the sides of the notebook in my hands. The action caused my fingers to ache and protest, so I loosened my grip while still maintaining eye contact with the instrument.

It was dead to me. *Dead!*

What a shame, too. It was my favorite drawing pencil.

I waited long seconds. Silence stretched on inside the room, but I knew he was still there. I knew he knew I was there.

I held my breath, hoping his obvious desire to not be seen would recognize the same desire in me.

After what felt like forever and my lungs were literally shriveling up beneath my ribs, I dragged in a ragged, relieved breath.

He must have left.

Slowly, I leaned back around, peering cautiously from behind the gumball.

My eyes met a pair of hat-shaded ones.

"Ah!" I squeaked and lunged backward.

He was still there!

four

Ten

I stayed late, an hour after the music department cleared out.

An hour wasn't long enough.

A huge crowd still gathered outside, waiting. People who couldn't get into the lecture and then the people who were inside and left, adding to the crowd.

I knew what I had to do. I was tired. I didn't feel like it. Sometimes putting on a work face or turning on the switch of the person everyone wanted you to be was exhausting.

I thought longingly of the beer my uncle kept in the fridge. I wasn't supposed to be drinking, but I did anyway. I didn't like when people told me what to do. It pissed me off.

Becca stepped into the room, walking with energy and purpose down the aisle toward the stage, where I was sitting on the edge.

"They're not going anywhere. They've got the front and back entrances staked out."

I nodded. I didn't even know why she bothered to look anymore. It was always the same.

"Ten, twenty minutes tops." She went on. I didn't know why she bothered to promise me amounts of time that were grossly under-exaggerated. It was like she thought I was fucking stupid.

I hopped down off the stage and rubbed a hand through my hair. It was longer than it used to be. I hadn't cut it since I went underground. I'd been hoping the longer hair and the new scruff on my jaw would make me a little less recognizable.

It didn't. Not really. At least not in places where people expected me to be.

It did seem to conjure up some press. What else was new? I was "letting myself go" and on a "downward spiral of despair." One online report actually said I'd given up showering and all hygiene.

Whatever.

Two bodyguards flanked me, and we made our way through the building as a unit. Becca followed along behind, reminding me the entire time how to be with the fans waiting outside.

I wanted to tell her that half those people out there weren't fans, but she wouldn't care. Image was image, no matter who was watching. In fact, according to her, I had to put on an even better show for my haters.

Before stepping outside, I adjusted the collar of my black-and-white flannel shirt, making sure it was slightly visible beneath the collar of the black leather jacket I wore. The shirt was open to reveal a white T-shirt, and I had a couple necklaces on dark cords draped against my chest.

After running my hand through my hair, making sure it was suitably disheveled, I nodded, and the guards opened the double doors.

The crowd went nuts. I smiled and waved. I shook people's hands, took selfies, signed autographs, and told girls they didn't need to cry.

News vans were nearby. Reporters had out their mics and cameras.

It was the same old, same old.

Some people got too handsy. The crowd started pushing in. Security ushered me away, back inside the building. I heard Becca thanking everyone for coming and announcing I was done signing autographs.

A lot of people moved on. Still, some lingered.

Luckily, they were all out front, hoping I'd come out one last time. One of the guards was able to go grab the Jeep and pull it up close to the back door. I slipped inside and drove off, all without anyone seeing.

I drove a few blocks, then pulled onto a side street and cut the engine at the curb. The first thing I did was shed the jacket, the black-and-white shirt, and the necklaces. Picking up a black baseball hat, I pulled it low on my head, allowing the brim to shade my face.

It was dark. The night air was cold and seeped into the Jeep through the ragtop and doors.

I needed to decompress, and even though the beer in Derek's fridge beckoned, I wasn't ready to go back to the duplex yet.

I thought about the girl, how envious I'd been of her walking down the street. Glancing around, out the windows and through the mirrors, I noted the street was empty. No one else was out walking. The occasional car would go by, but they might not know it was me. No one was expecting me to be here.

Without another thought, I got slid of the Wrangler and started to walk. I tried to imagine that I was some ordinary guy—a no-name college student—and this was just another night. Tucking my hands into the pockets of my jeans, I thought about going back for my jacket but decided against it. Ten always wore leather. It was basically a large neon sign of my identity. At the end of the street, I hesitated, glanced back at the dilapidated white Wrangler, and decided to keep going.

Turning the corner, I walked down the next street, this one looking a little livelier. Some of the buildings still had lights on in the windows, and as I walked, I wondered if maybe I should turn back to the street that was darker.

Chill. I was just a guy out walking. No one would think anything of it.

A little farther down the street, I passed by a coffee shop. The scents alone made my stomach rumble. I wanted to go in, but I knew better. I couldn't remember the last time I went and got coffee on my own.

Actually, I did remember. It made the news. I'd gotten my order, taken a sip, and made a face because, like a dumbass, I'd burned my tongue. Someone, of course, snapped a pic, and it made the front-page headlines.

"Ten disses local coffee shop."

"Worst coffee ever, according to Ten!"

No one wanted to believe that wasn't true. Not after all my other actual indiscretions.

As I passed, the door to the place opened and a group of college students spilled out onto the sidewalk.

My shoulder blades tensed, but otherwise, I kept moving.

"Is that...?" I heard someone whisper.

"No way," someone else whispered back.

"He was on campus tonight."

"Hey!" a deeper voice yelled.

My feet stuttered, but then I kept walking, ducking my head farther.

"Ten!" a female yelled. "It is him!"

The sound of pounding feet started up not far behind me. I glanced over my shoulder to confirm they were rushing toward me.

"Oh my God!" A girl gasped. She grabbed the girl beside her. "Ten!"

I bolted. Becca would have read me the riot act, but Becca wasn't there. I didn't want to perform for people who could later log online to brag they met me.

I started jogging. The people behind me started running.

Picking up my pace, I sprinted down the street and skidded around the corner. The students still pursuing. I heard them loud and clear. I had to think fast, get rid of them so I could double back and get the Jeep.

Being a regular guy on the street was nice while it lasted. For, you know, all four minutes.

Partway down the block, light spilled out from wide-open windows. I rushed toward it and inside the door without even pausing to see what kind of place this was. Quickly, I darted away from the windows, farther into the room, which seemed to be an art gallery.

A nearby doorway caught my eye, and I ran for it and slipped inside. There were a lot less windows in this room, and I breathed silently in relief. I knew I wasn't completely in the clear yet, so I plastered myself against the wall, away from the window, and listened intently for the students to run by.

Soft jazz played overhead, and I closed my eyes for long moments and relaxed. The voices of the people looking for me shouted, and I spun around instantly, pressing my back into the wall.

A low muffled gasp from inside the room (where I thought I was alone) made me forget about my stalkers outside.

I swung around in time to see someone disappear behind some giant sculpture, as if they too didn't want to be seen.

The plan might have worked if it weren't for the pencil.

I waited for a hand to reach out and snatch it back. None came.

Amused, my lips twitched. Did they really think I didn't know they were there?

I glanced at the window as the loud voices of the people on the street grew more muffled as they moved on in their search.

Now would be a good time to escape. I could rush outside and back the way I came, get in the Jeep, and have a longneck in my hand in under ten minutes.

I didn't do that.

Curiosity spurred me forward, closer to the white ball in the center of the room. I wondered how long the person would hide. How long until they would assume I left?

Not long.

I felt them move before I even saw them. After a few minutes, the top of a blond head appeared, and a pair of wide blue eyes collided with mine.

I don't know how I knew, but I did. Instantly. It was the girl from the street.

I didn't need to see any more of her to know. No, I didn't get a good look at her earlier, but I didn't need to.

I knew this was her. The nobody on the sidewalk. The girl I'd been jealous of.

The urge to stare at her now was the same thing that made me look at her as I drove past.

"Ah!" she gasped and retreated.

I stifled a laugh.

What the hell was she even doing lurking around in a darkened gallery?

Amused, I went forward, picked up the pencil, and stepped around the ball. She was plastered against it, her knees pulled into her chest. It was like she didn't want to talk to me.

Intriguing.

"You dropped something," I told her.

My voice seemed to startle her. The girl jumped up. The notebook in her lap was forgotten and tumbled to the floor. "Shit!" she muttered and glanced down to where it fell.

I chuckled. Instantly, her eyes shot to me. I waited for them to go wide, for recognition to slam into her body. I actually braced for it.

But hey, one girl was better than a gaggle of people chasing me down the street.

It didn't happen, though. There was no light bulb over her head. No indication I looked familiar.

"How'd you get in here?" she asked, breathless.

"There's this thing out there… It's called a door."

She rolled her eyes and muttered, "I would find the only crook who thinks he's a comedian."

I blinked, surprised. A grin split my face. "You think I'm a crook?"

"The gallery is closed," she said, lifting her chin in a haughty movement.

Her face was shaped like a heart. Her cheeks were red, and she wasn't wearing any makeup. I knew because she didn't look plastic or fake. Her skin tone wasn't flawless, and there were faint shadows under her eyes, like she was tired.

Call me intrigued times two.

"The door was open," I rebutted.

"Abella must have forgotten to lock it," she said to herself.

I assumed Abella was the person who owned this place.

"If the gallery is closed, why are you here?" I asked.

She crossed her arms over her chest. She had a good-sized rack. Probably a good handful. A strand of blond hair fell over her cheek, and she brushed it away as if it bothered her. "I'm friends with the owner."

"So am I." I lied.

"You are not!" She gasped.

Her indignation was adorable. What's more, she didn't seem to recognize me.

This was the first time that had happened, well... *ever*.

"If you don't leave, I'm going to call the police." She threatened.

Ignoring the threat, I bent to pick up the notebook she'd dropped. "What's this?" I asked.

"It's nothing!" she said, lunging closer to snatch it away.

I was taller, so I held it up out of her reach. She made a sound of dissatisfaction and tried to jump at it.

It was a drawing, all in pencil. Some sort of comic strip or cartoon. The paper was divided into a block of four scenes. It was amazing.

It was also about me.

"Did you draw this?" I asked, tearing my eyes away from the drawing for a second.

"Yes," she said. "Now give it back."

"In a minute." I brushed her off and studied it anew. Pulling my arm down, I tucked the bottom of the pad into my stomach and stared at it some more.

"This is awesome," I said, awe in my tone.

Her annoyance shifted, and I felt her stare. "You think so?"

I nodded, enthusiastic. "Is it about that singer... uh...?" I feigned stupidity. "You know, the one who was on campus tonight."

"Yeah. That's him."

"Ah, Ten, right?" I asked.

She made a sound. "Yep, the guy with a number for a name."

She thought my name was stupid.

"Something tells me you aren't his biggest fan." I goaded.

"Whatever gave you that idea?" she asked, batting her eyes.

I laughed and pointed to the drawing. "Um, this for starters."

She shrugged one shoulder, then reached out to snatch the book and flip it closed. "It's just a drawing. I thought it might be fun to poke fun at the people who literally flock to catch a glimpse of someone they don't even know."

"Not you, though," I said, settling a little more firmly into my sneakers. I liked this. This was the best conversation I'd had in a while.

She made a sound. "Definitely not me."

I hitched my chin at her. "So what do you have against him?"

She shrugged one shoulder and reached for her bag. "Besides the fact that he peed all over his own fans?" She snorted.

I stifled a laugh. "Yeah, besides that."

She glanced up at me after shoving her notebook into the bag. "How about you? I don't see you over on campus, climbing over the crowds to meet him."

"Guess I don't like him either," I deadpanned.

"I have to go," she said, moving as though she were going to step around me.

I felt a pang of disappointment and the sudden urge to stop her. "Wait."

She stopped and glanced at me curiously.

"What's your name?"

She tilted her head. "Why?"

"So I can look you up on social media later and stalk you," I replied without pause. "If you could tell me your first *and* last name, that would be great."

She rolled her eyes. "You aren't a stalker."

"How do you know?" I said, slightly offended. I could be a stalker.

"Thief, yes. Stalker, no." She went on.

I laughed. "You think I'm a thief."

"Well, your shoes *are* nice."

"There are these places," I told her. "They're called shoe stores. Some of them sell nice ones."

"So where'd you buy those?" she asked, crossing her arms over her chest.

Was she calling my bluff? This girl who seemed to have no idea who I was. This girl who thought I was a criminal.

I opened my mouth to respond, but then I realized I hadn't actually bought these shoes anywhere. They'd been sent to me. By a highly exclusive designer whose shoes usually retailed for thousands of dollars.

My lips snapped closed. I couldn't exactly say that. Well, I could. But I liked the fact she had no idea who I was.

She laughed. "See."

"I, uh, didn't buy them," I said, recovering. "They were a gift. From my mother."

"Oh." Her arms fell to her sides, and she glanced at them again, then back up to me. "That hat doesn't help you look any less like a vagrant." She pointed out. "I can barely see your face."

Ah. So *that* was why she didn't know me. The knowledge made me feel disgruntled. I thought about walking away, but something held me in place. Instead of leaving, I did something else. I called her bluff.

If you considered her asking to see my face a bluff.

I reached up and pushed the brim of the hat up so it was just sitting atop my head, not really on it.

"Better?" I asked and lifted a brow. Nerves coiled inside me. I waited for the reaction I always got.

She gasped.

A snarl automatically pulled at my lips. *Here we go.*

"Is everything okay?" she asked.

My eyes went wide. Confusion caused the angry snarl I was barely holding back to die. "Huh?"

"Is that why you were lurking around here, hiding your face with a hat? Were you running from someone?"

"Do I look like the kind of guy who runs?" I intoned. As if to challenge her to look at me closer, I stepped forward.

Never mind the fact that I actually had been running.

"Hmm," she said, looking me over. Her eyes touched on several places around my face. It was odd to be looked at as if I'd never been seen before. The sensation was oddly humbling. I wondered what she saw, what she thought of me—just a guy from the street. There wasn't a speck of recognition in her gaze, not a single glimmer.

She didn't answer my question. Instead, she stuck her hand out between us. "Violet."

I mentally high-fived myself. I passed whatever test she had given me and won the reward of her name. A beautiful name at that.

"Violet," I said, trying it out on my tongue. I wrapped my hand around hers, noting how small it felt in mine. "Hi."

"Hi," she said, ducking her head and pulling away. Suddenly, she was shy.

No one was ever shy around me.

It was endearing.

"Usually when you tell someone your name, they tell you theirs." She pointed out.

My face split into a grin. I began to introduce myself—but then stopped abruptly. I couldn't tell her my name. The second I did, she'd know. Plus, she already declared dislike of my name.

The thought of the way she was looking at me just then disappearing made me ache a little. Her shyness would evaporate. Hell, after the drawing I just saw, she would probably run. It was obvious I'd managed to find the only girl in town that didn't like me.

Oddly, that made me want to be around her.

I cleared my throat. "Stark," I said, thinking fast.

It wasn't necessarily a lie. Stark was my name. My last name. The media rarely used it. I was just Ten to everyone.

I didn't want to be just Ten to her.

"Stark," she repeated, and I nodded.

She was short. Short enough I had to look down when I looked at her. She wasn't tiny, though, not even small. Just little. I hadn't ever realized there was a difference between little and small until now.

She definitely wasn't at all like the girls I was used to. In looks or behavior.

"Well," she said, clearing her throat. "Since you aren't running from anyone and I know I don't have to protect you, I should go."

I barked a laugh. "*You* protect me?"

She drew back, offended. "I could be a black belt for all you know. I could kick your ass."

I pressed my lips together. "Are you?"

She paused. "Well, no."

I pulled the hat back down on my head and snickered.

"Whatever. Let's go." She motioned for me to go ahead of her.

I raised a brow. "I have to leave, too?"

Her button nose scrunched up, and she drew back, offended. "I'm not leaving you here with Abella. I'm not completely convinced you aren't thinking of doing something felonious."

Well. It definitely wouldn't be the first time.

Funny. She didn't know me, yet she kind of saw me.

I held up my hands in surrender. "All right, I'm going."

She didn't say anything, just motioned for me to get moving. Chuckling, I went, her following.

I wasn't sure if the people out on the sidewalk were gone. I sure as hell hoped so. This new Stark persona was someone I suddenly wanted to explore.

Abruptly, I halted. Partly because I wanted to buy some time. Partly because I wanted to talk to Violet.

I tossed a smile over my shoulder. "You're totally checking out my ass right now."

A laugh burst out of her. It was entirely genuine, and she slapped a hand over her mouth. Recovering, she said, "You're delusional."

I started walking again, putting a little swagger into my step. "Totally looking," I sang.

The large windows afforded me a view of the sidewalk, and what I could see was vacant. No sign of the students from earlier. 'Course, I still didn't relax. Just because I couldn't see them didn't mean they weren't there. The windows only showed so much.

I didn't hesitate when I got to the door, though. I pushed right through, telling myself that if I was outed, I'd just take off again, this time in the direction of the Jeep. The cold night air smacked me in the face, and my eyes watered slightly as I looked up and down along the block.

They were gone.

I breathed out a sigh of relief and turned back to Violet. She was still inside, though, holding the door open a bit. I heard her yell.

"I'm leaving, Abella! Don't forget to lock the doors!"

A muffled voice from somewhere inside the gallery echoed, and seconds later, Violet came the rest of the way outside.

The air ruffled her hair, pulling loose, light-colored strands so they waved around her face and cheeks. The rest was pulled into some kind of messy knot at the base of her skull. The strap of her messenger bag slashed diagonally across her chest, pressing the hoodie she was wearing against the front of her body.

She glanced up and down the street. Then her eyes came back to me.

"You go to BU?" she asked.

I nodded. I was just racking up the lies tonight.

"Me, too."

"I'm guessing art major?" I said astutely.

Violet nodded and stuffed her hands into the front pocket of the university hoodie. "Maybe I'll see you around sometime."

"You're walking back to campus?" I said as she started to leave. "Alone?"

She turned around, walking backward down the center of the sidewalk. Wind blew behind her, pushing all those loose strands into her face. "I can handle myself."

I frowned. Before I met her, I didn't like the idea of her walking around alone. Now that I knew her name and her obvious aversion to me, I *hated* it.

"I'll drive you." I decided out loud.

She stopped walking and glanced at the curb. "In what? You're imaginary mobile?"

"My Jeep is a street over," I explained, hitching a thumb over my shoulder.

"I'll pass." She turned and began walking again. "See ya later, Stark!" she yelled over her shoulder.

My name floated on the wind. *She just told me no.* The thought bewildered me.

I couldn't just let her walk away. She was a clean slate. A chance to have something I thought I never would again. Anonymity. She would have no expectations. I wouldn't have to be anything or anyone I didn't want to be with her.

At least for a little while.

Well, other than the fact she thought I was a criminal.

I grinned to myself. I definitely couldn't let this one get away.

She was far too entertaining.

I didn't stop her, though. Instead, I turned and jogged off in the opposite direction.

five

Violet

Most of the chaos on campus was over. No one was really out. The sky was dark, and the air was colder than I expected. I'd been in the zone at the gallery, staying later than I planned to. I got lost in the drawing. It happened a lot.

I didn't regret it, though. Even if I was questioning my decision to walk home alone in the dark.

My footsteps echoed against the sidewalk, my paint splattered Adidas sneakers glowing in the dark. A noise behind me caused my chest to tighten. I spun around, looking down the sidewalk, but nothing was there.

Burying my hands a little deeper into the front pocket of the hoodie, I kept walking, ducking my head against the cold air. Crossing the street, I started down the next block and thought longingly of a hot shower.

The sound of an engine rumbling in the distance didn't make me turn around, even as it grew closer and closer. The muscles between my shoulder blades began to cramp when I realized the vehicle had slowed and wasn't passing me. Instead, it seemed to be following.

I resisted the urge to look, though my footsteps quickened. That car legit sounded like something out of some horror movie. The kind where some beater van snatched people off the street, took them to some cave in the side of a hill, and carved out their eyes.

I shivered.

The car suddenly got louder, the engine revved, and a white blur shot forward, passing me. Lifting my head, I watched it, thankful it decided to move on.

Only it didn't.

Instead of speeding by like I thought, it pulled to the curb just ahead.

Like it was waiting for me.

Well, this is a problem. I liked my eyes where they were.

The white paint was worn, and there was a spot of rust on the back. The tire hooked onto the back was old and dirty, and the brown top vibrated against the wind.

I hesitated, not sure if I should rush past or turn and make a run for the gallery and hope Abella was still there.

As I debated, this low sound filled the air. Sort of like a zipper being undone. I stared, horrified, at the Jeep as the passenger-side window fell in.

I stopped altogether and stared, wondering what the hell was happening.

A terribly loud cranking noise burst out, and the Jeep reversed, stopping right beside me. My hand grabbed the strap lying across my chest and squeezed. My other hand went down into the pocket on the front flap and delved in.

"Need a ride?" a familiar voice called from the interior.

I squinted, trying to see inside. There was no light to illuminate the driver.

Again, something that would be found in one of those B-rated horror flicks.

"I try not to make a habit of accepting rides from strangers," I yelled.

A laugh drifted over to me. I knew that laugh. It was the same one that came after I was accused of checking out his ass just moments before.

"Stark?" I called out.

"I thought we already established I wasn't a criminal."

The tension in my body drained away. Stepping closer to the Jeep, I looked in. There he was, sitting in the driver's seat, the white T-shirt glowing and the top of his head in the shadows.

"I'm pretty sure I said I wasn't ready to make that assumption." I reminded him.

I liked the sound of his laugh. There was something melodic about it. A sound that made me want to close my eyes and put it on repeat.

"C'mon. Get in. I'll drive you back to campus."

I hesitated. What did I know about this guy, really?

He was good looking.

He had a nice ass (yeah, I looked).

His laugh made my insides quiver.

His shoes might or might not be stolen.

Yeah... I was thinking that wasn't enough information to accept a ride from him. I could end up on the next episode of *48 Hours*.

The sound of an extremely squeaky door brought me back from my internal reasoning. I watched Stark jog around the back of the Wrangler and onto the sidewalk in front of me.

"C'mon, Vi. You either get in the car, or I'm going to follow you all the way back to campus."

He called me Vi.

A nickname that suggested familiarity. A nickname he probably picked to get me to trust him.

God. I was such a moron.

It was working.

"Do you have heat in that thing?" I asked, gesturing to his ride.

Straight, white teeth flashed. "I'm pretty sure it barely works."

I laughed.

"C'mon," he said softly, reaching out and palming my elbow. I stiffened, and he pulled back. The frown on his face was clear. "I can't let you walk home in the dark alone. I'm just not that kind of guy."

The second the words left his mouth, he drew back like they surprised him.

I couldn't help but laugh. "Really? You seem pretty shocked by that."

Stark lifted the hat off his head and rubbed his palm all over the messy strands of dark hair crowding his head. "It's been a weird night."

When I didn't say anything, he glanced over at me. "You coming or what?"

He was impatient. Almost as if he couldn't believe I was still standing there and not jumping his bones.

In the front pocket of my bag, my hand curled around something, and I pulled it free. "Okay, yeah." I held up the bracelet that appeared to be made out of ancient telephone cord. It had a black whistle dangling off it. "But I'm warning you now. I have my rape whistle."

He blinked, glancing between me and the whistle I was holding up. "What the fuck is a rape whistle?"

"Guys have it so easy," I muttered.

That confused him even more.

"You know," I explained. "When girls enroll at college, we're all given rape whistles… you know, in case."

"Rape is that bad here?" He glanced down the street toward campus.

"I thought you went here?" I questioned.

"I do," he said, looking back at me. Then he screwed up his face. "How the fuck is a whistle going to save you if some scumbag is trying to rape you?"

I shrugged. "Beats me." A thought crossed my mind, and I placed the whistle between my lips and let it dangle. "Want to find out?" I smiled.

Horror stole his handsome features. He shot forward and snatched it out of my mouth. "Hell no! The last thing I need is someone thinking I tried to rape a woman!" His eyes roamed the street as if he were terrified someone might see.

Okay, so maybe it was a bad joke. I stepped closer, laying a hand on his arm. "Sorry. My sense of humor can be a little… off at times."

He glanced down to where my hand touched his arm, then back up at me. I wished the hat wasn't shading his face so much. I wanted to know the color of his eyes. I wanted to see if he was feeling the pulse of electricity where we touched like I was.

I could see his jaw, though. I was pretty convinced it could cut through steel.

"It's cool," he said and held up the whistle for me to take.

I took it and shoved it into my pocket.

"A rape whistle," he muttered, shaking his head.

"I thought everyone knew the girls were all given one." I wondered out loud as I followed him to the Jeep.

"Yeah, well, I thought men knew what the word no meant."

The silence between us was filled by the squeaking of the passenger-side door as he opened it up. I glanced into the Jeep warily. It was pretty basic. Noisy. And the corner of the brown ragtop was fraying.

I loved it.

Whatever hesitation I had known about accepting a ride from someone I just met was no longer an issue. Maybe it was the fact that he was offended when he realized women had to carry around whistles for protection.

Or maybe it was the fact he was gorgeous.

Like seriously gorgeous. I couldn't believe I hadn't seen him around campus before. A guy like him was definitely not one that would ever be missed.

"I'll just, ah..." he said awkward, fumbling with the window he'd unzipped to yell out to me. "Get this for you." It was almost as if he didn't know how to zip up his own window.

It was sort of charming.

BUTTERFLY

Better watch it, Violet, I told myself. *Guys like him aren't the dating type. At least not for girls like you. They're the love 'em and leave 'em type. Life's hard enough without adding that in the mix.*

The self-imposed warning had me sinking back against the vinyl seat. Maybe I should have taken my chances with the dark street.

Seemed accepting a ride from this stranger might be more dangerous.

Maybe I was a woman of danger. After all, my ass stayed firmly against the creaky vinyl. From my position inside, I watched his body flex and move beneath the white T-shirt as he held the window up and zipped it closed. He smelled good, like some pricey cologne. A scent that, after just one whiff, would forever remind me of him. Of this moment. It wasn't even that particularly memorable, yet here I was declaring in my brain that it would be there forever.

His dark hair was overly long and it stuck out from beneath the edges of the hat, the ends teased by the wind. When he was done, he slammed the door (making it quiver), then jogged around to hop in the driver's seat.

It was then that I realized I was sitting on something.

Delving my hand beneath me, I pulled out a roll of duct tape. I held it out between us, and Stark grinned. "Hold on to that for me, eh?"

I slid it over my hand and onto my wrist like a giant bracelet.

The Jeep made a groaning sound as he put it into drive and pulled away from the curb. It was loud in here, so loud I didn't bother speaking. If I did, I would have to yell. I couldn't help but notice the way he sort of lounged back in the seat. He made it look a lot more comfortable than I knew it actually was.

His body had this sort of... grace about it. Maybe it was confidence. Whatever it was, it acted like a magnet for my eye.

He caught me glancing at him, and a slow smile tugged at the corner of his lips. His hand shot out, and for a moment, I tensed, thinking he was reaching for me, but he wasn't. The palm of his hand hit the tall stick shift in the center and his fingers wrapped around the top.

I looked away, out the cloudy plastic window and toward the sidewalk. At least it was a short drive back to campus.

Seconds later, the Jeep began lurching, making a sound I was pretty sure cars didn't make, and then stuttered violently before shutting off completely. I felt my eyes round, and I glanced across the seat at Stark. "I don't think that's supposed to happen."

"Fuck," he muttered and steered it to the curb and threw the emergency break.

I hoped it worked. Nothing else seemed to.

Stark pulled the hat off his head and dropped it in his lap, running both his hands through his hair. When he looked at me, I was momentarily dumbstruck by the mess on his head and how perfectly he pulled it off.

"Stay here," he ordered and catapulted out of the interior.

I watched through the windshield as he popped the hood and smoke came floating out. I giggled. I didn't think it was very loud, but the next thing I knew, he was leaning around the open hood and glaring at me.

Pressing my lips together, I gave him a little wave.

A few moments later, he was knocking on the plastic window. I decided it was easier to just open the door rather than fight with the zipper. I cracked it open a little.

"Yes?" I asked.

"I need the tape."

I burst out laughing. "This I gotta see."

Bringing the tape, I met him at the engine. I could feel the heat radiating off the still-warm parts. "I'm pretty sure there's more tape in there than actual parts." I observed.

"No shit," he muttered. He leaned close to the dirty insides and spoke. "I think this is the problem."

I squinted, but it was dark. Reaching into my pocket, I grabbed my phone and called up the flashlight. It clicked on, illuminating everything with bright light.

"It looks even worse now," Stark cracked.

I grimaced. "I can walk the rest of the way."

"No," he growled and leaned back down to whatever it was he saw. Like a doctor in the OR, he held out his hand between us. "Tape."

Sliding the roll off my wrist, I slapped it into his palm.

I pointed the light while he applied. When he was done, his fingers were greasy and so was the roll of tape. "That should do it," he said, pulling back and dropping the hood.

After climbing back inside, he grabbed the key and glanced at me.

I crossed my fingers and made a face.

His chuckle was drowned out by the sudden rumbling of the engine.

I clapped. "I gotta tell you," I said. "You sure know how to use some tape."

"Stick with me, kid," he cracked and pulled back onto the street.

When my building came into view, I pointed to the street he needed to take. Then I pointed to the tall building up ahead. Stark pulled up in front of it, leaving the engine to idle. "I'm not gonna turn her off. She might not turn back on."

"Probably smart." I agreed.

We lapsed into an awkward silence, so I cleared my throat and reached for the door handle. "Well, thanks for not murdering me."

"It was the least I could do."

I climbed out of the ride. As I moved to shut the door, I leaned back in. "Hope you make it home."

His grin was fast. "Me, too."

My stomach dipped a little. Without another word, I slammed the door (there really was no other way to shut the thing) and gave him a little wave before rushing toward my building.

He didn't drive away until I was inside, and as I walked down the hall to my room, I couldn't help but wonder if that was the first and last time I would ever see him.

 Six

Ten

"Your plane is leaving in an hour," Becca said into my ear.

I jolted up from the mattress, the blankets falling to my waist. "What the hell, Becca? You couldn't have given me more warning?"

"You won't be on it." She finished as if I hadn't even been talking.

"What?" I asked, confused.

"You don't have anything scheduled. All your talks and interviews have gone well. It's time to move into phase two of your comeback."

There was a phase two?

"Which is?" I muttered, falling back against my pillows and rubbing a hand over my sleepy eyes.

"Lying low. Working on new music. Comebacks take a lot of preparation. Have you thought at all about the sound you want for your next album?"

"I wasn't even sure there was going to be a next album," I muttered.

Becca laughed. "Come on now. *Perfect Ten* sat on the charts for nearly a year after it released. Your last music video has well over a billion views online. You were the highest grossing artist last year. Did you really think there wasn't going to be another album?"

"I'm literally referred to in the media as Public Enemy Number One." I reminded her.

"I'm thinking that will be a great title for your next album."

"No one's going to work with me."

She laughed again. "Are you kidding? The label is already blocking out studio time, and I've got a few artists who want to collab."

"Who?" I asked, my interest piqued.

"Vein." She dropped the name instantly.

My eyes shot open. Vein was a DJ, and all the collabs he did soared right to number one.

"No way he wants to work with me."

"Did you forget, before all this drama, you were number one for a reason? You're talented. That much is obvious. But people like you, Ten. You had a good reputation with those in the industry."

"We both know the industry is fickle. Everyone turns on you at the drop of a dime." I sighed. I felt like rolling over and going back to sleep. "They only like you when you can do something for them."

"Yeah, well, there are some people who have longer memories than others. And those people are still supporting you. Besides, it's good business. Anything your name is attached to is going to be a chart topper."

I knew she was right. Like I said before, people liked drama, and they were all curious as hell. They would download my next song if only to criticize it.

When I didn't say anything, she cleared her throat. "I thought you were onboard with the comeback. Don't you want to be back on top again?"

"You know I do," I said. Music was my life. I wasn't sure who I'd be without it.

"Then let me do my job," Becca implored. "By the time your new material is ready to launch, everything that happened last year will be forgotten."

"Fine." I agreed. She knew what she was doing. Hell, she was the one who helped me get to number one to begin with. "What do you want me to do?"

"Lie low," she repeated. "I think staying in upstate New York is a good call. No one knows you have family here."

"But everyone knows I was here last night."

"Yes, which is why your plane leaving out of there and flying back to LA is going to be a headline."

The plane that I wouldn't be on. "A fakeout," I mused. A smile curved my lips. "I like it."

"Exactly. Everyone will think you're in California. No one will expect you to be where you are."

I liked that idea. For more than one reason.

"I'll do it." I agreed without any hesitation.

Becca paused. "That was way easier than I thought it would be." Another pause. "What happened?"

I rolled my eyes. "Nothing."

"Ten…" She warned.

"Nothing!" I yelled into the phone. Shit! She was like a damn pit bull with a steak. "I'm just glad for the break."

"Your uncle won't mind if you stay longer?"

"Nah, he won't care."

"Good. Well, I'm heading back out to LA. I'll work on things from there. Stay out of the spotlight. Out of the media. *Behave.* I can only do so much damage control."

"Okay," I said, ready to hang up.

"And, Ten?" Becca called as I pulled the cell away from my ear.

"What?" I grumped.

"No drinking."

I made a sound and disconnected the call. Damn, she was worse than my mother.

Nate pushed open the bedroom door and came in wearing nothing but a pair of boxer briefs. He was carrying a huge bowl of cereal and shoveling it into his mouth as he walked. "Oh, good, you're up."

"Don't you knock?"

"This is my room," he said, crunching the cereal. He sat down on his bed, which was on the other side of the room from mine. "Who was on the phone?" he asked, heaping another spoonful into his trap.

"Dude," I said, staring at him. "That was an impressive bite."

He grinned, revealing a row of teeth cluttered with chewed-up cereal in a rainbow of colors. "Thanks."

Fruity Pebbles. It was a fave of mine, too. "You pour the whole box in your bowl?" I asked.

"Of course."

I lay back but threw my middle finger up in the air at his reply.

"There's another box."

My gesture turned into a fist pump.

"So?" He reminded me.

I dropped my hand on my stomach. "Becca."

He grunted. "You leaving today?"

I propped myself up on one elbow. "Actually, I think I'm going to stay a while."

"Sweet. It'll be just like old times."

Nate and I used to be inseparable during the summers. Growing up, we'd been more like brothers than cousins. Even though Mom and I lived in the city and he'd grown up here, this place had always felt like a second home.

And since Mom had moved several times since I became famous, I had to admit this place now felt more like home than anywhere else. Even if it had been practically a decade since I stayed here.

"Think Uncle Derek will mind?" I asked.

Nate lifted the bowl to his mouth and began slurping the milk out of the bottom. When he was done, he lowered it, wiped his lips with the back of his hand, and burped. "Long as you don't out him as the media's favorite whipping boy's uncle, he'll be cool."

Sometimes I was still surprised people here had forgotten all the time I spent bicycling around this town when I was a kid. 'Course, that was years and years ago... Well, before I was even a blip on the music industry's radar. Plus, there was the added fact that this was a college town. People came and went all the time. It was easy to forget a face when so many weren't permanent.

"Wait a minute," Nate said, glancing across the room. "You didn't embarrass him last night, did you?"

I made a sound. "If I did, don't you think he'd be in here reading me the riot act already?"

Derek was the head of the music department at Blaylock University. It was a position he'd worked his way up to in the last ten years. My mom always said I got my love of music from him. She was right. Hell, if it weren't for all the summers I spent here, I never would have picked up an instrument or been exposed to much music.

When Becca called to see if he could get me in for a publicized lecture in his department, he'd agreed on the condition we not tell anyone he was my uncle.

He had his reasons:

1. It would look like he was giving me special treatment because we were family.

2. He liked his anonymity and the peace of not being hounded by the press.

3. He didn't want Nate subjected to the—and I quote—"corruption in the music industry"—aka: he didn't want Nate to be a fuck-up like me.

And…

4. He was embarrassed of me.

I told myself his lengthy list of reasons was understandable. I told myself it didn't bother me I was an embarrassment to the closest thing to a father I'd ever had.

"True dat." Nate agreed, setting the bowl on his nightstand and going to his closet to get some clothes. "How long you staying for?" he yelled.

"Not sure," I called back.

He came back out wearing a pair of jeans, but they weren't buttoned or zipped up. Nate was a little bigger than me even though I was almost a year older. He was taller, broader. I wasn't a small guy, but I wasn't that big either. What I lacked in size, my face made up for.

I had the perfect amount of baby face and sex appeal. It was one of the reasons I became so popular. I looked good on a poster, and all the girls liked to pretend I was singing to them when I crooned about love.

The clothes in his arms were dumped on his bed before he snatched up an old Blink-182 T-shirt and pulled it on over his head. "I have classes now. But maybe later we can hang?"

His mention of classes over on campus made me think of Violet. When Becca mentioned she was surprised I agreed to stay here so readily, the image of her sitting in my Wrangler last night, giggling over the fact I had to tape it back together to get home, flashed into my brain.

I wondered what my manager would say if I told her I'd been hanging out with a local, one who didn't even realize who I was.

She probably wouldn't believe me. Hell, even *I* wasn't convinced she wasn't pretending not to know me.

You know she didn't, I told myself. *That girl was totally clueless.*

And she hated you. Well, Ten.

Something large and semi-hard whacked me in the face and bounced off into my lap. "What the fuck?" I said, reacting after the fact. My hand fell onto the big pillow Nate had just thrown at me.

"Earth to Ten! Are your ears broke?"

I snatched up the pillow and whipped it back at him. It hit him in the center of the chest. "Asshole," I muttered.

Nate tossed the pillow down and pulled a wine-colored BU hoodie over his head.

"Hey, you know a lot of people on campus?" I asked, curious.

He shrugged. "Some."

"Girls?" My voice was skeptical.

"Are you kidding?" He scoffed and gestured to himself. "Chicks dig this."

I lifted one eyebrow. "You have a girlfriend?"

He blanched. "I like to keep my options open."

Nate strolled over to the mirror above his dresser and glanced at himself, adjusting one of the strings on the hoodie that was stuck in the neck. Then he took his hand and plowed it through his dark-red hair.

"You know anyone named Violet?" I asked, trying to not seem too interested.

He grabbed his backpack off the floor and slung it over one shoulder, then looked around to me. "Don't think so. She go to BU?"

I nodded. "I, uh, met her last night."

A large smile bloomed over Nate's face. "Was it love at first sight?" he asked, pretending to swoon.

What a dick. But I laughed anyway because he was funny. "More like hate at first sight."

"Tell me more," he invited.

I smiled and told him how I hid out in the art gallery and found her sitting there. "She was drawing some kind of cartoon strip that was totally making fun of me."

"Ooh. Burn!" Nate laughed.

"I gave her a ride home in the time machine."

Nate came over and offered me his fist. I smashed mine against his. "Mad props to ya, bro. You're the only guy I know that can find a girl making fun of him, then charm her into your car."

I shrugged like it was a given. But then I confessed. "Actually, she didn't know who I was."

Nate guffawed, then made a face. "You mean to tell me she didn't recognize you? Even as she sat there and drew your face?"

"Actually, the comic wasn't *of* me. It was just about me. Kind of a satire of everyone who was falling over themselves to see me last night."

Nate shook his head and made a sound. "Uh-huh. No way. She was playing you."

I shook my head, adamant. "She wasn't. I'd have known."

Nate wagged his eyes. "Was she hot?"

"Not bad," I replied, thinking of her blond hair, blue eyes, and imperfect skin. "Not my usual type."

"I thought your type was two legs and boobs."

I flashed a smile. "No, that's *your* type."

Nate spread his arms wide. "I don't discriminate. *All* aboard the Nate train." He gestured like he was tugging a whistle. "Woot! Woot!"

"That shit is why you're single," I deadpanned.

He cackled and headed toward the door. "I missed you, man. I forgot how much."

I swallowed, my throat suddenly kinda thick. "Hey, so can you find out about her?"

He stopped abruptly and turned around. "Find out about the only girl on campus who isn't obsessed with you? Shouldn't be too hard."

"I owe you one," I said and then told him what building I dropped her off at. "Oh, and she's an art major!" I called out as he left.

When he was gone, I flopped back down in the sheets and smiled up at the ceiling.

seven

Violet

Getting out of bed in the morning was a special task.

An unpleasant one.

The second consciousness came over me, no matter how deep I was still in sleep's clutches, I would internally groan. I was not a morning person, and I likely never would be.

I rolled onto my back, keeping the covers pulled up around me, and sighed. Slowly, I would begin to move my hands and fingers, flexing them in and out as they protested. Then I would rotate my feet and ankles around, wiggle my toes.

I didn't want to get up, but wallowing in bed all day just wasn't an option. I had classes and a life.

I slipped out of bed. The first brush of the morning air caused goose bumps to rise along my bare legs and

BUTTERFLY

arms. I shivered a little and reached for the oversized sweater lying across the foot of my bed.

Before tucking it around me, I felt the boxers and tank I was dressed in, making sure they weren't damp with sweat. They weren't, something I was grateful for. Night sweats weren't fun. Waking up with perspiration beading your skin, dampening your shorts and panties, and slicking your arms was not pleasant.

Usually, I would throw the covers off and let the night air dry my skin. Sometimes, when I was too wet, I'd get up, peel off the pajamas, and put on new ones before climbing back into bed, on the opposite side, where the sheets weren't damp.

I'd go from hot as hell and sweating to shivering with goose bumps because it was like my body had no idea how to regulate itself.

I didn't wake up like that every night, but it was at least a weekly occurrence. Familiar enough that when I woke and wasn't uncomfortably damp, I was grateful.

Once the sweater was around me, I walked across the room toward the bathroom. My ankles groaned and ached as I went. Glancing down, I noted how swollen my toes were and how pink they were around the nails.

I was swollen enough that it was noticeable, that walking wasn't as easy for me as it was for most people who'd just had a full night's rest.

In the bathroom, I did my business and washed my hands with cold water, taking note of my swollen fingers. They were stiff and didn't want to move the way I wanted them to.

Shuffling out, I headed toward the tiny kitchenette in the corner and dropped a pod into my coffee maker. As it brewed, I leaned against the small section of counter and thanked God I didn't have a roommate.

Coming to Blaylock had always been something I wanted. Living on campus didn't even seem as if it would be terrible, but having a roommate?

Not my thing.

So much not my thing that it actually began to put a damper on me wanting to come at all. Until my parents found out about a dorm hall that was filled with single-occupant rooms. A building that, of course, everyone wanted to live in. The extra cost didn't seem to matter.

There was a waitlist about a mile long, and the rooms didn't become available very often because the students who managed to get one often kept them their entire time at Blaylock.

My parents weren't deterred. They made some calls to the housing department and pulled a bunch of strings. One of the strings being my medical condition. It was something I *hated* to use to my advantage, because it wasn't an advantage. And because I despised people's pity. I didn't want to be defined by the fact my body hated me.

However, I wanted a solo room.

Having RA tipped the scales in my favor. When I started BU, I started with my own dorm room, which was more like a studio apartment.

The coffee finished pouring into my mug, and I grabbed some creamer out of the mini fridge and added a small amount. I took the coffee back over to bed and sat down. My loud sigh of relief filled the small space. It was nice to sit down.

I didn't have a TV in here. Even if I did, I probably wouldn't have turned it on. I didn't like the news. It was depressing and too real for me. Instead, I unhooked my phone from the charger and scrolled through Picgram as I let the caffeine chase away some of the fog in my head.

I languished as long as I could, then forced myself up. The swelling in my extremities wasn't as bad now. My fingers and toes moved easier than when I first woke up. It would take a little bit longer for them to go back down to normal, but just knowing they would made the process a lot less annoying.

After I rinsed out my coffee cup, I grabbed the little magic blender I used every day and stuffed a bunch of healthy crap into the plastic tumbler it came with before screwing on the blade. The loud whirring of the motor filled the space, and I stuck one finger in my ear to help block out the sound.

Once it was done, I carried the green smoothie into the bathroom, drinking it down and wrinkling my nose. I wasn't very good at making green smoothies. Actually, I was the worst at it. Or maybe it was just the fact I shoved in a bunch of "good for you" ingredients meant to help reduce inflammation in the body and others to help strengthen joints.

The result was still the same. Barely tolerable breakfast.

Yet here I was, choking it down. Every single morning.

Hey, at least I had coffee—my first love.

I wasn't even sure this green sludge did anything, but I'd do it because, if it helped even just a little with making me feel better on a daily basis, it was worth it.

Well, most days I thought it was worth it. Other days, I dreamed about coffee rolls, donuts, and stacks of waffles drowning in syrup.

But I didn't eat gluten.

Another no-no in the world of inflammation.

Not eating gluten (a.k.a. good stuff) actually did make a difference in my body and the way I felt. It was a lot easier to determine than the smoothies. About six months after I gave it up, I broke down and ate a chocolate cupcake. It had been soo good. Until my stomach got all bloated, and I woke up the next day with swollen hands—more swollen than usual—and a day filled with joint pain.

The water was nice and steamy in the shower, but I didn't linger. Once I was out and towel-dried, I pulled my hair down from the top of my head and brushed it out. It was long, dark blond, and thick.

After I smoothed on my face creams and downed more of the shake, I went in search of clothes. I wasn't a fan of getting dressed in the morning either.

Clothes felt restrictive. Not in the way like I wanted to join a nudist colony (ew, gross) and walk around with it all flopping everywhere, but I always seemed to feel uncomfortable.

I wasn't the thinnest of girls. In fact, I was outright chubby, overweight for my height. It sucked being a short girl, but not just because I couldn't reach stuff on the shelf at the grocery store. Every single pound on my body looked like two because there wasn't enough room for it all to stretch out.

I didn't have long legs, a long waist, or graceful limbs.

I had boobs, hips, and a butt. My arms were too round for my liking, and I never wore sleeveless tops because of them. My stomach wasn't flat, and the tops of my thighs rubbed together when I walked.

My body wasn't terrible; it had an hourglass shape, but I definitely could stand to lose like fifteen pounds.

And yeah, I'd tried. Tirelessly.

Remember when I said my body hated me? I wasn't lying.

It didn't matter how many healthy green shakes I drank, how many vegetables I consumed, or how many miles I walked a day, my weight clung to my bones like dog fur on a pair of black pants.

Somedays I accepted the fact I wouldn't ever look like a model, and I told myself it didn't matter. I wasn't defined by the size of my waist. It didn't matter I always wore some type of sweater or shirt that hid my upper arms.

I was still pretty, even if I wasn't the girl that got looked at first when she walked around campus.

Then there were the bad days. Those were the days I hated my body and myself. The days I would ask myself why I didn't try harder, why life was unfair, and why everything was such a freaking battle. And you know, the other usual thoughts of "why can't I look like her" as I stared at actresses.

I always regressed to the middle, a place I was usually comfortable. I knew the handful of medicines I swallowed every day made it hard to lose weight. I knew the limitations of my body restricted how hard I could exercise. I did everything possible to make sure I was healthy. It was just that my version of healthy didn't look like an underwear model.

I could still dress cute and be comfortable. I liked leggings and fabrics with some give because when my body swelled up a little or I became overwhelmingly tired, I didn't feel so constricted. I'd learned over the last year that being comfortable went a long way in making sure my attitude stayed positive.

Still, my battle with my wardrobe and the mirror waged almost daily.

Today I chose a pair of army-green leggings, the waistband coming up to the bottom of my bra. Seriously. Short girl problems. Clearly, the extra padding I carried around didn't negate the fact that I was a small person.

It was sort of an oxymoron. Small yet large? My life, folks. Every single day.

Anyway, after I tugged on the leggings and made sure the lace band of my bra was neatly tucked under the waist (bonus—it was kind of like wearing Spanx!) I pulled on a super-soft white tank top and a black T-shirt that looked like a tiger ripped part of it to shreds. Bits of white showed through the black fabric, and the neckline was ripped, which I thought was an interesting detail.

Next, I pulled on some low-cut socks and a pair of Adidas sneakers—of which I had several. Today's weren't the paint splattered ones. They were the traditional white ones with black stripes on the side.

After glancing at the clock, I quickly chugged the rest of the sludge, brushed my teeth, and pulled my hair back into a messy bun at the nape of my neck.

I didn't bother with makeup on a daily basis, even though I knew I would look better if I did. My skin had a lot of redness in it, and acne had a tendency to party on my face (without an invite, no less!). Not to mention I was quite pale, so the dark circles beneath my eyes always looked worse.

In short, I was a girl who would benefit from a concealer wand, some powder, and lip-gloss.

I didn't have time for that, not when I was trying to conserve my energy for walking around campus, going to classes, and drawing.

My hands got tired very easily. Actually, they were always tired. You know that feeling you get when you go to the gym and work out? Say it's leg day or arm day. You work until the muscles are spent. They quiver with exhaustion and feel like Jell-O, which makes walking or moving a little more difficult.

That's what I felt like every single day. In my shoulders, hands, knees, ankles… basically any joint on any given day. Sometimes all of them at once. Except I didn't get the rocking muscle definition because I hadn't been lifting weights.

Oftentimes, it became a choice. Doing my hair (seriously, holding a blow-dryer was not fun), my makeup… or art.

I'm guessing you know which one always won.

Besides, not only was art my true passion, but it was my job. I got paid for it.

In the grand scheme of things, it didn't seem so important that my zits might be out to party or that my face and cheeks always looked pink. Sure, I saw people look. Especially when my neck broke out. Ever have a deep cystic pimple on your neck? Be thankful if the answer is no. I looked like a leopard, and not a cute one. Thankfully, my hair could be worn down to cover it up.

It bothered me sometimes. Actually, more than I wish it did. At the same time, I knew I couldn't apologize for who I was and what I looked like. I did everything humanly possible to treat my RA and all the symptoms and side effects of it.

Such was life, right? I was lucky I could get lost in art and not think about it all for a while.

After slipping on a black, chunky-knit cardigan I went into the kitchen, grabbed my pill holder, and dumped the contents for today into my palm. After picking out the two huge horse pills and setting them aside, I shoved everything else in at once and downed it all with some water. Once those were down, I did the same with the remaining pills.

A minute later, I was out the door and walking out of the building on my way to my first class of the day.

So far, I was off to a good start. I was only marginally tired, and the only protest in my body as I walked was in my knees.

All signs pointed to it being a good day.

eight

Ten

What does one do with himself when he's lying low?

There were no expensive cars to take for a drive, no basketball court to play on, no pool, no gaming system.

Nothing but time to fill. Alone.

Nate was at class. Derek was at work.

After I ate an entire box of Fruity Pebbles, I got on my phone and quickly realized what a huge fucking mistake that was. People online were jerkbags. Everywhere I went was a negative headline about me, negative comments or predictions that the comeback everyone suspected was in the works would be an epic fail.

Pissed as fuck, I threw my phone across the room. Luckily, it landed on Nate's bed so it didn't shatter. I sort of wished it had. People had no idea the kind of pressure I was always under, the kind of life a person had when the spotlight was constantly shining on them.

Everyone made mistakes. But not everyone's were broadcast for the world to see.

Not everyone peed on an arena of fans either.

Or toilet-papered their neighbors house, a neighbor who happened to be a famous talk show host.

Or got arrested for a DUI.

Whatever.

Leaving my phone where it landed, I stalked across the room to the guitar Nate had leaning up against the side of his dresser. Sitting on the edge of the bed, I balanced it in my arms and struck a few chords.

After a few moments of fiddling, I began playing a tune I'd had in my head for a few weeks now, adding a few notes here and there as I played.

It had been a while since it was just me and a guitar. I didn't realize I missed it so much.

I sang a few lines, adjusted them, sang again. I had no idea what I was singing about yet or even if any of it made sense. I didn't usually write my own songs. Actually, I never had. Becca always went with writers, and I never really cared.

But maybe I cared now.

After finishing a few chords, I placed my hand over the guitar strings to silence the music. Loud clapping filled in where the music fell away.

I glanced up, surprised.

Nate was standing in the doorway, clapping his hands in the air. "You make me so proud, man," he said like a bad soap opera actor.

I laughed and set aside the guitar. "How long you been standing there?"

He wiped a fake tear from his eye and sniffled. "Long enough to know I'm in love with you."

I put a hand over my heart and stood. "Bro, I've been in love with you all my life."

We rushed at each other like we were about to hug it out. At the last minute, I shoved him away, and he fell onto the bed.

"But seriously," he said, sitting up as if we weren't just acting stupid. "That was pretty tight. I liked what you had going there."

"Yeah?" I asked, folding my arms over my chest. "I was just messing around. Had this melody stuck in my head the last couple weeks."

"How come you don't ever write your own stuff?"

I lifted a brow. "Who says I don't?"

Nate rolled his eyes. "Because if you did, your shit would be better."

My arms fell to my sides. "I'm not sure if that's a compliment or an insult."

Nate shoved up off the bed and went over to his. "It's just the truth. There's no denying you're one of the best. I'm just saying I think if you wrote some of your own lyrics, they would be better. They'd have more depth."

I cocked my head to the side. "Maybe I'm just not that deep."

Nate swung around. "You and I both know better." He turned back to his bed. "What the fuck is your phone on my bed for?"

I shrugged. "I missed you. I just wanted to remember the way you smelled."

Nate lifted his arm and came at me with his pit. "Here's an up close and personal whiff."

I shoved him back, laughing. "Put that shit away, man."

He cackled and pulled his hoodie off, tossing it on his bed. It was like we were nine and ten again, sharing a room and acting like idiots.

"I found your girl today," he announced.

All trace of reminiscing went out the window. "Violet?" I asked, my eyes sharpening on his face.

"I gotta tell ya. She's not what I was expecting."

Something warm and familiar filled my chest. "What the hell does that mean?" I growled. He'd better not insult her. Family or not, I'd kick his ass.

"It means she isn't a Victoria's Secret model."

"And?" I pressed.

Nate snorted. "And all you date are actresses and models."

I crossed my arms over my chest and glowered. "Are you implying Violet isn't pretty?"

Nate sat up abruptly. "Hell no! I think she's hot."

Now why did that answer only piss me off more?

"Did you talk to her?" I asked. I was hungry. Hungry for all info he had.

Nate scoffed. "Of course."

"Well!" I barked. "What did you find out?"

"Nothing."

I muttered a curse and paced away from him. "If you didn't find out anything, then what the hell did you talk to her about? The weather?"

His voice was smug when he answered. "I invited her aboard the Nate train."

Like hell he did! I spun. "You asked her out?"

Maybe he didn't notice the deadly quiet quality with which I snarled the question. He was too busy acting like he was the bomb.

"Sure did." Nate agreed. "She totally said yes."

I made a sound.

His eyes widened.

I rushed him.

nine

Violet

Remember how I said all signs pointed to it being a good day?

I'm thinking that thought was a little presumptuous. Or a lot.

Art history was interesting, as always, but the rest of my classes seemed to go on and on endlessly. In Drawing 204, my very eccentric professor announced a new project we'd be working on.

He wasn't eccentric because he often wore red pants with a patterned button-up shirt that didn't match. Or that those non-matching bottoms were always two inches too short, and instead of buying new pants, he just wore thick, white crew socks that he pulled up to cover his legs where the pants didn't.

Sometimes to top off his outfit extraordinaire, he wore a brown leather vest.

I didn't get it. I didn't think I ever would.

But his bad fashion choices weren't what made him eccentric. It was his teaching method. The art department would probably just say he was a creative thinker, a man who was a good example of outside-the-box thinking for art majors. He was good at art, he knew the ins and outs of drawing, and sometimes he would say something that really made something click inside me.

Most of the time?

Most of the time, I sat there cringing, hoping he wouldn't turn his artful wrath on me.

He was passionate. For him, that passion translated into yelling. I spent ninety minutes, twice a week, in a studio with about fifteen other students listening to him yell almost constantly. Except of course when we were all to be silently creating, a time he walked around and pointed out all the flaws in our work.

I wasn't sure if I preferred the yelling or the criticism.

Anyway, I noticed as the semester went on, I would always get a stomach ache before his class. A bit of anxiety would twist up my insides, and I would dread the one class I had looked forward to most when I made my schedule for the fall semester.

Aside from his habit of yelling, scolding, and unique teaching methods, he gave me the creeps. Like the actual heebie-jeebies.

It was a real thing because I felt it twice a week.

Artists were sensitive to the energy around them. Of that I was acutely aware, and his energy smelled. Bad.

Anyway, this new drawing lesson he announced? It made me want to drop the class.

Seriously.

Also? I was now legitimately thinking the dude was an old pervert.

We were going to be learning more about drawing the human form. Shade and light, contour, etc. So for this unit, we would have a model, one who would come in and pose for the entire ninety-minute session. The students would come prepared to work the entire time, and each of us would draw said model.

The caveat?

The model was going to be naked.

Butt-ass naked.

Look, I was an artist. Creativity was my jam. But looking at some girl's naked cooter for ninety minutes and trying to draw it?

Ew.

I had so many questions about this:

1. Was this model in that much need of money that she would stand on a podium, naked, for people to stare at her?

2. Did the professor post an ad for this? *Old teacher seeking naked model. References needed.*

3. As a naked model did you shave? Let it grow?

—This is a legitimate thought. I mean lady-scaping, or man-scaping, was a real thing.

4. Did the university okay this?

5. *Why* did the university okay this?

Of course, I didn't ask any of these questions in class because if I had, I would have gotten shouted at. I'd pass.

He already announced the model was a female. *Shocker.* Not that I was interested in seeing some dude's frank and beans dangling. I didn't want to try and draw *that.*

Obviously, as I trudged from the art buildings to my dorm room, I wasn't exactly present in the moment, instead focused inward on the cringe-worthy task I would have to undertake over the next few weeks. I was uncomfortable already.

This was why I didn't notice I was being followed.

Not until it was too late to go running in the opposite direction.

"Violet, hey," Ross said, stepping up beside me.

Giving him the side eye, I wondered if I could pretend I didn't hear him. He must have known what I was going to do (because I'd done it before), because he caught my wrist and held it.

I stopped walking and tugged it back. "Ross. Hey."

"I tried to call you last weekend," he said. "You didn't call me back."

"Yeah, uh, sorry about that," I said. "I wasn't feeling good, so I just stayed in."

A look crossed his eyes. "Still using that, huh?"

I bristled. "Yeah," I snapped. "I'm still telling the truth."

"Down, girl," he said, holding up his hands. "I was just kidding."

"Ha. Ha," I replied, sarcasm dripping from the words.

"So, hey," he reached out and tugged the front of my cardigan. "There's a party Friday night. It's at the Beta Phi house. It's going to be killer. I'll pick you up at eight?"

Did he seriously just insult me and then ask me out?

"You know that sounds, uh, pretty painful, actually. I think I'll pass."

Ross's already dark eyes darkened further. "Seriously?"

I nodded. "Yeah. Sorry. I can't."

"Why?"

"Because I don't want to," I snapped.

What was it with him? How many times did I have to turn him down for him to get a clue?

"This little game of playing hard to get is getting old," he intoned, stepping toward me. I didn't appreciate how he was trying to use the fact he was a foot taller as intimidation.

"I'm not playing. We had one date, Ross, and it was over a month ago. I think it's safe to say I'm not your type."

Translate that to: he's a moron with a big head and is an insensitive jerk-face.

"Of course you're my type." He gestured to me, as if that somehow proved his words. "C'mon, just come out with me. I'll make sure you have a good time."

I lifted an eyebrow and smirked. "You mean like the last time you made sure I had a good time?"

The good-natured, frat-boy attitude dropped, and what I knew was the real Ross appeared. He was already standing close, probably trying to make it look to those passing by that he was totally hitting on me and I was eating it up, but he moved in closer. His hand snatched up my arm, his fingers closing around my elbow.

"Let go." I warned.

"What are you implying, Violet?" he said low, his voice holding a note of warning.

"You know exactly," I spat and tried to pull away. I was done with this conversation. I was done with him.

He clearly thought otherwise and gave my arm a squeeze and pulled me back.

"Ow," I said. Pain radiated through my elbow and down my arm to my wrist. "Let go. You're hurting me."

"I'll see you Friday?" he asked, as if my agreement were the only way he would let me go.

"I'm not going to the party with you," I insisted, laid both my palms on his chest, and shoved.

His hand tightened before it released me, and I stumbled back. I stared up at him, breathing a little heavy, and reached out to cup my aching elbow.

"That didn't hurt." He scoffed, blowing off the way I cradled it.

Emotion swelled up in me. Embarrassment. Pain. Exhaustion.

"Hey, babe. Who's this?" said a voice close by. The next thing I knew, an arm was dropped over my shoulders and I was pulled gently into a side.

Startled, I glanced up, forgetting all about my elbow.

A guy I had never seen before smiled down at me, a little twinkle in his green eyes. Dark-red hair fell over his forehead.

Before I could open my mouth to ask him who the hell he was, Ross beat me to it. "What the hell is this?" he demanded.

"What's up, man? I'm Nate." Nate didn't offer a hand or anything. In fact, he just stood there, keeping his arm around my shoulders.

Ross glanced at me, his eyes angry. "You're dating someone?"

"Uh, no…" I stuttered. Nate squeezed my shoulder lightly, as if telling me to play along. "I mean, yes."

Ross crossed his arms over his chest. "Which is it? Yes or no?"

"It's new." Nate picked up the conversation. "First date is Friday. Going to a party."

Ross's eyes flared. "The Beta Phi party?"

"Yep, that's the one."

I wanted to stomp on Nate's foot. What the hell was this guy doing?

"This the reason you turned me down? You're cheating on me?" he roared.

"Babe, you told me you were single," Nate said, only mildly offended his date might have lied.

"I am," I intoned. Then I glanced at Ross. "I told you. I'm not interested. I went out with you. It sucked. I'm not doing it again."

Ross's face paled, then flushed red. He was pissed. It made me nervous, but this guy standing next to me gave me some extra courage. Besides, I was tired. Exhausted, actually. And I really wanted Ross to stop calling and texting. Clearly, this was the only way he would get the hint.

Ross made a sound, then turned his anger on Nate. "Good luck with this one, man. She's a real piece of work. Half the time, she's *too sick* to hang."

I bristled but decided it wasn't worth it. People like him were a dime a dozen. I didn't look sick; therefore, I was just a hypochondriac or lying.

"Maybe she's allergic to you," Nate offered.

A giggle bubbled up out of my throat.

"I'll tell you what." Ross reached into his back pocket and pulled out two twenty-dollar bills. He held them out in front of Nate. "You manage to get this chick to show up on your arm on Friday night, these twenties are yours. Not only that, but your cover to get in the door is on me."

"I'll take that deal." Nate agreed and held out his free hand for a fist bump.

Ross made an angry sound and knocked his fist away, then stalked off as though he were about to go steal some candy from a baby.

When he was gone, my shoulders sagged a little, and I pulled away from my rescuer.

"He just totally left me hanging," Nate said, glancing at his fist.

"He's a douche."

"You gonna leave me hanging, too?" He offered his fist. I touched mine against his. "Sweet."

"Who are you?"

"The guy you have a date with Friday night?" he said and grinned.

I rolled my eyes. "I'm not going out with you."

"What!" he exclaimed. "I just totally saved you back there."

"You did not save me," I muttered. "I was fine."

He gave a pointed glance at my elbow, which I was absentmindedly rubbing again.

I wasn't about to explain to him that my body was more tender than most. That certain touches, especially at my joints, were sometimes painful. He'd probably be just like Ross and several other men I'd tried to date in the past. Completely incapable of understanding.

"Thank you," I murmured. "Hopefully, he'll stop calling."

"He bother you a lot?" Nate asked, his voice turning serious for the first time since he stepped up to my side.

"Nah," I said, brushing him off. "He's just an asshole."

"An asshole who owes me forty bucks and cover to a frat party!" he said like he'd won the lottery.

"I'm not going out with you," I said again.

"A guy does a good deed, and look what happens…" He shook his head sadly.

I felt my lips twitch. "It's just forty bucks."

"I'm just a poor college boy." His mossy-green eyes widened, and I had to admit he was good at looking pathetic.

I shoved his shoulder and laughed. "Stop it."

"Aw, c'mon. How about it? It's just a party. I'll even pick you up and bring you home. I won't even expect a goodnight kiss."

"I'm not kissing you," I declared.

He smiled, sly. "But you'll go to the party?" I started to shake my head, but he hurried to say, "It will get that guy off your back, seeing you with me. He'll think you moved on."

I thought back to the last disastrous date I had with Ross and how much I would love if he fell off the face of the earth.

"She's considering it," Nate said. Some random stranger walked by, and Nate looked at them, pointing at me. "She's considering it!"

I laughed and grabbed his hand, pushing it down. "Fine. One party. Just long enough for you to get your forty bucks and to make Ross never want to call again."

Nate surged forward and caught me around the waist and lifted me off the ground for a quick, excited hug. "I'm rich!" he declared after I was back on my feet.

I shook my head, but couldn't stop the smile. "I'll see you Friday?" I asked. Maybe hanging out with him wouldn't be so bad.

For some reason, an image of Stark flashed into my mind. The way he looked partially concealed by the shadows in the driver's seat of his god-awful Jeep. And then again of the way he looked hunched over the engine with duct tape in his hands.

All of the sudden, going out with Nate seemed like a really bad idea.

"Eight o'clock," he answered.

"This is just as friends," I blurted, catching myself off guard. Then, to soften the harsh way I practically yelled it, I gentled my voice and said, "You know, to help each other."

Nate cocked his head to the side. "Ah, she's got her eye on someone else."

"No," I said, quick. Was it that obvious?

"Clearly, it's not that clump nugget." He thumbed in the direction Ross left. "And since you seem immune to my captivating charm, I'm thinking there's someone else."

"There's no one."

"But you want there to be." Nate gestured. "C'mon. Tell me his name."

I laughed. He was incorrigible. I liked him.

"Tell me your name?" he asked instead.

"Violet. So eight o'clock?" I told him. "Room ten. First floor." I pointed to my dorm.

He followed my finger, then pursed his lips. "Tell me who you had to kill to get a private dorm room."

I leaned in and whispered. "If I told you, then I'd have to kill you, too."

"Scandalous," he whispered back.

"See you Friday, Nate," I said, then backed away.

He waved, and I turned around. I shouldn't have let myself be talked into that party, but it was only for an hour or so. If it got me off Ross's radar, it would be worth it. Besides, Nate was pretty funny. He wouldn't be so bad to hang out with.

My thoughts drifted back to Stark. I'd looked for him today on campus. There hadn't been a trace of him in sight.

I couldn't help but wish it was him I'd be going out with on Friday.

the chapter

Ten (the person)

"You son of a bitch!" I growled as I collided with Nate and we both slammed up against the wall. Near his head, a picture rattled.

My forearms were pressed against his chest, all my body weight thrown into him. He was bigger, but I wasn't a wuss. My body was honed from all the dancing and performing I did during shows. I wasn't someone who couldn't hold his own.

"I'm kidding!" he choked out, breath whooshing from his chest.

The sudden anger I had subsided just enough to make me realize what the fuck I was doing. And also what he just said.

I shoved off him and forced my hands through my hair.

"What the fuck, Nate? You better be kidding."

"I am," he said, straightening his shirt. "Kinda."

I growled, and he held up his hands. "Down, boy!"

"Explain," I demanded.

"Shit, man," Nate swore. "Didn't know you take your ladies so seriously."

"I don't." I glared.

"Right," he said, clearly unconvinced.

I made an impatient sound, and Nate cleared his throat.

"I was sort of staking out her building. You know, hanging out, waiting to see if she'd show up."

"I didn't tell you to stalk her."

"Good thing I was," he said, not even bothered by the fact he was stalking. "'Cause some guy was hassling her, and—"

My shoulders tensed. "Wait. What?"

Nate nodded. "Some frat guy. Grabbed her a couple times."

I started to pace.

"Damn, Ten. I know you're a hothead, but cool down. She's fine."

"Just tell me what happened," I muttered, unable to "cool" down. Not until I knew she was okay. An image flashed into my mind of her sitting in the gallery against that giant ball, blond hair in her face.

"He asked her out. She said no, but he wasn't too happy about it."

It never even occurred to me that Violet might have a boyfriend. Or another guy in her life. The thought wasn't welcome. In fact, it made me jealous.

"So I pretended to be her date to the party. Gave her an excuse to give the goober the boot."

"So you only asked her out to get rid of the ass." I nodded. "Good call."

"Well, yeah, but then the dude bet me forty bucks and the cover for the party that I would show up with her."

I frowned. "Why would he do that?"

Nate shrugged. "'Cause she always made excuses to not go out with him."

Was this guy so hard up he had to badger her for a date? Why didn't he just accept the fact she wasn't interested?

"You told him to fuck off, right?"

Nate didn't say anything. My eyes narrowed, and he made a face.

"It's forty bucks, man."

I muttered some choice words beneath my breath. "I'm a fucking millionaire! If you needed cash, you should have asked me!"

Nate's jaw hardened. "I'm not taking your money."

"But you'll take my girl!" I burst out.

"She's your girl now?" Nate ribbed.

No, she wasn't. Not yet, anyway. But he couldn't have her. "I asked you to find out about her. For me. I didn't want you to fucking date her."

I sat on the bed, pissed at myself. Kinda pissed at her. Obviously, meeting me last night hadn't affected her at all. If it had, she wouldn't have so readily agreed to go out with my cousin. I had to admit it stung. Right there in the center of my chest. It was a feeling I didn't know very well, a feeling I didn't particularly like.

"It's just as friends, so I can win the bet and she can show up and get Ross off her back."

"Ross? That the guy who's giving her trouble?"

"I don't know if I'd call it trouble. She seems well equipped to handle that guy. That girl is a firecracker!"

I felt my cheeks rise with my grin. "Yeah." I agreed fondly. "She accused me of being a criminal."

Nate cackled. "I like her."

I stood up swiftly and stared him down.

He held up his hands. "Chill. You got dibs."

"Dibs? Are we in third grade?"

Nate smiled slow. I couldn't help it. I did the same. At the same time, we said, "Stacey Handler."

We'd both had a crush on her, but Nate always claimed dibs because he went to school with her, and I only saw her in the summer.

"Whatever happened to Stacey?" I mused.

"She married a marine and moved to California."

I smiled fast. "Guess neither of us got dibs."

"Look, bro. I was just trying to help her out. Didn't like seeing that guy hassle her. Then we got to talking... She's pretty cool. I figured if I kept our 'date,'" he said, using his fingers to put air quotes around the word, "then I could find out more about her."

"Where's the party?" I asked.

"Beta Phi."

"Lots of people gonna be there? Lots of booze?"

"It's a frat party," he said like it was a given.

"I'm coming with."

"Three's a crowd on a date, man."

I gave him a dry look. "You can stay home."

He appeared outraged. "I'm getting my forty bucks!"

I shook my head, bewildered. "I can't believe she agreed to go out with you." I think that bothered me more than anything.

She wasn't supposed to want anyone, not after she just met me.

I wasn't used to this. To actually having to work to see a girl. To get her to like me. If I was being myself right now (Ten), then I would already have won her over. Her counter would be filled with flowers, I'd have some expensive restaurant rented out, and I'd pick her up in my Lamborghini.

I couldn't be Ten, though. I had to be Stark. Stark, the guy who wasn't a pop star. The guy who wasn't hated by everyone, who was a broke college student and drove a piece-of-shit Jeep.

I had to win her over without any star power. Without any money. Without being the guy she clearly hated.

Why was I even bothering? All this work for some girl I spent less than an hour with.

A girl who doesn't know who or what you are. A girl who smiles at you anyway.

I mean, let's be serious here. How long could I realistically keep my identity from her? Not long.

I want to see her again.

"She told me it was just as friends," Nate said.

"What?" I asked, braking my thoughts.

Nate nodded. "She's totally into someone else. She made it clear."

"Who?" I demanded. Damn all these guys walking around on campus, tempting her.

"Wouldn't tell me. I'd be willing to bet my forty bucks it's you."

I couldn't keep the smile off my face. A thrill shot up my spine and danced around inside me. It could totally be me.

"I'm coming with you," I told Nate again.

It was a risk. There was major potential to out my own identity.

I was going to do it anyway.

I had a feeling she was a risk worth taking.

eleven

Violet

"I'll never forgive you," Vance announced into my ear.

I made a sound. "Can't you just write to his fan club and get one of those signed pictures of his face?" I half whined.

I forgot one very important detail when I defiantly stayed away from campus the night Ten was there. I hated when my brother was mad at me.

He made sound of distress. "Everyone knows those pictures don't even have his real signature on them."

I pulled back from the mirror, mascara wand paused in the air. "Really?"

He made a disgusted sound. "How do you even get through the day without me?" Even though Vance was a year younger, he was more like a big brother than a little one.

"Maybe if you were here, I wouldn't have gotten myself roped into a fake date in order to get Ross off my back," I muttered, leaning close to the mirror and making a strange face as I finished applying the mascara.

I figured if I had to go out, I might as well look nice.

"I told you to report him." Vance's voice went hard.

"I don't have the energy for Ross's drama."

"Well, now you have to have the energy for a date."

"A fake date." I corrected.

He made a tsking sound. "Girl, why can't it be a real date? Is he unfortunate-looking?"

I laughed. "No. He's actually kind of cute. He has red hair."

Vance gasped so loud my lip-gloss wand fell out of my hand and clattered into the sink. "A ginger! Girl, those are rare breeds!"

"He's not a horse." I admonished, fishing out the wand. "And it's dark red, not like carrot red." Was that still considered a ginger?

"So who's the guy?" Vance interrupted my inner ponderings.

"His name is Nate."

"Not the limited edition." His voice was impatient. "The other one."

"What other one?"

"Don't play games with me, V. I've known you all your life. There's another guy. And he must be good, so spill."

"He drove me home from the gallery the other night." I confessed.

My brother's interest was piqued. "He has a car?"

I laughed. "Sort of. It's being held together with duct tape."

"So what you're saying is he's hot as hell."

"He's not unfortunate-looking," I chimed, echoing his words.

His growl came through the speaker on my phone, and I grinned. I loved torturing my brother.

Abandoning my makeup bag, I leaned against the counter and sighed. "Dark hair, scruffy jawline, and broad shoulders."

"Name?"

"Stark."

"Sex on a stick."

"More like sex in a Jeep." I sighed.

My brother's laugh filled the bathroom. "You got it bad."

"I literally spent less than an hour with him."

"He ask for your number?"

"No." I pushed back and looked in the mirror. "I'm totally not his type."

"Don't make me drive up there and kick your ass." Vance threatened as if it were actually a threat. I'd love it if he came to visit. I couldn't wait for next year when he was enrolled.

"I'd date you. If you weren't my sister. And I wasn't gay."

I pressed a hand to my chest. "Oh, stop, you flatterer!"

"I just want you to know I'm giving you the finger right now."

"I have to get dressed," I said, picking up the phone and carrying it out into my room.

"Dark jeans, a low-cut top, and heels," he instructed.

I translated that into a T-shirt and sneakers.

"I'm serious, V. It might be a fake date, but you can still look good."

I made a sound. I was already tired. Going out was just not my thing. And I hadn't had time to eat, something that maybe wasn't that big of a deal, except for the fact I had to take my weekly meds on an empty stomach. *Not good.*

"Maybe you'll see him."

I glanced up from my dresser. I hadn't thought of that. Okay, fine. I had. That's why I put on makeup and left my hair down.

I said I was tired, not dead.

"Who?" I feigned, even as I stood there and imagined running into Stark at the party tonight.

There was a knock on the door. My head whipped up, and I made a sound.

"Oh my gosh!" I said. "He's here, and I'm not even dressed."

"Be safe and call me tomorrow!" Vance sang, then disconnected the call.

There was another knock. I rushed to the door and pulled it open just enough to stick my head out.

Nate grinned down at me. "I'm about to be forty bucks richer!"

I rolled my eyes. "Give me a minute?"

He nodded, and I shut the door in his face and raced back over to my dresser. I pulled out my favorite jeans (just because I preferred leggings didn't mean I disavowed jeans). They were mostly made of faded cotton and had a little stretch in the material. There were several rips in each leg. The one highest on the thigh had a silver glittery patch.

Once those were on, I yanked out a slouchy, dark-blue T-shirt with a glitter pocket on the left breast. As I shoved my feet into a pair of white Adidas with silver-studded toes, I jammed the front end of the T-shirt into my jeans, leaving the rest untucked.

If I didn't do it, then the shirt would hang down past the tops of my thighs and I'd look even shorter than I already was.

It was a casual outfit, but the glitter added something extra, right? Besides, who went to a frat party dressed like it was prom?

Before rushing out the door, I tucked my phone, dorm room key, ID, and a twenty into my back pocket.

Nate was lounging against the wall across from my door when I stepped out, tugging the door closed behind me. "Sorry," I said. "Thanks for waiting."

He pushed off the wall. "Looking good tonight, Violet."

"Thanks," I answered self-consciously.

Nate stepped up close to me, offering his elbow. "Shall we?"

A light laugh fell from my lips as I hooked my arm in his. "Lead the way.

"So, hey, what are you studying?" I asked as we made our way down the hallway toward the doors.

"Music. What about you?"

"Art."

At the door, Nate went ahead and held it open for me. The night air was cold, and instantly, I regretted not grabbing a jacket. "Did you drive?" I inquired. If we were walking, I was totally running back inside for something.

"*I* didn't," he answered, and it sounded a whole heck of a lot like it wasn't as simple as that.

"But?"

"You know how you said this date was just as friends?"

I felt like my stomach got kicked in. I mean, really. Was I so bad that even my fake date was going to dump me? I swallowed. "Uh, yeah," I said cautiously. Being a third wheel on a fake date was just beyond insulting.

"I sort of brought someone with me. My cousin."

"Oh," I said, not as put off. At least it wasn't some girl, him thinking he was going to walk into the frat with a girl on each arm and collect double his money.

"He drove." Nate finished.

We were nearing the parking lot now. I glanced up at him. "So where's he parked?" I asked, suddenly apprehensive. I hadn't thought this through. Here I was on a Friday night, about to get into some strange car with not one, but two men I didn't know.

48 hours, *here I come.*

My steps stuttered, and I quickly tried to come up with an excuse as to why I suddenly couldn't go.

Nate was a few steps ahead of me now, so he gestured with his chin. "Right over there."

My gaze followed his direction. I did a double take.

It couldn't be.

As I watched, a brown, flimsy door popped open, and a guy with long, jean-clad legs and too-nice sneakers stepped out. His head was covered in a black baseball cap. When his chin lifted, my heart skipped a beat.

I'd know that jaw anywhere.

"That's your cousin?" I said, my mouth going dry.

I didn't look away from him. Even though his eyes were shadowed by the brim of that damn hat, I felt ours connect.

"That's him," Nate said from somewhere beside me.

I forgot all about trying to get out of this date. I forgot all about how tired I was. Suddenly, I felt like this was the best fake date I'd ever been on.

Still gazing at Stark, I smiled.

twelve

Ten

She smiled at me.

A genuine smile of what I seriously hoped was affection.

It might not seem like that big of a deal, a smile. But for me, it was everything.

She didn't want an autograph, a picture, or an interview. Her eyes didn't glitter with calculation or greed. There was no hidden agenda in the way her lips curved upward, in the surprise that lit up her eyes.

She was happy to see me. *Just me.*

I didn't really know her. Not really. Still, possession unlike anything I'd ever felt before rose up inside me as we stood there yards apart and stared at each other. Chemistry electrified the air, having begun crackling the second we saw each other.

"We meet again," I called out, tucking my hands deep into the front pockets of my jeans.

Violet's steps restarted. As she moved forward, the ends of her long blond hair floated out around her like light-colored ribbons against the night sky.

Her movements were mesmerizing. I couldn't help but admire her body and all the curves my hands desired to learn. She was so different from all the girls I'd dated in the past. From all my one-night stands. Not just in looks, but in the energy that surrounded her. I couldn't quite explain it, though I sorely wanted to. I wanted to know why I was utterly drawn to her. Beyond the obvious that she didn't know who I was.

I had to spend more time with her.

Starting now.

"I see you made it home the other night," she quipped, glancing at the Jeep.

I flashed her a smile. "If duct tape can't fix it, nothing can."

"Is that a guarantee?" Her eyes sparkled, just like the pocket on her shirt.

She was flirting, and just the notion of it made me feel a little giddy.

I shifted closer, about to make some witty and charming reply, when Nate crashed into the moment. "You two know each other?"

"We've met," Violet answered, then wagged her finger between Nate and me. "You two are cousins?"

Before coming to get her, we decided it would be better to pretend this was a giant coincidence and seeking her out wasn't something I asked him to do. What I *didn't* ask was for him to ask her out. Or butt into what could have been a flirt-fest.

"Since birth," Nate quipped.

I rolled my eyes. "His dad is my mom's brother," I explained.

Her blue stare turned back to me. Every time it brushed over my face, it felt it like a caress. Like she touched me without even lifting a finger.

Her lips pursed, distracting me for long moments. "This seems like an awfully large coincidence."

"What does?" Nate asked, once again butting himself into my conversation.

"Pretty crazy, right?" I answered, wanting her eyes back. "Nate came home the other day and told me he had a date with a girl named Violet."

"I almost died." We both glanced over at Nate as he quite dramatically wrapped his hands around his throat and pretended to choke.

Violet gasped. "You attacked him!"

"No," I said at the same time he said, "Yes."

"Shut the hell up!" I growled, giving Nate a light shove.

Violet crossed her arms over her chest and regarded us both as though she were a school teacher and we were naughty students. "Well, which is it?"

My body rotated toward hers farther. I was totally digging the whole sassy vibe she had going. "He's still alive, isn't he?" I drawled.

Nate scoffed. "Yeah, that's because I told him about the forty bucks."

Violet laughed, and I glared at him. Was he trying to ruin my chances with her?

Her laughter died down, and she looked at me, cocking her head as if waiting for an explanation. So I gave her one. "The only date you're going on is with me."

The whites of her eyes stood out when they rounded in surprise. But she recovered quickly, and I stood there in anticipation, hoping she'd bring that sass back.

I think I had a thing for sassy.

Violet didn't disappoint. Her fists slid off her hips, expression narrowed. "First you attack your cousin, and now you're telling me what I can and can't do?"

"Well, this escalated quickly," Nate chirped.

We both gave him wilting glares. He held up his hands. "I'll be in the Jeep."

Before he went, he sidled up alongside Violet and leaned into her ear. My back teeth snapped together just seeing him that close. Before I could tell him to back off, I heard his words.

"He the guy?" he whispered, loud.

"What guy?"

"You know," he said, as if he were trying to be quiet when he really wasn't. "The guy you're into."

Violet quickly glanced at me, her face flushing.

I feigned surprise and then pointed at myself. "Me?"

"You're supposed to be in the car," she finally told Nate, pointing at it as if she were sentencing an animal to the corner.

Nate moped off, and I smiled wide like someone just told me a huge secret.

"You're into me," I said when Nate was in the backseat.

Violet sniffed. "I don't even know you."

I stepped closer, so close the toes of my sneakers bumped hers. She had good taste in shoes. "Do you want to?"

Peeking up from beneath some impossibly long lashes, her smile was enigmatic. "Maybe." Her small fingers reached out to tug on the white string of the Blaylock University hoodie I was wearing.

My stomach actually fluttered. The sensation momentarily stunned me because it was something I hadn't really felt before.

"Just say yes," I quipped, snatching her hand out of the air when she pulled it back, lacing my fingers through hers. "I always get what I want."

"Is that so?" she asked softly.

Letting my eyes roam her features, I nodded.

Oh, I liked her. She was like a shot of the highest label scotch, burning all the way down to my belly then instantly making my head a little light.

Nate's loud voice echoed from inside the Jeep. "This is my date. Why am I sitting in the car?"

Violet giggled. I loved the sound as much as I loved a perfect beat in the studio. "It *is* his date." She reminded me.

"Like hell," I vowed. "The second he collects his forty bucks, you're all mine."

"Can we go?" Nate called.

"He's such a third wheel," I bantered.

Her hand slipped out of mine, and her laughter carried back to me as I watched her climb into the beat-up time machine.

The large colonial-style house was nearly spilling out with bodies, all the main rooms crushed with people. Looking around, I realized this was my first frat party. Though I was college age, I'd never had any college experiences. I thought it was just an extension of high school—you know, trudging to and from boring as hell classes with a bunch of people who didn't want to be there any more than I did.

And maybe it was like that most days. However, I was getting the impression Blaylock was more than that. I'd been worried about being identified the entire day leading up to our arrival. Hell, I was still paranoid. But as we pushed our way through the crowd of people dancing, yelling, and drinking, I realized these people couldn't care less about me.

They were in their own world, a world I wasn't a part of. A world where no one expected to see me. It was a little humbling actually, realizing if I wasn't famous, if I hadn't become public enemy number one, *this* would be my world. I couldn't help but wonder what I would be like, what my life would be like today if I hadn't been discovered and then rocketed to fame.

Nate and Violet were in front of me, with me trailing along behind. Like the third wheel. I'd never been a third wheel in my life. It sucked ass. But as Nate so loudly pointed out, this was technically his date. At least until he won the bet.

I had to hand it to him, though. He didn't just find out information about her. He paved the way for me to see her again. The least I could do was let the guy get his forty bucks.

Nate slung his arm around Violet's shoulders and guided her under the archway leading into another room. She glanced up and him and laughed, and I knew jealousy.

There wasn't really anything to the way he casually touched her, but I hated it. Usually, I was the one with the ease, the charm. I was known for having women eating out of the palm of my hand within minutes.

Yet here I was. Trailing behind, watching them, dumfounded.

Violet made me nervous. Nervous to the point I almost didn't know how to act. I didn't want to treat her the way I treated other women in the past. She was different.

Nate glanced around at me. I lifted my chin so he could look at me beneath the hat. "Beer!" he shouted.

I cupped my hand around my mouth and yelled, "Hit me!"

A moment later, I managed to wedge myself beside Violet so she was sandwiched between me and Nate. There was a large crowd there because this was where the kegs were. Nate filled a red cup close to the brim and passed it to me.

I accepted it, immediately putting it to my lips and swallowing. As I did, I felt a tingle of awareness and noted Violet watching me. I stopped mid inhale. It occurred to me I was being an asshole.

Pulling the beverage from my mouth, I held it out to her. "Do you want a beer?"

Her nose wrinkled and she shook her head. Not seeing her refuse, Nate slid a cup identical to mine beneath her nose. "Liquid courage," he announced.

"No thanks!" she called out.

"You want one of those girly drinks, don't you?" Nate surmised and pointed to a blue, plastic baby pool filled with ice and longneck colorful drinks. "A pink one?"

I chuckled. She glanced at me, and for the second time since I picked her up, her cheeks flushed. Looking away and back to Nate, she said, "I, um, don't drink."

Nate laughed, thinking she was joking. But she wasn't. I read it off her body language and the way she shifted slightly, uncomfortable and embarrassed.

Switching the beer into one hand, I slipped my arm around her waist. It settled into the dip above her hips as if it were meant to be there. Pulling her into my side, I leaned down, using the volume of the room as an excuse to bring my lips closer to her ear. "Out of your element, aren't you?"

She turned her face quickly. Our noses nearly collided, my lips so near to hers. "Is it that obvious?" she asked.

I shrugged one shoulder. "I think it's cute." Moving back out of her personal space, I lifted the cup to my lips, all the while holding her stare.

"Blue," she said.

"What?"

"I've been wondering what color your eyes are. They're blue."

She'd been thinking about me. Wondering.

Good.

"You sure you don't want this?" Nate asked, waiving a pink wine cooler in her face

She shook her head, adamant.

"Give me that," I said and snatched it out of his hands. I shoved the bottle back into the icy pool and fished around until I came up with a water.

I held it out to Violet, and she accepted it with a smile.

I think she was the only person I'd ever met that didn't drink. Especially at a party. It's like she wasn't even tempted by the kegs, pool full of wine coolers, and Jell-O shots going around.

Drinking more of the beer, my eyes surfed the room. No one was paying me any attention. The Blaylock U hoodie I was wearing, along with the hat, must have concealed me well enough. And judging by the number of drunk people, no one could probably see straight anyway.

I drained the rest of my glass and passed it over Violet's head (which was very easy to reach over) for a refill. Soon as it was out of my hands, I noticed Vi struggling with the cap on the water bottle. She seemed to be turning it as hard as she could, but the thing wouldn't budge.

Grunting, I reached out and snatched it out of her hands. "This is a man's job."

The cap unscrewed on the first twist. I frowned a little as I handed it back to her. It hadn't been on there very tight at all.

She scoffed. "I loosened it for you."

When she tipped it back to her mouth, I noticed all the condensation rolling off the bottle and the way it dripped over her hand. I snatched it out of her hand again.

"Hey!" she yelled.

Using the hem of the T-shirt beneath my hoodie, I wiped it all off so the bottle was dry, then handed it back.

Violet seemed surprised by the action. A soft smile pulled her lips, and she ducked her head slightly, tucking a strand of hair behind her ear. "Thanks."

The simple appreciation made me want to do more. Be more. I didn't want her to be surprised when I did something kind for her. I wanted her to expect it.

"There he is!" Nate said, leaning over Vi's shoulder and pointing into the other room. "That dude that owes me forty bucks."

Violet's face darkened a little; an air of wariness wrapped around her.

I turned and looked. "Who?" I called back, not sure where the guy was.

"Guy with sunglasses on his head," Nate answered.

I disliked him instantly. He was tall, thin, and had an air of superiority about him, and I was pretty sure he had tiny dick complex. I mean, why else would be feel the need to wear a pair of Ray Bans on his head during a party at night?

Or maybe it was the fact that I knew he'd been hassling Violet.

"Hold my hand," Nate said, drawing my attention. "That will send this guy a message!" He held out his hand to Violet, offering it up.

I growled and smacked his hand away. "Hell no!"

Both my cousin and Violet looked up at me.

"We're family. I wouldn't move in on your girl." Nate made a face like he was offended. "It's for the bet,"

"No," I said again, unbending.

"I'm not his girl," Violet announced.

"Yes, you are," Nate and I said at once.

She nearly choked on her water while Nate and I pounded it out.

"I'm getting another beer," I announced. "Go get your cash."

"Hold this." Violet pushed her water bottle into my chest. I took it, making sure our fingers brushed.

The flicker of electricity that registered on her face was satisfying.

After getting a new beer (who knew what Nate did with my last one), I spun in time to see Nate put his arm across her shoulders again as they walked through the crowd. The guy, whose name I didn't know, blanched when he saw them and nearly choked on his drink.

The second his initial surprise wore off, I watched his eyes narrow on Violet. Something dark passed behind them. Tightness bunched in the back of my neck. I knew his type. Asshole. I saw guys like that nightly when I was on tour.

Moving through the crowd, I drank my beer, kept my hat pulled low, and watched the exchange. I didn't want anyone to recognize me, but if someone fucked with Nate, I wouldn't hesitate to get in the middle of a fight.

The douche said something, and Nate retorted. All the people standing around them laughed. Except Violet. She didn't laugh. She looked like she wanted to get the hell out of there.

A wad of cash was slapped into Nate's hand. He slipped it into his pocket without a word. When they turned and walked away, I was glad Nate put an arm around her shoulders. I hoped it sent a silent message to the douche and his Mickey Mouse club that she was off-limits.

If not, I was going to have to send the message myself.

Nate's eyes swung around. I motioned for him, and he angled Violet in my direction. Leaning down, he spoke in her ear. Her eyes found me instantly, and there was a distinct echo of relief in her gaze. I smiled, oddly wanting to reassure her (of what, I wasn't even sure) and wished I could take off my hat so she could feel the full weight of my stare.

The three of us met up a few moments later in a room toward the back of the house. There was a set of large slider doors that were open. The party continued outside.

I gestured to them with my chin. "Outside?"

She nodded aggressively, and I laughed. After giving her back the water bottle, I held out my hand for hers. Without hesitation, she surrendered it.

I led the way out back, keeping firm hold on her fingers while she followed. At the door, cool fall air rushed in around us, proving just how warm the inside of the house had been.

There was a large square patio behind the house, all concrete with lights strung up around the perimeter. Music pumped through the dark, and people danced and yelled.

"Beer pong is my jam!" Nate yelled, pointing at all the guys playing a drinking game a few feet away.

They all cheered, and Nate glanced at me.

"See ya," I said, amused.

He raced off, and though he was family, I was glad to see him go. I led Violet past most of the people to the edge of the patio, where it gave way to grass and trees. I positioned myself with my back to the yard so I was facing the house and people. Violet was in front of me, all her attention focused away.

"So what's with the water?" I asked, casually shrinking back into the shadows created by the trees.

"It's wet," she said and took a drink.

"You gonna tell me why you don't drink?"

"Nope."

"Okay, then tell me about the guy." I looked toward the house so she knew who I meant.

She sighed heavily. "His name is Ross. I went out with him once. I'd rather chew glass than go out with him again."

"He's not too happy about that, I take it?"

She shrugged. "It's not me he's even interested in. He doesn't like being turned down." Her eyes skirted away, focusing down on her shoes.

"What else?"

"Hmm?" she said, as though she had no clue what I meant.

"What else did he do?"

"Why do you think he did something?"

"You were uncomfortable back there. Almost timid. I know from first-hand experience that's not how you usually are."

"Very observant," Violet mused.

Unable to stop myself, I fingered a strand of hair falling over her shoulder. "When it comes to you? *Very.*"

"I don't come to parties like this very often. Almost not at all," she told me, ducking her head. "I'm not really one for crowds."

"Me either," I murmured, thinking about the last time I was in a huge crowd. I'd been drunk with a full bladder.

The thought made me chug some more beer.

"Really?" Her voice was surprised and curious.

I grinned. "That surprises you."

"Well, duh. You're cocky, charming, and good looking. I would think a place like this was like your mothership."

A slow grin transformed my face. "You think I'm good looking?"

"And cocky," she reiterated. "To a fault."

I chuckled warmly. "I like your bluntness. You don't try to kiss my ass."

"I don't ass kiss. It's a waste of energy."

Hiding another smile, I drained my cup.

"So what's your deal?" she asked, point blank. "Why aren't you over there being the life of the party like I know you could be?"

Crushing the cup in one hand, I leaned in. "I'm not here to be the life of the party. I'm here for you."

"Why?" she probed, folding her arms over her chest.

"You're real," I said simply.

She drew back, clearly not expecting me to say something like that. She probably expected some cheesy line, of which I had about fifteen in my back pocket. Violet was better than a pick-up line.

It took her a minute to digest that. As she did, her lips wrapped around the bottle and water slid down her throat.

The noise of the party became muffled, as if it were far away and she and I were the only two people out here. The glow from the string lights illuminated her blond hair when she moved, and occasionally, the glitter patches on her jeans would catch the light and draw my attention to her thighs.

I meant what I said. She was real. Probably the realest thing I'd seen in a long time. In a way, meeting her was like letting oxygen flood into a tank where before it had been airtight.

I didn't just mean real in terms of the world I came from either, though there, someone like her was literally unheard of. It was here, too. In the middle of an art gallery when she was drawing a satirical cartoon making fun of me. When she accused me of being a criminal and let herself be suckered by my cousin into a fake date.

Here, now, at a raging frat party, she was raw with genuineness. Everyone else around her acted like sheep. Doing what the crowd was doing, involved in only themselves.

Yet here she stood, next to the fakest guy in this place, drinking her bottled water and hiding out near the tree line.

I opened my mouth to say something more, but I was oh so rudely interrupted by a voice that wasn't hers.

thirteen

Violet

"Did you show up here just to humiliate me?"

The familiar voice actually made my skin crawl.

Forcing myself to not react, I turned slightly and glanced over my shoulder at Ross. Clearly, he was drunk. Or stoned. Hell, maybe both. Inebriated Ross was not someone I wanted to be around. I learned that lesson once before.

I turned away. "I know it's hard to believe, but not everything I do is about you." Pausing, I reconsidered my statement. "Actually. Nothing I do is."

It was too much to hope he'd just go away, wasn't it?

His hot beer breath blew against my ear when he leaned over my shoulder, and I shuddered a little, moving my head away. "I'm supposed to believe that *you*, a girl who never comes to our parties, a girl who has every excuse in the book to never hang out, just happens to show up *here* with a guy because it isn't about me?"

"Pretty much," I replied, keeping my back to him.

I was very aware of the way Stark stood by, watching the exchange with rapt interest. I didn't even think Ross noticed he was there, between his focus on spewing his drunken words at me and Stark being well concealed in the shadows. He hadn't acknowledged his presence at all.

"I'm talking to you!" Ross spat, grabbing me roughly around the upper arm and yanking me so I would have to look at him.

Energy sizzled behind me, the kind that oozed with quiet strength. It caressed along my back, almost enveloping me, offering me support to stand my ground. It also held promise. Promise in the way it pulsed that it wouldn't take much for him to intervene.

"Fine!" I spat, ripping my arm away. "I came here to send a message. Leave me the hell alone."

"And if I don't?" He threatened, taking a step forward.

He was so close I had to dip my head back to stare up at him. My stomach clenched. Memories from the night I made the mistake of going out with him made me want to cringe.

"If I don't, I'll make sure everyone knows what kind of man you really are." It wasn't the strongest of threats, but hey, at least I stood my ground.

Ross laughed, but it wasn't a humorous sound. I saw the intent in his eyes just seconds before he moved. The plastic cup in his hand hit the grass with a thud when he threw it aside, and both his hands latched onto my upper arms and dug in as he towed me close.

"Where's that date of yours now?" he growled. "Collected his cash, then left you to rot." He snarled.

"Her date's right here." A low, angry voice eclipsed everything else. A fist came rocketing in from the side, plowing into Ross's cheek. The hit was so solid Ross stumbled, which made him release my arms.

I tripped backward, but Stark filled my sight as he reached out to steady me. Anger glittered in his eyes, his steely jaw jumping with tension. "You okay?" he asked low, looking me over as if he might have missed something that could cause me harm.

"Watch out!" I shrieked as Ross appeared ominously behind his shoulder.

With barely any effort, Stark kicked out behind him, planting his foot solidly in Ross's middle. Ross fell back, doubling over and heaving. Some of the alcohol he consumed made a second appearance all over the grass and his shoes.

It was very unattractive.

"Lightweight." Stark scoffed and turned to face him.

Ross looked up, swiped his arm over his nasty mouth, and straightened.

"Vi, move," Stark instructed, keeping all his attention on his opponent.

I dashed off to the side, no longer behind him, as Ross dropped low and charged. Stark barely even readied for the hit. I yelled his name, because, you know, me screaming on the sidelines would totally help.

Stark had the situation under control, though. Instead of bracing for impact, he stepped out of the way at the last second, and Ross stuttered forward, surprised. As he went past, Stark kicked him in the ass, and he fell, practically doing a belly flop on the grass beneath the tree.

I thought it was over, but Stark had other ideas.

Instead of walking away, he surged forward, grabbing Ross by the shoulder and flipping him over. Grapping a fistful of his T-shirt to yank his upper body off the ground, Stark punched him again.

I flinched. The sound of flesh hitting flesh made my stomach roll.

People were noticing the commotion and were coming closer, gathering around to watch.

"Touch her again and I'll kill you," Stark growled, his voice low and shiver-inducing. It was the first time I saw it—the restrained anger that lurked somewhere deep beneath his hoodie and baseball hat.

Ross twisted, disengaging the grip Stark had on the front of his shirt. "You can't threaten me," he slurred, starting to rise.

Stark punched him again, and he fell. He raised his fist again, and I winced.

"Whoa!" Nate burst through the crowd and rushed over to Stark. "It's over, man. You win." I sucked in a breath when Nate put his hand on Stark's middle and pushed him away from the situation.

Stark gave him a look, then made a sound and shook out the hand he used to pummel Ross. He turned, noticing how the crowd had gathered and everyone was standing around, silently watching.

Murmurs started moving through the gathering, low rumblings about what just happened. I heard a few people ask, "Who is that guy?" and my forehead wrinkled.

Adjusting the brim of his hat so it was pulled down even farther, he stalked the few feet to where I stood and reached for my hand. I stiffened, and his eyes flashed up to mine.

"C'mon. Time to go."

Behind us, Ross was on his feet and glaring between me, Stark, and Nate.

Even though I was suddenly apprehensive about going with him, I nodded because honestly, leaving with him was preferable to staying.

Besides, he'd been defending me.

At least at first, he had been. But after the second time Ross hit the ground and Stark kept going, I had to wonder if maybe something else took over. Something gloomier. Something like anger.

It scared me.

The last thing I wanted or needed was a repeat of my one and only date with Ross.

More voices erupted, the noise level rising. Stark's grip tightened on my hand, and he towed me along, moving fast as Nate created a path through the crowd. The second we broke through, Stark picked up his pace, and we started running across the lawn, past the house, and around front.

Nate ran, too, as if maybe they were afraid Ross would get some buddies and come after us. Honestly, even if they did, I'd still put money on Stark. Crap, he barely broke a sweat knocking Ross on his ass. Twice.

Nate and I jumped into the Jeep as Stark fired it up. The engine turned over once, and he cursed low, glanced at the rearview mirror.

"C'mon," he murmured and tried the engine again.

This time the Jeep fired right up, and he pulled out onto the street in one second flat.

"What the hell was that about?" I said, turning in my seat to face Stark.

He glanced at me, then back at the road. His jaw was clenched. The muscles working in it made my stomach do funny things.

"He put his hands on you." He spoke angrily.

I drew back.

"Wasn't the first time either, was it?" He went on, shifting the Jeep aggressively. The poor thing made a wretched sound.

I glanced back at Nate, hoping he would bring some of his usual sarcastic wisecracks to the conversation and lighten the mood. His eyes flickered at me, and he frowned. Then he shifted to look at his cousin. "Grabbed her the day I met her," he intoned, his voice not light at all, instead hard and serious.

What a traitor! *Thanks for the help, Nate.*

"That was the last time," Stark vowed, shifting again.

I slumped against the seat, not really sure what kind of response to give. On one hand, I was sort of glad Ross got his ass kicked. The guy deserved it, and as much as I hated to admit it, I just didn't have the kind of physical strength it took to do it. On the other hand, that kind of physical strength intimidated me.

Maybe because I didn't have it.

Maybe because it had been used against me before.

We turned onto some unfamiliar street, heading away from campus. I sat up, pressing a hand against the plastic window. "Where are we going?" My voice was slightly higher than normal. Anxiety tended to make me sound like a soprano.

Stark's palm covered my thigh and gave it a gentle squeeze. "It's okay. I'm just taking Nate home. Then I'll take you back to your dorm."

I glanced between him and his hand. The darkness of the interior seemed to swallow both of us whole. But the energy that sizzled around—even darkness was no match for that.

I swallowed thickly. "Don't you try anything," I said, steady. "I have my whistle."

Oh my God. I seriously needed to get a better weapon than a whistle. This was embarrassing.

Some of the intensity pulsating around him dimmed. I felt him stifle a laugh. His face turned toward me, and his hand gave my leg another squeeze before pulling away. "You're safe with me, Vi."

Those were some pretty words. So pretty nervous energy coiled low in my belly. I liked what he said. Feeling safe was something I often sought out. It was one of those qualities I instinctively wanted.

"Your words are pretty contradictive to your actions back there," I said, trying to remind my heart that my head was the one in control.

"No," he refuted, turning down another side street I wasn't familiar with. Though, to be fair, I wasn't familiar with many streets off campus because I didn't go out much. "What I just said is proven by how I reacted back there."

I turned around, peeking into the backseat. Nate was sitting in the center of the bench, just taking in the conversation. "You're awfully quiet back there. Nothing to say?"

He shrugged. "Not my date anymore."

A minute later, the brakes squeaked as the Jeep slowed and then turned into a paved driveway. I gazed out the windshield at the brick duplex. It was dark, so there really wasn't much I could make out.

Stark pulled the emergency brake and got out, pushing up his seat for Nate to climb out of the back. "Don't wait up for me." Stark's words floated into the car.

I leaned forward and called out, "Actually, you can wait up. He won't be long."

Nate cackled. "Turned down! How's that for your once-spotless record?"

Stark smacked him in the back of the head, and Nate made a sound. Then, to my surprise, he stepped up to his cousin and adjusted the hood on the sweatshirt and patted his face. "I forgive you. It's been a hard night."

Stark smacked his hand away but softened the words and his action with a smile. "You're an asshole."

The driver's seat flopped back into place, and Nate leaned in. His fist appeared over the center console. "Best date I've been on all year!"

"It wasn't a date," Stark muttered darkly.

A laugh bubbled out of me, and I smashed my fist against his.

"I'll see ya around." He started to pull back, then stopped. "Oh, and be gentle with our boy here. He's out of his element."

Before I could ask what the hell that meant, Nate was gone and Stark was sliding back in.

I watched Nate jog up to the front door of the brick home and let himself in. "Do you live here, too?"

"Yep," he replied. "Nate's my roommate."

For some reason, that made me smile. "You and Nate share a room?"

"Always did, ever since we were kids. So when I came back here, it was sort of the natural thing to do."

"When you came back for college, you mean?"

He nodded. "Uh, yeah."

"Where are you from, then?" I asked.

"The city."

I guess I could picture him as a city boy. He definitely had some mystery about him, sort of the way I always thought of the city. I mean, seriously, have you ever tried to park in NYC? Or get really good tickets to a show? It was a damn mystery to me how it was done.

"Nate's dad lives here, too?"

"Yep. Just me, Nate, and my Uncle Derek. He's actually the head of the music department at Blaylock."

"Oh, wow," I said, gazing back at their side of the duplex.

"So I guess I'm not invited back to your place?" he said ruefully, smoothly steering the conversation away from his living situation.

"I just watched you beat up some guy. I'm going to go with no."

Stark had been backing the Jeep out of the driveway. After I spoke, he left it to idle right in the center of the road, turning his full attention to me. As if he knew the hat pulled low on his face somehow kept distance between us, he pulled it off and tossed it into the back.

He rubbed a hand over his messy hair, somehow artfully arranging it into a bedhead style. His eyes, which I knew were the bluest of blue, settled wholly on my face. "Did he hurt you?"

I so wasn't expecting that to be the first thing he said.

"No," I replied, the word a little breathless.

"Would you tell me if he did?"

I swallowed. My spit was suddenly very thick. I nodded.

"Let me see your wrist."

I blinked. Hesitated.

Stark made a sound and held out his hand. "The one he grabbed," he motioned. "C'mon, give it to me."

Extending my arm, I put my hand in his. Warm, smooth fingers wrapped around my hand, enveloping me with quiet strength. Gently, he pulled my hand toward him to study my wrist, which was free of bruises.

The Jeep stuttered a little as it idled. But then it caught and rumbled back to normal. Stark leaned down. The messy, long strands of the front of his hair tickled my arm, but the sensation was short-lived. He brushed a soft kiss over the inside of my wrist, letting his lips linger with the faintest of caresses, before pulling back and tucking my arm back into my lap.

I had nothing. Words failed me. All there was inside me was my heart, stuttering just like the Jeep had before rumbling back to life.

In that moment, I felt I'd just run a marathon. My heart was still pounding a mile a minute, and the only breaths I could take in were shallow.

Oh my. What a conundrum Stark was.

One minute he was beating the crap out of some lowlife frat guy and the next tenderly kissing the inside of my wrist as if his lips were the cure for any ailment I might have.

They may be, my heart whispered.

I pretended not to hear.

"So," Stark said, turning back to the steering wheel and the road. "You like ice cream?"

My brain couldn't keep up. "Wh-what?" I stuttered.

He smiled as if he knew exactly how slow my brain was running. "Milkshakes," he replied. "I'm taking you to get one."

"Oh," I replied. The inside of my wrist still tingled. "Actually, uh…" I grimaced to myself. God, this was going to sound so high maintenance. First, I don't drink, and now this. "I try not to eat dairy."

He glanced at me quickly. "No beer *and* no ice cream?"

I sighed. Might as well get it all out now. "I don't eat gluten either."

The Jeep slowed when he yanked his foot off the gas pedal. "No bread!"

I shook my head.

"How do you survive?" He was completely horrified.

I was used to the reaction, but his face made me laugh. "On the blood of my enemies," I intoned.

He scoffed. "That, I do not believe."

"It could be true!" I insisted.

"What the hell can you eat?" he asked, not even entertaining the idea.

How insulting.

"I like smoothies," I said.

"Like with fruit and shit?"

"You make it sound so appetizing." I giggled.

He smiled. It was the kind of goofy, genuine grin that made my belly flop. "Okay then, a smoothie and a milkshake coming right up."

I knew I should have told him to take me right home after everything that happened. Hadn't I just been thinking practically the same thing like five minutes ago?

Thing was I didn't want to go home.

I was pretty positive all those words my heart whispered to my head hadn't gone ignored after all.

fourteen

Ten

"Is this legal?" Violet asked from the passenger seat.

"Huh," I said thoughtfully. "Hadn't really thought about it."

I felt her incredulous reaction and turned my face to glance at her.

"What?"

"Tell me you're kidding," she replied, pulling the straw away from her lips. It was too dark inside this Jeep. I wished I could see her more clearly. Her very presence commanded my attention.

When I didn't readily laugh or confirm that I was actually just playing around, she reached across the car and smacked me in the arm. "Being arrested in not on my to-do list for tonight."

Huh. Maybe it was that lack of thinking about these kinds of things that got me hated by the press and most of my fans. I was never actually arrested for any of the shit I pulled, so maybe that's why I didn't think of it now. I'd gotten away with a lot of shit. In a twisted sense, my name and status protected me.

Until my name and status turned on me.

"We're not going to get arrested." I assured her. "We aren't doing anything."

"Trespassing is something." She pointed to the large chain-link fence I'd just parked directly in front of. The headlights illuminated a large metal sign.

No Trespassing.

I couldn't help it. I grinned. "Semantics." I shut off the engine and killed the lights. "They mean on the other side of the fence. This is a safe zone."

She made a sound. "We're getting arrested. Why couldn't we just stay at the ice cream place like normal people?"

Because I'm not normal. Because I'm not ready to tell you who I am.

"Where's the fun in that?" I scoffed. "I haven't been out here in years."

"The airport?"

I nodded. "Derek used to bring me and Nate out here a lot when we were kids, and we'd watch the planes take off and land." Glancing through the windshield, I saw the blinking lights of a plane overhead, circling and preparing to land.

"C'mon." I motioned with my head and got out.

We met at the hood, both of us holding large white cups with lids and straws. I considered it a win that the ice cream place we went to also made smoothies.

I was still hella shocked this girl didn't eat ice cream. Or bread.

Setting my chocolate malt on the hood, I grabbed her hand and led her around to the side near the front tire. Once there, I leaned down, offering my hands as a step ladder.

Her face turned dubious.

"View's better up there," I explained.

"Are you sure it can hold us?"

I laughed. "Relatively. Good thing I brought my duct tape."

She made a sound but wedged her foot in my hands. I lifted as she went, giving her a boost up onto the hood.

"It's still warm," she said, pressing a palm to the metal beneath her.

After settling beside her, I picked up the shake and took a long pull. "Plane's coming in." I pointed to the one readying to land.

"You ever fly before?" she asked.

I thought of my private plane and all the places I'd traveled. "A couple times," I replied. "How about you?"

She shook her head. "No. What's it like?"

"Well, when there isn't turbulence, it's pretty cool. It's kind of like being in your own little world, you know? Like everything happening on the ground doesn't matter for those minutes you're in the air."

As she listened, she nibbled on her straw, switching between sucking up the smoothie and chewing the plastic as she considered my words. I liked her.

So much.

She was real. Probably the realest person I'd met in a long time. She wasn't calculated in any kind of way. She didn't try to be someone she wasn't. She chewed straws, wore sneakers instead of heels, and told me in no uncertain terms I wasn't coming back to her place.

"Sounds peaceful," she answered.

"You gonna tell me why you don't eat anything that tastes good?" I teased, elbowing her gently.

"This tastes good!" she insisted.

"You're telling me that your pineapple smoothie is better than a chocolate shake?"

"I do like chocolate," she murmured.

"Doesn't chocolate have milk in it?" I inquired.

"Semantics," she echoed, and I laughed. "Try it." She thrust the drink in her hand near my mouth.

I looked between her and the straw, then lowered to take the offered taste. The sweet, distinct flavor of pineapple hit me first. It was thicker and creamier than I thought it would be. There were hints of banana and something else fruity, but I didn't know what.

"Hey, that's pretty good." I concluded.

"I know." She was smug, returning the straw to her lips.

I wanted to kiss her. Right then, she probably tasted like pineapple.

The plane I'd been looking at earlier rumbled close, the sound overpowering everything else, including our conversation. We both turned toward the long runway as it gracefully lowered, still suspended by air but preparing to join the rest of us on the ground.

The wind around us picked up once it hit the pavement and rolled quickly by as the pilots worked to slow it down. I'd forgotten how cold the autumn nights here got. I was too used to living in LA, where winter didn't seem to exist.

Beside me, Violet shivered. She folded in on herself a little, brought her knees up to her chest, and wrapped her arms around them.

"Cold?"

She smiled, chin balanced her knee. "I didn't really dress for trespassing."

Balancing the cup on the hood between us, I tugged the hoodie off my body. Cold air brushed over my bare arms and against the black T-shirt I wore.

"Here." I held out the sweatshirt.

"But you'll be cold."

"I'll be fine." I pushed the hoodie a little closer.

Setting aside her drink, she took the offered jacket and pulled it down over her head. The hood was oversized, so it sort of framed her face, drawing attention to her jawline and eyes.

The length of her light hair was still stuck into the neck, but a few shorter, thick strands had come loose and bordered her face.

"Thanks," she spoke shyly as she burrowed down in it.

My body heat was wrapping around her right now. Soaking into her pores and giving back the warmth she'd lost.

"You're really beautiful." Both of us looked at each other, caught off guard. Sure, I'd been sitting here thinking it, but I never intended to blurt it out. Usually, I was much more in control of the way I acted around women.

A small smile pulled at her lips. She ducked her face and pulled her hands into the sleeves of the sweatshirt until they completely disappeared.

She didn't respond, instead gazing out across the airport. Off in the distance, a plane was flying down the runway, preparing to take off.

"So what's the deal with that dirt bag from the party?" I asked, leaning back against the windshield.

"He's an asshole."

Well, now he's an asshole with a black eye and a busted lip.
"There's more to it than that." I pressed.

She sighed. Keeping her back turned, still staring out across the pavement, she answered. "I'm not really that social. I mean, I do stuff and have a few people I will hang with from time to time, like go to the gallery or the movies. You know, regular stuff."

I didn't really know. This was the most "regular" stuff I'd done in so long.

"But mostly I just hang in my room, draw, and talk to my brother."

"You have a brother?" I asked.

She nodded. "He's my best friend, but he's younger than me so he's still at home with our parents. He's going to come to Blaylock next year, though. I'm excited."

"He like to draw, too?"

"Yeah, but not the same kind I do. He's really into fashion and wants to be a designer." She turned to look over her shoulder, blond hair partially concealing her face. "My brother is gay."

"Being into fashion does not make you gay." I scolded her.

She laughed. "No. But being totally in love with Ten and being convinced he can somehow make him switch sides does."

I choked on my shake. Like full on had a coughing fit right there. I hacked and coughed so much my eyes started to water.

Violet made a sound of distress and pushed to her knees. The metal buckling a little under her movements didn't stop her. She moved to my side and started banging on my back.

"I don't know CPR!" she told me. "You better not die."

The cough turned into a laugh, which sort of sounded like I was dying.

She banged on my back some more as I sucked in some air, partially doubled over. Eventually, I got control of myself and lifted my head. My eyes were still watering, so I wiped them with the back of my hand.

"Wrong hole," I said, my voice hoarse.

"According to my brother, there is not wrong hole," she deadpanned.

I started hacking again, and she started banging on my back again.

"Damn, woman," I said, getting control of myself. I twisted and grabbed her hand, the one she was beating me with. "Are you trying to save me or kill me?"

"Well, since you aren't dead, we can assume I saved you."

I threw back my head and laughed. This chick was hilarious. Keeping hold of her hand, I tugged on it. "Sit with me."

Her butt plopped down, and she leaned against the windshield, mirroring my position. I kept hold of her hand even though she glanced down at it pointedly, then back at me.

I wasn't done holding it.

"Back to dirt bag." I reminded her.

Her face turned in my direction. "You don't care my brother is gay?"

"Should I?" I asked quizzically.

"No." Her voice was firm.

"Okay then." I didn't care. Not at all. There were a ton of gay artists (out and not out) in the music industry. Sexual orientation wasn't something I cared about. Though, I had to admit I was shocked as hell her brother seemed to have a hard-on for me.

That might make Thanksgiving a little awkward.

Wait. What? Why was I thinking about spending the holidays with Violet and her family?

"I do have one question, though," I said, pushing aside the thoughts of family holiday meals.

"What?"

"Does your brother know you were making fun of his… crush with your drawing?" *And how the hell can you not know me if your best friend is like obsessed?*

She made a sound. "He knows I really could care less about Ten or any other recent music artists. I listen to classical, something he thinks is insane." She shrugged. "He didn't speak to me for days when I refused to go to the music department to try and get Ten's autograph for him."

"Uh-oh," I said, grinning. I couldn't help but wonder what her brother would think about his sister hanging out with Ten.

She rolled her eyes. "His idea of not speaking to me is texting me in all emojis instead of words."

My chuckle was drowned out by another plane coming in for a landing. Neither of us said anything as it filled the night with loud sound. Instead, we just sat there, me holding her hand, and watched it roll by.

My chest felt funny, like my heart couldn't decide whether it should speed up or beat slow. What resulted was an uneven rhythm that wasn't altogether unpleasant.

"Ross asked me out a few times. The first time, I brushed it off, figured he was just trying to get some. I'm not really the type that frat guys ask out."

I stiffened. "Why not?"

"Because I don't look like a model. I'm not popular. I don't party."

I frowned. I didn't like that answer or the opinion she seemed to have of herself.

"But the second time he asked, he seemed really sincere. I figured maybe I'd give him a chance. Maybe I'd have fun."

"What happened?" I asked darkly.

"Well, when our date night came, I was sick. So I called and cancelled. He wasn't too happy. Thought I was faking, trying to stand him up." She glanced at me. "He's such a moron. If I was going to stand him up, I wouldn't tell him about it first."

I smiled. She was a feisty thing. "You have a point."

"Anyway, I promised I'd go out with him the next weekend. So when it came around, we went to some frat thing his house was sponsoring. He made fun of me for not drinking, insulted my sneakers, and told me I should wear my hair down, not up."

"You left, right?" I asked, agitation making it hard to sit still.

"I tried," she said, her voice growing quieter. "He was drunk, something I'm starting to think is a permanent state for him. As I was leaving, he grabbed me, pushed me up against the wall, and told me I owed him a goodnight kiss." She shuddered, and the hand not holding hers clenched. "I tried to shove him away, but he has me beat in size and strength. So after a few moments of sloppy, gross kissing, he went for my chest."

I shot up, anger buzzing inside me.

"He tried to force me up to his room, but I told him to forget it and kicked him in the balls."

I smiled widely. "That's my girl."

She returned my smile with a fast one of her own, but it faded too quickly. "I ran out of the house while he was clutching his boys and moaning. I made it almost to the street before he caught up with me. Grabbing my arm, he shoved me down into the grass and climbed on top of me." Her throat bobbed. "His hands came around my throat, and he started to squeeze."

Her eyes lifted to mine. "For a minute, I really thought he was going to kill me."

I palmed the side of her head, stroking her silky-soft hair. "I should have killed him tonight."

Her eyes cleared. "But a group of people came out of the house, and I guess he realized what he was doing. He released my throat, and as I lay there gasping for air, he slapped me across the face and told me if I told anyone what happened, he'd make my life hell."

"Then what?" I demanded.

"Then he ran off into the dark. I got up and walked back to my dorm."

"You called the police, right?" I demanded, my heart thumping hard against my ribs. I was so angry with how he treated her I was shaking.

I wanted to jump off this hood, drive back to that party, and choke him out myself. I didn't, though. I remained rooted in place. For the first time in a long time, my anger didn't control me. I was controlling it.

Or maybe Violet was.

She was the reason I was sitting here cradling her head in my palm and hunching my body close like a protective shield.

"No, I didn't. I just wanted him to leave me alone. I didn't want any drama, and I thought if I said nothing like he asked, he would stay away."

"He didn't leave you alone, though."

"No. He didn't." Her voice was hoarse. "If anything, I think my silence made him think I would put up with it." Her eyes met mine. "I feel sorry for any girl who ever dates him. He's a walking domestic violence case."

"So you agreed to go to the party with Nate." I surmised. I wished I'd been there that day. The day Nate saw them and came to her rescue. I wouldn't have pretended to be her new man. I'd have pummeled the pecker right there on sidewalk and made damn sure he got the message.

She was innocent to think a date with another guy would make this one back off. It scared me for her.

"It's so stupid," she muttered. "Girls shouldn't need the presence of another man to get one to back off. Unfortunately, sometimes they do. Sometimes we *are* the weaker sex." The last statement was whispered, and I heard the shame in her voice.

"Hey." I released her hand to use mine to lift her chin so she could meet my eyes. "That's not your fault."

Really? I couldn't come up with anything better to say? What the fuck, man?

Truth was I couldn't. I was too busy getting lost in her eyes.

"I don't think Nate scared him away," she told me.

"I sure as hell did," I growled.

"You scared me, too." The words rushed out in a whisper. "Why do you have so much anger inside you, Stark?"

I drew back, feeling as if she slapped me with the words. My face stung. My insides stung. "Me beating up some jackass who is physically violent with you is not me having anger issues," I refuted.

She reached for my hand, pushing her fingers through mine. "You didn't know he was violent to me then."

"He grabbed you."

"I saw it, Stark. I felt it. That might have started as protecting me, but the aggression changed."

I didn't like this conversation. It was stupid.

It was too close to home.

I started to pull away. She tugged me back.

Looking down at our hands, I noticed how much paler her skin was in comparison to mine. How much smaller her hand was. One of her knuckles was crooked.

"What happened to your hand," I ground out, pointing at the knuckle as though it had done something offensive. Had Ross done more to her than she'd admitted? Rage bubbled up inside me like water in a boiling pot.

Violet yanked her hand from mine and tucked it inside the sleeve of my hoodie. "Nothing."

"I want to know," I snapped.

"Well, I want to know why you have such a horrible temper!" she snapped back. Without another word, she spun around and slid down off the hood of the Wrangler.

"Vi," I groaned and followed her.

"Don't call me that." She warned.

"Why not?"

"Because."

I crossed my arms over my chest. "That's not a valid answer."

Her hand grasped the handle on the door. "I'm tired."

I sighed heavily and went to her, gently grasped her shoulders, and nudged her around. "I'm sorry I yelled at you. I just don't like thinking of him touching you." She didn't say anything. "Did he do that to you?"

"No!" she said, her head lifting rapidly. "He didn't."

The coiled tension between my shoulder blades relaxed. Without thinking of her reaction, I pulled her into my chest, wrapping my arms around her.

I felt her surprise at first, but then she went lax against me, and her cheek pillowed against my chest. My hand cupped her head, cradling it close so she wouldn't pull away. I wasn't ready to let her go. Not yet.

As I held her, she shifted, lifting her arms to tuck them between our bodies, pressing her palms flat against my chest.

I hunched in around Violet, a natural instinct, a need to get even closer.

I'd never felt like this before. I'd never been so internally moved by a hug. By another human being.

This wasn't a hug, though. It was more. It was me trying to make her understand. Me trying to silently tell her all the things I couldn't actually say out loud.

Her fingers closed around the fabric of my shirt, clutching. Not pulling away.

My heart flipped over.

Eventually, she eased back, blue eyes lifting to meet mine. I wasn't exactly sure of what I saw. I just knew that I liked it.

Holding her face in my palms, I leaned in and pressed a kiss to her hairline. "C'mon, Vi. I'll take you home."

She didn't tell me I couldn't call her that.

fifteen

Violet

I woke up sticky with sweat, clothes clinging to my skin, and my underwear feeling as if I'd gotten caught in the rain and forgot to change.

After stripping them off, I showered and changed into a pair of fresh PJs. Shuffling out of the bathroom toward my coffee maker, it dawned on me the shower didn't really wash away the crap way I felt when I woke up.

The headache that plagued me yesterday was still here to play. Not only that, but my hands were stiff and puffy and my ankles protested with every step I took. Glancing down, I noted the dark redness around my nail beds and sighed.

I was tired, even though I slept all night. My body felt unrested, something I might be used to but hated just the same.

In the kitchen, I made my coffee, grabbed a water, and carried my pill holder with me over to the coffee table. Sinking down into the small sofa I managed to squeeze into this room, I stared off into space for a while.

I guessed it was going to be one of those days.

At least it was Sunday and I didn't have anywhere to be.

I took my medicine and reclined on the couch, propped up my feet, and pulled out my laptop. Netflix and chill. That was today's plan. Of course, my version wasn't exactly like everyone else's, but whatever.

I didn't think about the fact that I didn't feel good or worry that maybe I was having a flare as I pulled up a list of shows.

All I could think about was Stark and how he hadn't kissed me the other night.

How I wished he had.

sixteen

Ten

For the first time in my entire life, I didn't kiss the girl. I wanted to. More than I ever wanted to kiss any woman ever.

But I didn't kiss her.

Actually, I did. On her *forehead*.

Who was I? When I looked in the mirror this morning, I looked the same as I had last week.

But something was definitely different.

I was different. On the inside.

I didn't fucking kiss her.

Regret was a metallic taste on my tongue. I couldn't get her out of my mind, or the fact that she somehow saw me for more than I was.

Perhaps because I was lying to her?

Because she didn't know my real identity?

Even without it, she felt the aggression I carried around. She saw the darkness that lurked beneath the surface of what I knew were raging good looks.

I wanted to see her again. I knew the "rules" to getting a woman good and interested.

1. Wait at least three days before calling.

2. Five days between dates is golden.

3. Don't answer any text for at least a couple hours.

4. One-syllable words are the best answers to all questions.

5. Keep your options open.

The rules always worked, and they'd always been easy to follow.

Until now.

It had been one day. One freaking day since I'd dropped her off at her dorm and drove away. I hadn't called or texted (probably because I didn't have her number). I wanted to see her again. So much she was practically all I thought about. I wanted to talk to her… and not just with one-syllable words. Of course, I had options, but none of them appealed.

More than anything, I wanted to rectify the mistake of not pressing my lips to hers.

Derek and Nate were in the kitchen when I wandered out to get some coffee. It was already after ten a.m., but I was just getting up. Might as well sleep in when I was having some off time. It wasn't like I had to be anywhere.

Nate was inhaling some cereal, and Derek was reading the newspaper.

"They still make newspapers?" I wondered out loud as I poured the black brew into a mug.

"Some of us prefer to get our information from reliable sources and not the internet," Derek replied, dry.

"The internet is totally reliable, Dad. I just saw an article on the birth of an octopus with ten arms. It's a scientific breakthrough!" Nate chimed in.

"You better not have eaten all of the Fruity Pebbles," I told him, joining them at the table.

"Left you half a box," Nate said around a mouthful.

"You boys can do the grocery shopping today," Derek said, turning the page on the paper.

"I might get recognized in the grocery store," I said.

Nate nodded.

"Didn't you both go out Friday night?" Derek asked without missing a beat. "I'm assuming by the lack of your face on the front page here, no one noticed you."

"I wasn't really in public." I hedged.

"Ten managed to find the only girl on Earth who has no clue who he is." He cackled.

Derek folded the corner of his paper down and looked at me. "You were out with a girl?"

"It wasn't really like that."

"He wants it to be," Nate cracked. "Poor guy's been friend zoned."

"I have not!" I argued.

Nate retorted, "Did you kiss her?"

I balked.

Nate and Derek laughed.

"Whatever," I muttered and drank some coffee. "I was trying to be a decent guy."

"Since when are you ever decent?" Nate quipped.

I gave him the finger.

Derek laid the paper flat on the table and gave us a look. "I think it's wise you don't do anything to call attention to yourself while you're here. It's supposed to be a secret."

"Friend zoned." Nate ribbed again.

Shit. What if by not kissing her, I did friend zone myself? I didn't want to be just friends with Violet. It wasn't enough. It was nowhere near enough.

Without saying anything, I sat back and drank the coffee, my mood dark just the like liquid.

"I'm just playing with you, man," Nate said good-naturedly. "You know I like Violet. She's pretty cool."

Derek grunted. "Cool or not, playing with some girl's emotions and not telling her who you are is *not* the way your mother raised you to behave."

"I'm not playing with her emotions." I defended. Just the idea made me sick.

"He likes her, Dad. Like for real."

Derek heard the words and glanced at me for confirmation. I nodded once.

"All the more reason to stay away," he replied.

Ugh. I hoped I wasn't such a stick in the mud when I was a dad.

"Becca could call any day now, and you could be on that fancy plane of yours back to your life." Derek went on.

I pushed back from the table. This conversation was shit. And so was the fact that deep down, I knew Derek was probably right. Leaning over, I grabbed the coffee around the top of the mug, something in the paper catching my attention.

"Hey," I said, abandoning the mug and picking up the section of paper. "It's Violet's drawing."

"The one where she makes fun of you?" Nate asked, standing up to glance at it.

It was a comic strip-style illustration, one of several, but hers took up the most space on the page. Like it was the most popular.

This one was four cell blocks, more detailed and polished-looking than the night I'd seen it in her sketchbook, but absolutely hers. *Four stages of a Fangirl.*

"She drew that?" Nate said, pointing.

"Yeah," I replied, unable to take my eyes off it. Pride filled my chest. She was amazing.

"Which comic?" Derek asked from the table.

I turned it around so he could see.

"That's the girl you were spending time with?" he asked, surprised.

I nodded.

"She has a weekly strip in the paper. It's the most popular of all the strips they run. I knew the girl behind it was a student at Blaylock... but I didn't know you knew her." He said the last part to Nate.

"I just met her last week. But she's Ten's girl."

I slapped the page down on the table and carefully ripped out the strip, making sure not to rip it anywhere near the edges of her work.

"I wasn't reading that or anything," Derek muttered.

I folded it carefully in half and moved to slip it into the back pocket of my jeans. Then I realized I was only wearing boxers.

"Thanks, Uncle Derek," I called out, going into the bedroom to get dressed.

Screw the rules. I wanted to see her.

Now more than ever.

seventeen

Violet

I ignored the first knock on the door, thinking it was for the girl who lived in the room next door. When the noise repeated, I lifted my head off the pillow and glanced at the door, like looking through the wood would somehow be possible.

I got up, grouchy and grumbling, crossing the room on slightly unsteady ankles. It was probably the resident advisor. I was just going to have to tell her coming 'round on Sundays was not cool.

I didn't bother to hide my grouch face when I opened the door only enough to stick my head out. Hopefully I scared her.

"Hey." A voice that was most definitely *not* the resident advisor's greeted me.

Behind the door, my hand tightened around the handle as my eyes went wide with surprise. "Stark," I squeaked, straightening a little.

"Bad time?" he asked, his eyes searching my face.

Oh shit. I looked like crap. Probably worse than crap.

"How did you know my room number?" I stammered, still worrying about my uncombed hair and pajamas.

"Nate told me."

"Right."

He gestured to my door with his chin. That damn hat was pulled low on his face again. "Is there a guy in there?" he demanded.

"What!" I gasped.

"A guy," he replied, voice hard. Next thing I knew, he flattened his palm on the door and pushed.

I let go, allowing the door to swing wide. "Do I look like I have a guy in my room?" I muttered, pointing at myself.

He grunted and walked right into my room. "You look like you were rolling around in bed."

I wanted to laugh. He was acting territorial. And stupid.

Rubbing my temples, I sighed. "I was lying on the couch." I pointed to the blanket, pillow, and open laptop on the coffee table.

His demeanor changed instantly. His body rotated around, eyes sweeping me from head to toe. "What happened?"

"Nothing," I said. "I'm just not feeling well."

"You're sick," he mumbled and came forward, worry drawing his mouth down. When he reached me, his hand automatically pressed against my forehead as though he were feeling for a fever. "What hurts?"

"Everything."

A soft sound vibrated the back of his throat. The next thing I knew, he swept me up into his arms, carrying me the short distance to the couch. No one had ever carried me before.

"I'm going to hurt your back." I warned. I didn't want to show how much I reveled in this.

Plus, for realsies, I was going to hurt his back.

"You calling me some kind of sissy?" Stark sat down, keeping me sideways in his lap.

"I could be highly contagious, you know." I pointed out.

I didn't feel good, and he was holding me.

Oh God, I hoped he didn't stop.

Comfort wasn't always easy to find, but I felt it now.

"I don't care," he murmured, pressing my cheek into his shoulder.

I sighed.

After a moment of us just breathing quietly, his hand stroked up my back. "Stomach bug? Flu? Tell me what I'm dealing with here."

I smiled into his chest. "Nothing that serious. I just have a headache and feel like I might be coming down with something."

I knew I wasn't, but I wasn't sure how else to explain it.

Stark tucked his arms around me, and I felt surrounded. If I was comfortable before... now it was even better.

Almost as if I'd found where I belonged.

"What you watching?" he rumbled over my head, pointing to the laptop.

"Netflix," I answered. "A series called *Strange People*."

"I think I've heard of it," he said, thoughtful.

"I just started it this morning. It's a binge watch kinda day."

"Want some company?" he asked.

"Sure," I said, trying not to sound surprised, excited, or any of the fifty other emotions I was feeling at the same time.

"Did you eat today?" he asked, settling a little farther into the couch.

"Not yet," I said. "I couldn't face my green shake this morning."

"Green shake?"

"It's good for me," I explaining.

"So it tastes like shit." He surmised.

I giggled. "Yeah."

"You gotta eat, Vi." He scolded.

I didn't mind. I actually kinda thought it was sweet.

"I'll go get something later."

In one movement, Stark slid me off his lap and stood. The sound of car keys jangling made me look up. Guess he decided hanging out with my sick ass wasn't as fun as it sounded.

"Pineapple or strawberry?" he asked, spinning the keyring on his finger.

"What?"

"What flavor smoothie do you want?"

I sat up a little straighter, amazed. "You're going to get me a smoothie?"

"You need anything else while I'm out?" he asked, glancing around. "Tissues or something?"

I pressed my lips together, suppressing a smile. "No, I'm good."

He leaned down and pulled the blanket over me. I felt his lips in my hair. "I'll be back in a few, baby. Just rest."

I stilled, wondering if he realized what he'd just said. He was already moving across the room, though, keys in hand.

"Stark?" I called out.

His body tensed, but didn't turn around.

He knew. He was just as caught off guard as I was.

"Yeah?" he answered.

"My keycard to the building is right there on the dresser. Take it. Then you won't have to wait for someone to let you in."

He sidestepped, snatched it off the top, and slipped it into the back pocket of his jeans. Jeans that hugged his ass in a very nice way.

I might be sick, but I sure as hell wasn't blind.

"Don't watch any more of that show without me," he instructed, then let himself out of my room.

I blinked at the closed door, then glanced down at the blanket he'd covered me with. He was going to get me a smoothie. He'd held me in his lap. *He picked my chubby, round ass up and didn't even act like I was heavy.*

He called me baby.

I was playing with fire with this one.

It was the first time in my life I might have been anticipating getting burned.

eighteen

Ten

Instinct is a tricky bastard.

Instinct told me to get the hell over to her place and kiss her senseless. There was no way on God's green earth that I was going to get friend zoned.

Ah, hell no.

When she opened the door looking like she'd just been laid and might still be in there with some guy's hands all through her silky blond locks, instinct screamed to make sure she, the guy in the room, and anyone else in the vicinity knew she was mine.

I'd spent only the measure of several hours with this girl out of my entire twenty-one years. My head told me to slow my roll. But instinct, the tricky bastard he was, overruled all.

I was drawn to her. Almost as though I'd known her far longer than anyone else. I acted first, thought second.

And my actions? They spoke of much more familiarity than my thoughts.

That was why, when what I really went to do was kiss her, to claim her, I ended up calling her baby and running out to get her a smoothie. The very same instinct that demanded I claim her also very ardently wanted to shield her. The image of her lying on her couch, sick and alone, twisted my stomach.

I wore sunglasses with my hat and went through the drive-thru. Then I did the same at a sub place nearby. The show she was watching, I feigned not knowing it. Really, I'd heard of it. I'd been to the set. A buddy of mine was one of the actors. At least saying I hadn't watched it wasn't a lie. I'd never had time to sit around and watch Netflix, not really.

Rehab didn't allow television or media of any kind, and my everyday life was usually too busy to get caught up in a series. Normally, I'd just watch a movie, then move on.

I anticipated the act of doing nothing with her beside me. Not having to be Ten. Hiding out in a dorm room where no one would even think I would be. Of course, I still wanted to kiss her. So much it hummed in my blood, tingled my skin, and teased my lips.

I would kiss Violet.

But not until she was better.

Some things were just more important.

See that right there? Those thoughts? New. Foreign. Kind of ridiculous.

I'd never thought I'd put anything above physical gratification, especially when it came to a woman.

Yet here I was, being played by instinct.

Worst part was…

I liked it.

When I made it back to her room, I didn't knock. She'd given me a key, so I used it. The second I pushed the door open with my foot and strolled inside, my eyes searched for her.

She was in the same spot I'd left her, head resting on the arm. Her sketchbook was open on the coffee table near her, but there was no pencil in her hand.

"How's my favorite girl?" I asked.

What the actual fuck? Those words kept popping out of my mouth. Those feelings. It was as if I had no control over my own mouth, my own brain.

She smiled, and my inner dialogue took a backseat. Frankly, I was glad. The inside of my head was becoming worse than a commercial for hemorrhoid cream.

Violet sat up. The blanket fell to her waist, revealing the baggy T-shirt covering her upper half. The scooped neckline was askew, showing off a whole lot of creamy, pale skin on her neck and chest. Blond, rumpled hair fell around her face and over one shoulder. The dark smudges under her eyes bothered me, not because it made her look less perfect, but because it made me worry.

"You came back." She mused.

I dropped the bag of subs on the table, set down my soda, and then parked my ass on the table directly in front of her. "Sorry it took so long. I had to go get a copy of your room key made. You know, so I could come back and murder you later."

"Thanks for the warning. I'll be sure to put a weapon under my pillow tonight."

We sat there grinning at each other without saying a word.

The moment was broken when she yawned and leaned back against the cushions.

"Were you like this yesterday?" I asked, concerned. Those stupid fucking dating rules. I should have called. I should have checked up on her.

Oh shit, I didn't have her number.

"I was okay," she replied, not elaborating.

"Where's your phone?" I asked, glancing around.

"Why?"

I saw it, scooped it up, and pressed the screen. It was fingerprint enabled. I held it out to her. "Let me in, Vi."

She reached out, laid her finger on the sensor, and the screen came to life.

"Who the hell is that?" I demanded, holding the phone out to her. Her wallpaper was a photo of a couple smiling. Her with some dude and his arm around her.

"That's Vance," she replied, dry. "My brother."

Right. She told me about him. He was in love with me.

I made a sound acknowledging her words and then flipped to her contacts to create one. "I'm putting my number in here, in case you need it."

"Why would I need it?"

I glanced up. Her eyes were twinkling, little brat.

"In case you need a smoothie." I winked. When I was done, I handed the phone to her, and she glanced down at the info I'd punched in.

She burst out laughing. "You put your name in as #1?"

"It fits, don't you think?"

"I don't know what to think," she said, setting it aside and sighing.

I held the smoothie out to her. "Think later."

I watched her take a sip of the drink. The pink liquid crept up the straw as she sucked. After a few moments, she pulled back and smiled, shy. "Thank you."

"I got wraps, too, from that place down the street. You might live off smoothies, but I sure as hell don't."

"Wanna sit?" she asked, patting the cushion beside her.

I stood, and the motion knocked something off the coffee table. I turned to see what it was and frowned.

"What is this?" I asked, staring down at it and then back at Violet.

"It's a pill holder," she said, leaning down to try and reach it.

I beat her to it and lifted it. The pills in each compartment for the week rattled. There were a lot of pills. "This is yours?" I questioned.

She nodded and held out her hand.

I remembered something from the other night when we were at the frat party when Ross was running his mouth at Vi. He said she always *pretended* to be sick. She said herself at the airport that she'd cancelled her first date with him.

She wasn't pretending right now.

Refusing to give her the plastic container, I sank back onto the table in front of her. "You don't just have some kind of bug, do you?" I half whispered.

She shook her head.

"What's wrong with you?" The words rushed out, a chill moving down my spine.

"It's really not that big of a deal. I don't like—"

"Violet," I growled. "Answer me."

BUTTERFLY

"I have RA."

I searched my mind, but it came up blank. "What is RA?"

She made a soft sound. "Sorry, I forget a lot of people don't know what that stands for. It's rheumatoid arthritis."

I drew back. "Like what old people get?"

She smiled. "Sort of. It's more severe, and you don't have to be old to get it."

"What do you mean more severe?" I asked, worry clenching my heart.

"I just mean it goes beyond having achy joints. It's a condition that never goes away. There is no cure."

No cure. Never goes away. "I need you to explain, Violet."

"Basically, my body attacks itself. For no reason. Well, it thinks it has a reason." She went on. "No one really knows why, but my immune system thinks my joints are foreign and attacks them, like it would if I had a cold."

I tried to digest that. "Your body attacks itself?" That was fucked up.

"You know what they say," she said, smiling. "The only thing strong enough to kick my own ass is me."

"That's not funny," I deadpanned.

"I think it is," she grumped and drank more of her strawberry smoothie. She looked so cute sitting there bundled up in front of me.

I clutched the pill holder in my hand. "Does that hurt?"

"Every day," she replied, no hint of humor in her voice now.

"Tell me more."

177

"I have a lot of inflammation in my body. Mostly in my joints, which makes them weak, achy, and stiff. Some things are difficult for me. Stuff most people do during the day that they don't think twice about. I get tired very easily. Sometimes my throat hurts, or I just feel like you might if you were coming down with the flu."

"And today?" I prompted.

"Today, I'm just having a bad day. My joints are achier than usual, my throat is sore, and I have a headache. And I'm tired because I didn't sleep that well."

"But why? What makes you have a bad day?"

"Sometimes there's no reason."

I was having trouble digesting this. Violet wasn't sick. She didn't look sick.

As if she could read my thoughts, she replied, "I don't usually tell a lot of people. It's not like it's a secret. It's just not something I bring up. I don't usually look sick or act sick, so people think I'm lying. Or being dramatic. It's easier to just live with it, not make it my entire life."

"Ross thought you were lying."

"I didn't tell Ross I have RA. I don't owe him an explanation. But yeah, when I said I was sick, he didn't believe me."

My eyes lifted to hers. "You told me."

"You make it hard not to."

"I believe you," I said.

Something passed behind her eyes. Something close to relief and something deeper—appreciation.

Just that brief look speared me right in the center of my heart.

I couldn't sit across from her anymore. I couldn't not touch her. Shifting, I went from in front of her to beside her. My side pressed along hers. Without hesitation I put an arm around her, drawing her close.

She pillowed her cheek against my chest.

"So all these pills?" I held up the container. "You need them?"

"Yeah. It's quite a cocktail every morning." She mused, reached out, and took them from me to set them aside. "Some of them are vitamins, though. You know, to help boost my immune system since it's being suppressed."

"What do you mean suppressed?"

I felt her head tilt up. I gazed down. "You really care about all this?"

It was an easy answer. An instinctual one. "I really care."

Her face ducked into my chest again, hiding those expressive blue eyes. "One of the medicines I take isn't in that container. I only take it once a week. It's called methotrexate. It suppresses my immune system because it's on overdrive attacking my joints and organs."

"Your organs!" I shot out, alarmed.

Her arm slid around my waist as if trying to reassure me. "RA can attack the organs. Mine are all okay, though. I get bloodwork every three months or so to check all my blood counts, the inflammation levels in my body, and to make sure all the medications I take aren't damaging my liver."

I was overwhelmed. In some ways, she kind of downplayed it. Acted as though it were just a fact of life. Hell, she probably wouldn't have said anything at all if I hadn't seen the pills. But then she told me details. About the things she had to deal with. Worry about.

I'd never in my life had to even think about something even remotely this serious.

It made me feel like a complete ass. Here I was a millionaire at the age of twenty-one. I'd traveled the world three times over. I had fame, fortune, and an entire team (well, I had a team until they all quit) to do shit for me.

And how did I act?

By literally pissing all over it. By being ungrateful. By being selfish.

Meanwhile, there was this girl. This girl who was quite literally everything I wasn't and got served up a shit deal in life.

She went through her day with pain even after swallowing a handful of pills and getting a shitty night's sleep. People treated her like a liar because she didn't have a wheelchair or show any signs of disease.

Even still, she was the snarkiest, most creative, beautiful girl I'd ever seen.

In spite of it all.

I cleared my throat. "So the meds are helping?"

"For a while, they weren't controlling it well enough. That's why they added the methotrexate. I tried for a long time to go without it. It's a pretty serious drug. But I can't. It takes a long time to start working, but it finally is. I feel better than I used to."

"Not today," I muttered darkly.

I felt her smile against me. "Actually, I feel better now."

I gathered her closer, tucked the blanket around us both, and gestured toward the laptop, still paused on the show she'd been watching. "Tell me what I missed so we can hit play."

BUTTERFLY

We spent the rest of the day on her couch. She was still in my arms long after the sky went dark.

She fell asleep against me, and I pondered for a long while just holding her all night. In the end, I worried about her comfort, about making her body lie in such a position the entire night. I carried her to the bed and tucked in her sleeping form. I knew I should go, but as I stared down at her, a rush of emotion so powerful overcame me, nixing the very thought. She was small, yes, but so much more fragile than I realized.

I couldn't leave. Not after hearing her tell me the reason she didn't feel good. Not after holding her most of the day.

Instead, I went back to the couch and flopped down. The laptop was still open, so I pulled it into my lap and pulled up the net.

As I waited for the page to load, I glanced across the room to where Violet lay sleeping.

I hadn't kissed her yet. But really, it was like I didn't even have to.

A kiss wouldn't change what I felt about her. It wouldn't make it any more intense. If anything, when I finally kissed this woman, it would be concrete proof of what I already knew.

nineteen

Violet

I woke up as I always did—slowly. But as soon as enough consciousness came over me, my eyes sprang open as if I'd had a bad dream.

Shoving up on my elbow and pushing at the hair in my face, I glanced a few feet over from the bed to the couch.

Oh my God! It hadn't been a dream. Certainly not a nightmare.

Stark was here. He'd spent the night.

His body was sprawled out on the couch, one of his legs dangling off, his foot on the floor. His face was turned toward me, and he was sleeping. Ignoring the protests of my body, I sat up in the center of the bed to stare at him.

I didn't remember coming to bed. I'd fallen asleep on the couch, with him. Part of me was disappointed I wasn't still over there, that the arm casually draped over his lean midsection wasn't draped over me instead.

He had a sort of boyish look to him. Softer, I guess. It made me realize how on-guard he always was when his eyes were open.

What is it you're always anticipating?

Gazing at his features, his dark hair and lashes, the fullness of his lips, I had a slight tinge of recognition. Like maybe I knew him from somewhere.

It was a strange sensation. I peered at him a little closer, tugging the blankets closer into my lap. His cheekbones were just as fierce as his jawline. I mean, seriously, dude had good bone structure. The dark hair falling onto his forehead was disheveled and endearing, so much so I wanted to creep over there and run my fingers through it.

The stubble shadowing his jaw was dark and soft-looking. I'd never kissed anyone with facial hair. That thought drew my eyes to his mouth. Stark's lips weren't overly full, yet they enticed me. I couldn't help but wonder what they would feel like on mine.

A soft sound vibrated his throat, and his head turned away.

I jolted, embarrassed, like I'd been caught ogling him. I had been, but he didn't know it. What the hell was I doing anyway? Sitting here daydreaming about kissing him.

What I should be doing was feeling shocked he was still here. I couldn't believe he spent the night, that he hadn't gotten up and snuck out while I was sleeping.

Sliding out of bed, I crept across the room and silently shut myself in the tiny bathroom. Usually on Monday mornings, I walked around like a zombie with uncombed hair, PJs, and no bra, trying to prolong the morning before I had to get my ass in gear and report to class. Normally, I definitely wasn't wide awake and in the bathroom, staring at myself in the mirror.

But, girl, I needed to get myself together!

Stark was all kinds of gorgeous, and I wasn't about to have him open his eyes to Hagville. I'd fallen asleep accidentally last night, which meant I hadn't done any of my usual nighttime routine.

As I was brushing my teeth, I stared in the small mirror over the sink and considered my hair. It was going to have to be a ponytail day because letting it air-dry yesterday after my shower had done me no favors. Once I was rid of the morning breath, I leaned down and washed my face and hands. After applying some lip balm and moisturizer, I brushed my hair into a high ponytail, grimacing a bit at the red blemishes marring my neck.

It was a good day for a ponytail for my hair. Other parts of me? Not so much. Maybe I would wear a scarf.

Before leaving the bathroom, I swiped on some extra deodorant because, you know, there was a hot guy on my couch.

A hot guy who spent the night.

Why did he spend the night?

Oh God, I hoped it wasn't awkward when he woke up and realized he was still here.

Stark was still asleep when I snuck close to peek over at him. My skin prickled with goose bumps against the morning air, so I went and grabbed my fuzzy cardigan on the other side of the room. As I was pulling it on, I noticed my laptop on the coffee table near Stark's head.

It was partially open.

Frowning, I stepped between the table and the couch. The second I pulled the screen up so it was open all the way, it lit up. I glanced over my shoulder at Stark, still sleeping. Had he been on my laptop last night? What in the world for?

Turning back, I noticed the internet browser was open. It looked like some long article with a lot of words.

Well, at least it wasn't porn.

It was always a good thing to know the guy who spent the night in your place wasn't a raging perv.

Dropping down in front of the screen, I focused on the words, scrolling up to the top of whatever he'd been reading.

Shock rippled through me. I blinked, then looked again to make sure I was actually seeing what I thought I was seeing.

A small sound ripped from my throat as I scrolled through, skimming the article, looking at some of the images toward the bottom. I noticed the open tabs at the top of the screen. I clicked on those. It was more articles, more information.

Oh my God.

A small noise off to my side made me stiffen. My ponytail whipped around with the force of my movement when I glanced around at Stark.

He was awake.

Looking at me.

The blue of his eyes was deep and sleepy. I got lost for long moments just staring into them.

"Who are you?" I whispered. I was kinda, sorta in awe of him right now.

The blue flared, sleepiness evaporating. "What?"

I gestured over my shoulder to the laptop on the table. "You researched rheumatoid arthritis," I whispered.

His eyes went to the screen and then back to me. The alarm gave way to something else. The corner of his mouth kicked up. "Well, yeah."

"But why?" I murmured, turning a little so I could face him.

Stark pushed up so he was partially sitting, leaning against the back of the sofa. His legs were spread, one foot on the floor and one up on the furniture. As he adjusted, I ended up sitting between them.

"I wanted to know more about it. About you."

Unfolding from the floor, I stood but then dropped right back down on the edge of the couch, still between his legs. I was shocked. "You stayed the night?"

"I wanted to be here in case you needed me."

I blinked, a heavy sensation settling on my chest. It made it hard to breathe, yet I didn't want the feeling to go away. My belly trembled; a million butterflies filled me up.

I pulled in a shuddering breath, overwhelmed by everything.

"Hey." There was genuine concern in his voice. He leaned forward, brushing the pad of his thumb along the side of my jaw. "You still feeling sick?"

I lifted my eyes to meet his. I was in trouble. *So* much trouble.

"No one's ever looked up my disease before." The words rushed out of me. "No one's ever sat with me when I was sick."

His body moved closer, his chest leaning nearer. "I'm here now." He assured, and something inside me broke.

Yes. Yes, he was.

And if he kept looking at me like that, if his thumb kept gently stroking over the side of my jaw, I was never, ever going to want him to leave.

I met him halfway. It wasn't even a question as to whether or not I was going to kiss him. It just was. It was like being pulled toward a planet with the strongest force of gravity ever recorded. Even if he hadn't moved, I would have.

Our lips fused the second they brushed together.

The shock of how right he felt made my eyes spring open and my body freeze. Stark reacted, but not by pulling away. His eyes opened, too, and I was left with only the view of the bluest eyes I'd ever seen, the most intense gaze I'd ever known—both of which were focused solely on me.

My hands began to tremble. Curling my fingers into my palms, I hoped he wouldn't notice. Stark retreated just slightly, enough that there was just a breath between our lips. My eyes stayed locked on his, his on mine. As he stared, he cupped my face. His palms were full of warmth, and it seeped into my skin.

Still watching me, he lowered again, bringing our mouths back together.

My eyes slid closed, and I practically melted. A low sound vibrated in his throat, and then he was kissing me. Expertly moving across my lips as though he were telling me the juiciest secret that would ever be told, and I answered by gulping it down.

I had no idea how starved I'd been. How utterly lacking my life truly was until his tongue stroked over mine.

I stopped kissing long enough to sigh heavily, making his fingers tighten on my face, and I felt him smile. A low buzzing sound filled my ears, and I went back for more.

In one swift movement, Stark moved, pulling me beneath him, pressing me into the couch and covering me with his body.

My arms slipped around his waist, my trembling fingers digging into his back. The sensation of his body, the weight, the way he moved provocatively against me was indescribable. The kiss went on. His tongue made love to mine, and even when, eventually, he pulled back, his lips still lingered dangerously close.

"I've been wanting to do that since you called me a felon," he said, his voice sounding as if his vocal cords had been roughed up by sandpaper.

I didn't say anything. In truth, I was totally in awe. Of him. Of the fact I'd opened my eyes to find him still there, as if he'd been keeping watch while I slept.

I brought up a hand, gently pushing back the dark strands of hair falling into his face.

"I have morning breath," he murmured.

I smiled. "I know."

With a chuckle, he ducked his face into my neck.

I sighed. "It was still my best kiss ever," I whispered.

Stark's head lifted. The hair I'd just brushed back fell over his forehead again. "Really?"

I nodded.

He kissed me again. This time, a flush suffused my skin and desire unlike anything I'd ever felt filled my limbs. His hand slid up my side, caressing the outline of my body. It slid up and up until I thought he was going to cup my breast.

Suddenly, he froze and lifted his head. His eyes swept over my face, a look of adoration deep in his stare. "Not with you," he whispered, almost to himself, and then pushed off me to stand.

I was left shocked. But not by the quiet words. By the lack of his weight, his heat, and the absolute devastation of losing his kiss. Hell, I could barely think, let alone ask what the hell he meant.

In that moment, I didn't give a damn.

"I want to come back over there," he growled, pacing in front of me.

"I won't tell you no," I answered.

A noise rumbled out of him. It was reckless and sexy.

"If I kiss you again, right now, I won't be able to stop."

I glanced at the screen of his phone lying on the table. "I have two hours until class."

Blue flames ignited in his eyes, and he took a menacing step forward. I shivered under his intent. But then he stopped, closing his eyes as if to scorch the flame. "Not with you."

I pushed up onto one elbow. "What the hell does that mean?"

He glanced up. "It means you're too good for me to just take you on the couch." His smile was quick and rueful. "And I'm gonna need more than two hours."

Desire curled my toes.

"Don't give me that look, woman." He grimaced. "You're testing my resolve."

A slow, enticing smile curled my lips.

Stark shoved forward and covered the distance between us in one second flat. My back hit the couch when his body pressed into me. His head dipped, lips crashing against mine. I opened for him instantly, allowing our tongues to dance. Lifting his head, he switched direction and assaulted my mouth anew. I shivered beneath him. The way he surrounded me was unlike anything I'd ever experienced.

Pushing my fingers into the hair at the back of his neck, I massaged against his scalp, pulling him closer as the soft strands curled around my skin.

Stark tore his mouth from mine to trail warm kisses across my cheek until his teeth captured my earlobe and tugged.

I made a sound and whispered his name.

His head lifted, half-focused eyes staring down. I leaned up and kissed him quickly, just because I could. He blinked. A small smile curved his mouth, and I rubbed a hand over the scruff on his jaw.

"I like this," I nearly purred.

"I like you," he rumbled. The words were a direct contrast to his action of pushing up off me for a second time. "So much that I'm going to feed you breakfast before class."

That made me think. "Do you have any early classes?"

He glanced away. "Um. No. I like sleep."

I laughed. "Me, too."

"C'mon. You need to eat with your meds." He held out his hand.

"How do you know?" I inquired, surrendering mine.

"I read things," he said, glib.

"You really read all that?" I asked as he pulled me to my feet. I was still shocked he would do something like that.

"Why didn't you tell me that medication you're on is basically chemotherapy?"

I grimaced. Clearly, he actually did read all that and wasn't just trying to impress me. "Would it have mattered?"

"Yes. No." He raked a hand through his hair. "I don't like this."

"It's overwhelming. I get it. And if you read everything I think you read, then yeah, you're probably freaked out. Good thing is," I said, moving past him, "it's really not your problem."

He caught my wrist and pulled me back around. "The fuck it isn't."

I sighed. "You spent the night. We kissed. That doesn't make me your responsibility."

His eyes searched mine. Gently, his knuckles grazed the underside of my jaw. "It's more than that... Tell me you feel it, too."

Oh, did I ever. Our chemistry practically sucked the oxygen out of the room. It nearly suffocated me. Instead of verbally agreeing, I lifted onto my tiptoes and kissed him softly on the mouth.

When I pulled back, he smiled. "You drink coffee, don't you?"

"Coffee is one thing I will never give up." I confirmed.

He chuckled, a thoughtful glint in his eyes. "The no dairy, gluten, and beer, is that because of the RA?"

I nodded and went to the mirror on my dresser to fix my crooked ponytail. "Yeah. Gluten is really inflammatory. I went off it to try and control some of my symptoms, and it helped. When I ate something with it a few months later, it made me sick for days. It's not worth eating. I don't drink because I take so many meds. My liver has enough to process, you know?"

"And the dairy?" he inquired.

"Same with the gluten, though it doesn't make me feel sick. I just know it's better to keep it out of my diet." I grimaced and glanced at him. "I'm not the best at that one, though. I cheat sometimes because, well, ice cream and cheese."

Stark nodded, taking it all in. I'd never really told anyone this much about my disease, except, of course, my family. It still astounded me he seemed to care.

Once my pony was fixed, I yanked open a drawer to fish around. I felt better today, thankfully. Maybe Stark was good medicine.

I felt his touch on my elbow, and I jerked up, startled. "Hey," he murmured, stepping up close. So close our feet bumped together.

He was in my personal space, something I never liked. Until now.

Without another word, he kissed me softly. His lips felt like butterfly wings flitting over my mouth, caressing. Teasing. Making my heart beat unevenly. His lips were damp when he pulled back and smacked me on the butt. "Get dressed, gorgeous. I'll take you for some coffee and breakfast before you have class."

Quickly, I threw on a pair of black leggings, a white-and-black-striped loose top, a chunky-knit gray sweater, and then because I was self-conscious about all the red bumps on my neck, I grabbed a grey, red, and navy-blue plaid scarf. After stuffing my pill holder and a bottle of water in my messenger bag, I nodded, ready to go.

As usual, I didn't bother with makeup, something that also made me feel self-conscious, especially since my skin was far from perfect and the man with his palm at the small of my back most decidedly was.

But I wasn't willing to spend time in the bathroom when I could be with him. Besides, he'd already seen me as I was. Multiple times.

He kissed me anyway.

Holy moly, he kissed me.

"You mind if we hit a drive-thru?" he asked when the Wrangler pulled out of the parking lot. The gears were screeching, and the heat didn't work.

I didn't care because Stark was driving.

"In addition to my morning breath, I haven't showered, and I look like I slept in my clothes."

"It's a good look for you." I observed. Even if his hat and sunglasses concealed too much of his face for my liking.

He winked at me. "Drive-thru it is."

We had lattes and gluten-free breakfast sandwiches— something he'd never tried. After he inhaled the entire thing, he declared he probably wouldn't get it again. We ate in the Jeep in the parking lot in front of the art building.

The radio didn't work, so we filled the silence with conversation.

The air was cold, so he held my hand.

If people stared at us hanging out in a duct-taped old Jeep I didn't notice because he was all I saw.

When I finally had to leave him for class, it was hard to walk away. The only thing that kept my feet moving was the promise I would see him again.

twenty

Ten

The melody in my head was still there. It was getting stronger. It was sort of like having the same dream for a week straight. Except, of course, I was awake.

There was something about this persistent tune that felt different. Special. Like it had meaning in a way no other lyric ever had.

I messed around on the guitar for hours, trying to come up with more than just the few chords that replayed in my mind.

I ended up with more lyrics, though. Words that seemed to tumble out.

There's a fine line between love and hate.
People turn their back on a dime.
Sometimes it seems like this is all a waste of time.
You don't see me,

BUTTERFLY

Only the mask I wear
No one bothers to look beneath it.
I'm not the man I am anymore, just someone they all want me to be.
Trapped.
Caught.
Ensnared by a web.

Nate walked in the room, and I made a frustrated sound, relaxing my fingers off the strings.

"Still working on that song?" Nate asked, dropping his bag in the middle of the floor.

"It's more like a few chords and a melody. Can't seem to put any music to the words."

"You got words?"

I held out a sheet of paper lying on the bed beside me. He took it to read over the few lines that had found their way onto the paper. It was a weird thing, letting someone read something you wrote. It was like giving them access to part of your mind, part of your innermost workings. It made a person feel vulnerable.

Nate glanced up. I couldn't really read his expression, and my stomach sort of dropped.

"This is what I was talking about. You should write your own stuff. It's good."

"You think it's good?" I echoed, slightly surprised.

"Yeah." He sat down beside me on the bed. "It's about all this bullshit, right? Of how you became public enemy number one."

"What the hell happened to me, man?" I said, setting the guitar between my legs.

"I wondered that a lot too over the years." Nate tossed the paper down.

"It was just stupid shit, me blowing off steam… I've just been so pissed off."

"I'm not talking about TP-ing the neighbor's house. Although, dude, that shit was funny."

We both snickered.

"His house could have been an ad for Charmin," I told him.

"I'm not talking about the fights, the shit with the fans… You just stopped coming around, man. You were my best friend. My brother. Then one day you were famous and just… gone."

I'd never really thought about it from Nate's point of view. Or anyone's, for that matter. I spiraled down into a place where everything was about me. Who I was. What I could do for other people. What other people wanted from me.

It wasn't me anymore.

It was Ten.

"The first couple years went by in a giant blur. Becca and my team, they own me. They tell me where to go and what to do. Hell, they even pick out my clothes. I was basically property of the label, a huge money-maker. I know it looks all glamourous on the outside, like I'm riding high and living in my castle on the mountain, but this business…" My words trailed off, and I dared a glance at my cousin.

He nodded as if he wanted me to continue.

"It eats you alive. By the time I realized, by the time I missed what I'd been missing all that time, it was too late. Uncle Derek doesn't even want people to know I'm his nephew. He wants a normal life without being hounded. If I had come here, it would have dragged you all into it."

"You could have called. Texted. Sent a postcard from your glamourous travels," Nate said. "I, personally, would have liked a selfie of you at the Eiffel Tower."

I gave him a WTF look.

Nate laid his hand on his heart. "I could have taped it to my headboard and thought of you at night."

I shoved him, and he cackled. Then he turned serious again. "Seriously, though. You could have called."

"Yeah, I could have."

"I missed you." He admitted.

Looking around the familiar cramped room, I nodded. "I missed you, too."

"Brothers gotta hug!" Nate exclaimed and then launched at me. With an, "Oomph," he wrapped his arms around me.

Chuckling, I hugged him back. A feeling of homesickness punched me in the gut.

When he pulled back mere seconds later, he lifted the guitar into his lap. "So let's work on this song."

Surprise rippled through me. "You write songs?"

"You're not the only musically inclined person in this family," he commented. "You think I just have a guitar around here for shits and giggles?"

"Your dad is the music department head." I pointed out.

"I'm a music major, jackass."

I drew back. Wow. How the fuck did I not know that? I was selfish.

A selfish bastard.

"I'm sorry," I said, suddenly feeling I didn't have the right to even be sitting here.

My uncle and my cousin offered me shelter, a place to hide from the press and the mess of my own making, and I didn't deserve it. I hadn't even said thank you.

"For what?"

"For being a complete dick."

Nate laughed. "Better to be a dick than a vagina."

"Dude. No," I said, a smile pulling at my lips. But then I turned serious again. "Seriously, though. I've been self-absorbed. Thanks for not forgetting about me." *The way I forgot about you.*

"We're family," he said simply, then turned back to the instrument.

The sounds of the exact tune I'd been messing around with filled the air. "So that's what you got," he said, glancing over at me.

I nodded, not bothering to conceal my surprise. He was good, and he picked that up after hearing it only twice.

"So what if we add something like this?" He went on and started adding to the song.

No.

He *made* it a song.

Passion for music and the energy I hadn't buzzed with in a long time came flooding back as if a great dam had burst.

For the first time in a long time, I felt music and I were the same.

We were still playing around when my cell phone rang a while later. Glancing at the screen, I saw Becca's name and answered.

"The groundwork for your comeback is aligning," she said without any kind of greeting.

"I'm good, thanks. How are you doing, Becca?" I responded.

"I'm busy," she said, tart. "I take it from the silence on the media front, you're doing what I told you and staying out of sight."

"Don't I always do what you tell me?"

She made a rude sound. "If you did, I wouldn't be working double time for a comeback you wouldn't have needed."

I leaned back on the bed. "You like the game."

"I'm sending your plane back for you day after tomorrow. I want you back in the studio the end of this week."

"What?" My voice rose with surprise, and my body reacted by sitting up straight.

"Your exile is coming to an end. You can remain out of sight here in LA while getting a new album together."

I glanced over at Nate while she was telling me this. The guitar was still in his lap, and he was looking down at the sheet with my words on it, making a few notes about the chords.

"We have a lot of good press to put together, appearances, a new music video, where to debut it all… and of course, a press conference where you will have to promise—"

"I'm not ready," I said, cutting her off.

Her words stuttered. A beat of silence rang into my ear. "What do you mean you aren't ready?"

"I'm not ready to come back to LA. I like being here, away from everything," I explained. "And I'm working on a song—"

"A song!" Becca exclaimed. "We have people to do that for you. LA is where you're needed."

"I need more time," I said, just as stubborn as her.

"What's this really about, Ten?"

"I just told you. I like being where the press isn't hounding me."

"No," she answered definitively and made a sound to back it up. "I know you. There's more to it than that. What's happened?"

I resented the fact that she thought she knew me so well. How could she? Especially when, lately, it felt as if *I* didn't even know me that well.

"No, there isn't," I said, firm.

"Is there a girl?" she asked suddenly.

What the fuck? Was she a mind reader?

"Why would you think there was a girl?" I asked.

Nate widened his eyes and grinned.

I gave him the finger.

"Because you're twenty-one years old. Your hormones control your life."

"I'm pretty sure you control my life," I snapped. I mean, seriously. What the fuck business was this of hers? She was my manager, not my mother.

She was on my payroll, but she acted like she was the boss.

It never bothered you before, a voice in the back of my mind whispered.

Well, it sure as fuck bothers me now.

"I'm just looking out for you. You know you're my favorite client."

"I'm your most profitable client." I clarified. Even when I was considered persona non grata in the entertainment world, I still made more money than most.

"What's her name?" She cut to the chase.

"I told you—"

"Cut the crap, Ten. The only reason you wouldn't want to hightail it back to sunny LA and out of that primitive New York town is because you're getting laid. Now what's her name?"

"I'm hanging up now. I'll come back to LA when I'm ready."

"You want a couple extra days, fine. Take them. But let me remind you of your career. A career that literally teeters on the cliff of ruin right now. I'm the only reason you haven't fallen off that cliff, Ten. Cozying up to some nobody girl who has stars in her eyes because she's in bed with a pop icon is a bad idea. The second you're back on that plane, she will be at every tabloid's doorstep, selling whatever story she can for a payday. It won't hurt her. But you. You, it could destroy."

Her words didn't scare me.

They did the opposite of what she likely intended.

That anger that lived so firmly inside me rose up.

"She's not like that," I growled, a dangerous new tone in my voice. Almost as though I were daring Becca to even hint that Violet was anything other than what I knew her to be.

I felt a ripple of unspoken surprise on the other end of the silent line, and then I disconnected the call.

twenty-one

Violet

Days. That's how long it had been since Stark stayed the night and we ate breakfast in the barely working Jeep.

Even though I kinda didn't want to admit it to myself, the truth still stared me in the face.

I missed him.

He texted, though, every day. He would ask if I was feeling okay, something I wasn't used to. Not on a daily basis anyway. I mean, sure, my parents called every few days to check in, and I talked to Vance every night. But Vance didn't ask about my RA unless he could sense I was having trouble. That's one of the reasons he was my best friend.

He got it. He understood it was serious, but he also knew there was more to life than what was wrong with me. Instead, we talked about classes, clothes, and designing. I sent him my weekly comic strip, and he kept me updated on everything in my hometown in Pennsylvania.

Stark's concern was nice, though. In fact, every time my phone went off, little butterflies would swirl around in my midsection, and I would have to hold myself back from diving on my phone in anticipation it might be him.

I mean, really. It was kinda pathetic.

I still did it, though.

It was sweet how he seemed so interested in my wellbeing. Baffling, though, he was interested in me. I mean, let's be honest here. We weren't exactly a likely couple. If this were high school, we'd be voted most likely to never date.

Not that we were dating.

You know what I mean, though. He was good looking and smooth. He was confident and had this air of rhythm about him.

And I was—well, me. Soft, kinda squishy, with imperfect skin and an imperfect body (inside and out). I wasn't saying I wasn't pretty. I was, in my own way. I had pretty eyes and hair. I was talented with a pencil, and I was kind to people. At least I tried to be.

Some people, though… some people I wanted to stab with my drawing pencils.

I mean, if I didn't actually stab them, I could still consider myself a good person. It was all about balance, right?

I sure as hell hoped so.

All these thoughts floated through the back of my mind as my hand worked over the page. I was working on a new comic, but I wasn't so sure if I would submit this one to the paper. It was more… personal. Submitting or not, though, I felt compelled to create it. That was art. Some emotions, some visions swirled beneath your skin, created a fog in your mind, and pushed out everything else until you succumbed to giving them life.

Once I got this finished, I planned to pull out a project I hadn't worked on in a while.

Another project that was just for me.

One I hoped might someday see the light of day, just in a larger capacity than the local newspaper.

That will only happen if you get your head out of your ass and make it a priority. I scolded myself.

I set aside the pencil, scrutinizing a section of the drawing, and then went at it with my finger, smudging and blending the lines I'd just made.

My attention was thwarted by a sudden and unexpected knock on the door. I pulled out the one earbud in my right ear and dropped it on the couch.

The sketchbook lay abandoned on the coffee table when I padded across the room in my slippers. My hands trembled a little because you know exactly who I was hoping it to be. Before I pulled open the door, I shook out my hands, as if it would somehow shake free the sudden jitters I had.

Strands of my hair flew back over my shoulders with the force of me yanking open the door. I stopped and blinked, my brain trying to catch up with what I saw.

Right there front and center staring at me was a ripped-out section of last week's newspaper. The section with my comic strip on it.

I had two reactions:

1. Laughter, because that comic was seriously funny.

And

204

2. Excitement. Not for the comic, though, but for the boy holding it.

"What's this?" I said, an obvious smile in my voice.

The paper crinkled a little when he yanked it down and grinned widely at me. "You didn't tell me your work got published on a weekly basis."

"My work gets published by the local paper every week in the form of a comic strip," I reiterated.

Stark made a sexy sound, the kind of sound that made me forget we were having a conversation, and rushed me. His body plowed into mine, his arms wrapping around me, making sure I didn't fall as he basically bulldozed us back into my dorm room.

The door made a definitive sound when he pushed it closed with this foot. The paper he'd been holding fluttered to the floor, and his hands were suddenly buried in my hair. All the oxygen in my body whooshed out of me in surprise but also in expectation of the lips so quickly lowering to mine.

Oh, could he kiss.

Stark had the kind of lips that made a girl forget she needed air. The kind of tongue that erased away entire worlds and an overall presence like a drug that created addicts after only the smallest of hits.

His hand was so big it cradled my head, his thumb stroked along my cheekbone, and his body curled around mine. My hands clutched his biceps until they were too weak to actually grip him.

As if he knew I was in danger of melting right at his feet, Stark grabbed both my hands and guided them up and around his neck. The movement brought my body fully against his, and I sighed dramatically into his mouth.

He laughed even as he kissed me, changed direction, and assaulted me all over again.

Oh, it wasn't fair. How easily I came apart in his arms. How fast heat suffused my skin and made my limbs tingly and heavy. I knew I probably couldn't make him melt this way, but I wanted to try. Even if I was fifty percent successful, I would call it a win.

Tightening my fingers at the base of his neck, I pressed closer. The sound of our ragged breathing between each desperate kiss filled the space and only added to my desire. Pulling back just slightly, I licked over his bottom lip and then sucked it into my mouth. His arms, which had wrapped tightly around my waist, slid down, down until his palms were filled with my ass.

I sucked a little deeper, and he groaned. Emboldened, I released his lower lip and went after the upper. After I tormented it the same way, I licked across his mouth and smiled.

"Hot damn," he rasped. The hat always on his head was ripped away, and his forehead found its way against mine. "I'd ask you how you feel." He smiled slowly. "But I already know." His hands flexed against my ass. "One hundred percent fine as hell."

I lifted my chin, inviting him in for another kiss.

His eyes flashed to mine. Something that looked a whole lot like tenderness filled his gaze before he dropped and pressed a soft caress to my offered lips.

"So," he said, easing back so he could look me over. "If I go outside and knock again, would I get another greeting just like that one?"

I giggled because the answer was probably yes.

"Working on something new?" he asked, lifting an eyebrow in interest, noticing my sketchbook on the table.

He went for it, but I was faster, beating him to it. Quickly, I lifted the book and flipped it over, hiding what I'd been working on.

He gasped and pressed a hand over his heart. "Your secrecy wounds me."

I rolled my eyes. "It's not done."

He bent and swiped up the comic he'd brought over. "This one wasn't either when I first saw it."

"I didn't want you looking at that one either." I reminded him, smugly crossing my arms over my chest.

He grinned as if he'd gotten away with something.

I was very, very worried it was more than just a glimpse at an unfinished drawing.

I thought he was running off with my heart.

"Not even a little peek?" He cajoled.

"No," I said, stubborn.

"Fine." He agreed and turned to walk across the room. "How about you tell me about some of your other stuff?" He gestured to the small part of the room that had canvases leaning against the wall, pastels exploding out of a box, and various other supplies scattered around.

He stopped in front of the largest canvas on display. It was a butterfly. Actually, I'd done a series of butterflies, ranging from a caterpillar all the way to the transformation into the butterfly. Noting how he seemed really struck by it, I pulled a few of the others from behind it, lining them up in order.

"They tell a story," he murmured.

"A caterpillar to a butterfly." I agreed. "Just when he thought his life was over…" My voice faded.

"He transformed," Stark replied, still staring at the main image. He moved closer, lightly running his finger over one of the wings. I'd chosen orange and black with small pops of white for the wings. I thought it was a striking color combination.

His eyes moved from the canvas to me. "This is beautiful."

I felt shy under the weight of his praise. But it felt good. "Thank you."

He glanced back at it, taking in all the canvases again. Something about the way he studied them pulled at my heart.

Clearing my throat, I asked, "You came over to ask me about my art?"

He turned around, bestowing upon me a wicked smile. My heart rate accelerated. "No. But that doesn't mean I don't want to know."

I shrugged and moved to stand beside him. "Drawing is my main passion. I like the comic style, the cartoonish art. It's not very respected in the art world, though. It's considered sort of mediocre."

"Are you shitting me?" He scoffed. "Let me guess. The ones who make the rules are hoity-toity suit types that probably don't even create anything other than facial expressions to make themselves appear interested and knowledgeable."

I laughed. "I've had similar thoughts," I remarked, then snickered.

"Have those dudes never seen *Journal of a Wimpy Student* or any of the other comic-style novels taking over the shelves? I mean, shit, even the Hollywood scene is all about that life. Look at all the movies they're turning out based on the books."

I glanced over at him, startled.

"What?" He held out his hands. "I know shit."

Something about his impassioned little speech, the way he scoffed that my work might not be considered legitimate, hit me in all the right places. Places I was trying to keep from him. Not only that, but the passion in his voice, the hint of knowledge.

"You've seen that trend in books?" I asked, interested.

"Do I live under a rock?" He mocked.

"Well, you aren't exactly a middle-grade reader." I grinned wickedly. "Although, your maturity level is questionable."

"Ha. Ha," he said and poked me in the ribs. I squealed and twisted away. Looking smug, as though he'd gotten the better of me, Stark rubbed the back of his neck. "I'm actually not that familiar with the books, but I know of the movies they're making."

I nodded. Made sense. Movies were advertised more.

"Why do you look like you have a squirrel running on a wheel in your brain right now?"

I made a face. "Ew."

He gestured because apparently that was an actual question that required an actual answer. "I'm trying to decide how much I trust you," I replied seriously.

Stark turned fully to face me, something in his eyes shuttered. It made my stomach clench. "Why?"

"I want to show you something. Something I haven't showed anyone before."

His shoulders relaxed, and a smile softened the wary look in his eyes. "Is it your boobs?"

A laugh burst right out of me. I covered my mouth with my hand, still giggling. "Seriously!" I said when I was able. "Do you think of only one thing?"

"When you're standing in front of me and I haven't been able to scratch that insanely scratchy itch? Um, yes."

My head ducked automatically. His response made me blush, and it was embarrassing. After I recovered, I lifted my face. "I hate to break it to you, but the girls have been—"

"Stop right there," he intoned, holding up a hand. "I don't want to hear about anyone looking at you. Anyone that isn't me."

Geez, he was intense sometimes. Heaven help me, I liked it.

Clearing my throat, I went over to a nearby drawer and pulled out a special notebook, carrying it over to where he was.

"I've been working on this, kind of as a hobby. Kind of as a dream…" I held out the heavy spiral-bound book, and when his hand closed around it, mine had trouble letting go.

"I can't open it unless you let me," he said soft.

I let go and then stared as he opened up the cover and stared down. He was quiet, probably more silent than I'd ever heard as his eyes traveled over the pages I already knew so well. Then he would flip to another and then another.

At one point, his mouth kicked up in a small smile. His eyes glanced up at me and then went back down to devour more of the pages.

My thumbnail found its way into my mouth, and I started chewing it. I had a nasty habit of biting my nails when I was nervous. Without looking up, Stark reached out and pulled my hand away from my mouth.

Finally, he glanced up. "You did this?"

I nodded.

"It's a freaking book," he said, awe in his voice. "Like the kind we were just talking about."

"Well, it's not as good."

"No." He agreed. "It's fucking way better."

My eyes widened. "What?"

"It's a complete story, and the images you've drawn, the two go seamlessly together."

"It still needs some work," I said, not willing to accept such high praise. "And I haven't written the ending."

Stark's blue gaze finally released the pages before him to capture my eyes instead. "This is too good to be sitting in a drawer, Vi."

"You think it could get published?" I asked, voicing something I wanted so much, but never allowed myself to think was possible.

"Not even those hoity-toity art critics could deny the talent in these pages," he told me. "I mean, you not only created a story with words, but you added the perfect visual. Kids are going to love this."

"Well, it's for older kids, like middle grade-ish…" I said, worrying suddenly I'd made it too young.

He nodded enthusiastically. "Totally."

My heart fluttered, and happiness filled me. It was the first time I'd ever taken a chance and showed someone what I was working on. The first time I told someone about my dreams beyond drawing for a newspaper.

He liked it.

It meant so much to me.

Carefully, almost reverently, he closed the cover and handed it back to me. "You need to finish that and then send it somewhere. Get a manager."

"You mean an agent?" I said, wrinkling my nose.

"Yeah. One of them." His head cocked to the side. "But not a bossy one, not one who thinks they can run your entire life and tell you what to do."

"That is, um… very specific." I pointed out.

He grimaced, and I went to put the book away.

"So if you didn't come here to see my art…" I began. "Why did you come over?"

"I reached my limit," he said simply.

"Your limit?"

Stark's stare found mine. "The limit of days I could go without seeing you."

"Frankly," I informed him, "I'm offended it took so long."

A low predatory growl filled the room. He stalked over and pulled me gently into his chest. His kiss was like before… all consuming.

Chemistry and desire sizzled my skin, and I grasped his face to pull him even closer.

We kissed until air was absolutely essential, and both of us were gasping for breath when we finally pulled away. The second my lungs were full, I glanced at him and laughed.

"What?"

"You have pencil on your face." I held up my finger, the one I'd been using as a tool.

He grunted like he didn't care. I leaned up to rub it off with a clean finger, and those sparks that never seemed to die down crackled once more.

"I like you better without a hat," I confided as I brushed the last of it away. "I like being able to see your eyes."

"Come out with me tonight," he said abruptly.

I pulled back and looked at him with a question in my eyes. "You want to go out?"

He nodded. "With you."

It wasn't even Friday yet. I had class tomorrow.

"A real date," he invited, but it was more of a dare. "I'll dance with you."

Or maybe it was a bribe.

I was tempted. *So* tempted.

"I don't like to dance," I stuttered, even though I was mentally kicking myself.

"Everyone likes to dance," he refuted.

I shrugged one shoulder. I wasn't going to argue. I already stated how I felt.

He moved directly in front of me, slipping along my body like he knew it. Like his body belonged there. "If you don't like to dance, it's because you've never had a skilled partner before."

And then he started to move.

He oozed confidence. Purpose. He knew exactly where his body was and where he wanted it to go. He anticipated a beat only he could, following along with it like perhaps he wrote all the chords.

He used his limbs like a fine-tuned instrument, made music where there was none.

He felt solid against me.

Sure.

There was something about the way he moved, the way he felt plastered close that caused the bottom to fall out of my stomach, and a soft buzzing sound began in the back of my head, slowly blocking out everything else.

His hand slid around, cupping my hip, but not stopping. It curled around until he was full-on palming my ass. He wasn't feeling me up, though; he was dancing. Using my body as an anchor for his.

"Like this," he urged. I swore his voice dropped about twelve octaves. Chills broke out over my arms. "Move with me."

He pressed against my ass, brought his other hand around and flattened it out there to. With both his oversized hands cupping the roundness of my butt, my body obeyed him, undulating under the direction of his hands. I knew when I started moving the way he liked because his fingers spasmed against my ass.

"Come dancing with me," he said again.

Of course I said yes. My body spoke before words could even form on my tongue. It was the only answer to give.

twenty-two

Ten

Becca pissed me off.

Sort of like being away from her for even just a week or so was an exorcism that cleansed my life of her management.

Management = dominating my life.

Everything she said on the phone smelled like rotten eggs that came out of a decaying boar's ass. I don't know why now, all of a sudden, all her domineering behavior bothered me.

Actually, that was wrong. It *always* bothered me. Hell, it was probably why I was angry half the time. It was quite a realization.

Almost as if I were becoming Yoda.

Wise me being.

Except I was better looking. Naturally.

I just never really cared up until this point. Things were changing, though. It was sort of like waking up from some dream that lasted years. Like coming back to Earth after a trip in space.

I cared now. About how I lived my life. About *having* a life.

For the first time in what felt like half my life, I felt somewhat normal again. I wasn't consumed with success, how to make other people happy, money, traveling... following orders.

Coming back here to what Becca referred to as a "primitive" town was a wake-up call. What was the point of having huge success and a fat bank account if I didn't enjoy it? If I didn't have a life?

If I didn't feel like I earned it?

I knew that was a bit of a stretch. Obviously, I earned all of my millions. Some of those dollars were hard-gotten gains. This life wasn't easy. Maybe that's why somewhere along the way, I switched into autopilot and let Becca control it all.

And now I was here.

She said the only reason my career hadn't crashed and burned completely was because of her. I was beginning to think the reason it crashed at all was because of her.

No, she didn't whip it out and piss on a crowd. She didn't get in fights or snap at fans. She didn't do any of the shit I'd pulled... but she certainly didn't make my life any easier on me.

Maybe if I'd been more active in my own life, in my own career and decision making, I wouldn't feel so cornered by it all.

Cornered, yeah. That's exactly how I felt.

I loved music… I loved performing. But the business of it all was killing me. Squashing my passion and making it harder and harder to thrive.

These were thoughts I'd never really entertained before coming here. I'd been too busy, too drunk, or too passed out to ponder anything.

Then I stepped into my old summer room. I realized Nate went on living a life I knew nothing about. Derek welcomed me back, but I saw the apprehension, the way he almost wanted to protect his son from me. As if he didn't know me… as if I weren't like his second son all those years ago.

He was embarrassed of me.

I was ashamed.

Then there was Violet. The biggest catalyst of them all.

She didn't know me. Not my name. My career or the shitty things I'd done. She thought I was some broke-ass college student who drove a Jeep with more tape than parts, shared a room with my cousin, and had underlying darkness inside me.

She liked me anyway.

She didn't like me for who I was, just how I made her feel. For how I treated her when we were together.

Standing in the shadows was an interesting place to be. For someone so used to being in the spotlight, it was quite amazing to realize just how eye-opening the dark could really be.

I wasn't ready to go back to LA. Back to the life that I wasn't even sure I wanted anymore. The thought of leaving Violet made my chest ache.

I didn't deserve her. Hell, I was lying about everything. How could I tell her the truth? How could I look someone so beautiful in the face, someone who had a real reason to be angry, to be mad at the world but wasn't, and admit I had more than she could ever dream of, and I fucked it all up by being a selfish bastard?

When Becca demanded I give up my piece of ass because she was only using me, sickness climbed up the back of my throat.

It wasn't Violet who was using me. It was me who was using her.

Me, the guy sitting here thinking about how I wanted to be better. Do better. Yet what was I doing? More of the fucking same.

Still cornered. Just by different demons of my own making.

I wanted her. I wanted Violet so bad my heart beat with that desire. I stayed away while the war raged inside me. I wanted to see her desperately, but I knew it was wrong.

I carried the cartoon of her indirectly making fun of me in the pocket of my jeans. I kept it on the nightstand when I went to bed, and I looked at it when the ache inside me was almost a gaping hole.

Every man has a limit, though. Mine didn't take long to meet.

I had to see her. To touch her. To show her (and maybe myself) I was the man she knew... regardless of my actual name.

The second she pulled open the door, I could barely contain myself. The pull I felt to her was undeniable, unexplainable. Eventually, I was going to have to tell her exactly who I was and what I was really doing in town.

But not tonight.

Not now.

I wanted time with her. I craved it.

I was damn well going to have it.

There was a rave on the edge of town. Nate told me about it, said Blaylock was famous for having some huge, all-night raves. He'd never been since it wasn't on campus or at a frat. But it appealed to me. Raves were notoriously dark, with lots of people. You could easily disguise yourself.

Plus, music.

I missed the loud bass of a good song and the way it vibrated everything beneath your skin. I missed moving my body to the beat and just losing myself.

Seemed like a no-brainer to go get Violet and bring her with. Nah, she wasn't really a party girl, but she was a *me* girl.

I could say that because she was currently riding shotgun as I pulled into what looked like an abandoned part of the old business district on the edge of town. Abandoned buildings and warehouses lined the streets. Everything seemed kind of bare here, the sidewalks empty and cracked. The buildings were rundown with broken windows and marks of graffiti on the brick.

It reminded me of New York City, of the places I grew up.

"You're sure there's a party here?" Vi asked, totally doubtful.

I laughed low. "If Nate said it, then it's true."

"Are you sure Nate knows what he's talking about?"

"I can hear you," Nate retorted from his position in the back.

"Well, I wasn't whispering," Violet told him, turning to glance in his direction.

"It's the old warehouse at the end of the street," he said. "There's a rave there a couple times a month."

"If this turns out to be some gang hangout where everyone is shooting up with heroine, I will never forgive you." Violet sniffed and turned back around.

Laughing, I reached out and patted her leg. "I'll protect you from the gang, Vi."

"I'd never do you like that, Vi," Nate said, poking his head between the seats.

I released her leg to shove his face back where it came from. "That's Violet to you, ass."

"I feel so unloved," Nate announced.

"I think this is it," I said, downshifting. There were cars everywhere. The tall, dark building was glowing from the inside, neon light flashing through some of the windows. Music, loud and heavy, pumped out and could actually be heard over the Jeep.

"How is this place not crawling with cops?" Violet asked.

"I'm thinking they look the other way," Nate replied, sticking his face back between the seats. "Because everyone on campus knows about this place."

"I didn't." Violet looked at me. "Did you?"

Considering I wasn't actually ever on campus, the chances were slim. "Once or twice," I mumbled, not sure what to say.

"That's because you're a good girl," Nate told her.

"Does that make you a bad boy?" she asked cheekily.

BUTTERFLY

"The baddest."

I rolled my eyes. He was delusional.

"There's a spot down there," he said. I followed the direction and wedged the Jeep between two cars down the block.

Nate got out on my side, and then I went around to help Violet because she was lingering in the car.

"Are you sure about this?" she asked, biting her lower lip and making me think about kissing her.

"I'm sure I want to dance with you." I enticed. "And paint your body with some of that glow-in-the-dark paint I know they have going on in there."

"Can I paint you, too?"

"Oh, sweetheart, that's a given."

She held out her hand, and I pushed it away, instead leaning in to lift her out of the Wrangler, placing her on her feet.

"I don't know how you do that," she murmured.

"What?"

"Act like I don't weigh a ton."

I made a face. What the fuck was she talking about? "Have you looked in the mirror, Vi? You're tiny."

She made a rude sound. "In stature, yes. But we both know I have a little extra padding."

Again, I made a face. "Just what the fuck are you implying?"

"Nothing," she said and started past.

I caught her wrist, taking care not to squeeze too tightly. I knew she was more delicate than most. "Hey."

Violet turned back.

"Don't you say negative shit about yourself. Ever again." I released her arm so I could palm the sides of her

221

waist in the exact spot where it curved in on each side. Coaxing her closer, I stared down from beneath the brim of my hat. "I like the way you feel in my arms." My voice was low, the words only for her ears. "And the way you fill out your clothes, the way my hands fit right here." I flexed my fingers. "I know you have lots of reasons to be at war with your body, baby. But the shape and size of it ain't one."

She seemed stunned I would say that. Her eyes went round when I spoke, now blinking several times, as if she were trying to process the words.

I didn't wait for her to reply. I didn't need one. Instead, I leaned closer, kissed her forehead, and then tugged her along with me onto the sidewalk.

The three of us weren't the only people on the sidewalk. There were several groups and pairs walking in.

The girls were all wearing the kind of shit I saw in LA at the clubs and parties. Short. Tight. See-through. I liked it. I mean, I was a guy. What guy didn't want a sneak peek at the merchandise?

Usually, the way they flaunted their bodies turned me on, and I ended up going home with one or two on my arm.

Not tonight. Tonight, I looked at them and didn't feel desire. I felt kind of sorry the only thing they thought they had to offer was their body.

Thank God Violet wasn't dressed like that. If she had been, I probably would have ended up in more than one fight.

I didn't want men looking at her the way I looked at women back then. Just the thought of it made me sick.

"Looks like there's a cover," Nate said, his steps hesitating.

I glanced at the sign propped up by the metal door as we stepped up in line. It was fifty bucks a head.

"I got it," I said, reaching into my pocket and pulling out two hundred-dollar bills.

Violet's hand jolted in mine. "Who just walks around with two hundred dollars in their pants?"

Actually, I had about five hundred in cash on me. But I wasn't about to tell her that. I shrugged. "Using duct tape saves me a lot of money."

"You sure, man?" Nate asked. He was the only friend of mine that ever seemed hesitant or even disinterested in my money.

I respected that.

"Hell yeah," I said. "This was my idea."

"Next!" a large guard at the door called out.

The three of us moved up, and I slapped the money into his palm. "No change," he said.

I rolled my eyes. "How about a couple of those paint tubes?" I pointed to some glow-in-the-dark paint sticks in a plastic tub by his feet.

He grunted but grabbed a few tubes (yellow, orange, and green) and held them out.

"I want pink," Violet said.

"She wants pink," I told him.

Nate took the three tubes, while the guard fished around for a pink and handed it to Violet. After that, he pointed for us to get out of his sight.

We moved into the warehouse, and I was pretty fucking impressed. This was like a full-on rave. Right here in the middle of what Becca referred to as a "primitive" town.

The wide-open space was basically made of concrete with a huge window on one side with about fifty small window panes. At the far end of the space was a stage where a DJ was set up, and a bunch of glow-in-the-dark balloons hung over his head.

The only light was from the black lights, and everybody in here was painted with neon-colored glow paint.

The music, some sort of techno, trembled my insides and made it hard to take a deep breath. The crowd was loud. Bodies mashed together in the center, and more bodies scattered out around the perimeter, drinking and laughing.

We passed by a large card table covered in glow-in-the-dark props. Glasses, bracelets, necklaces. There were even masks, rings, and hats.

I stopped and snagged a neon-orange fedora and switched my baseball hat out for it.

Violet smiled and adjusted it a little, leaning up to yell, "That's a good look for you."

Pulling apart the plastic adjuster on the back of the baseball hat, I gestured for Vi to hook it onto the belt loop on my jeans. As she did, I snagged a yellow glow-in-the-dark whistle (she loved her whistles) and put it around her neck. Next, I picked up a glowing pink ring (it looked like one of those candy ring pops) and held it out.

She laughed and held out her pointer finger for me to slip it on.

After I added a pair of neon-green glasses to my face, we both turned to glance at Nate. Both of us burst out laughing.

He was wearing a glow-in-the-dark mustache, three bracelets, and an oversized pair of neon-blue glasses.

Violet went back to the table and came back, holding out what she'd gotten to Nate. He nodded enthusiastically and bent so she could fasten it around his neck.

It was a freaking bowtie.

This dude was so over the top.

When he was suitably dressed, he gave us both a thumbs-up.

A girl appeared, a girl who was quite literally covered in body paint, and grabbed Violet's hand. Startled, Vi let out a squeal, and I reacted instantly, rushing forward to get in the middle of them.

"Hair paint!" the girl yelled, not offended at the way I was about to literally take her out.

Woman or not, no one got to grab Vi.

I glanced at Violet, and she grinned. So I stepped back and watched this glowing girl paint streaks of neon pink, orange, and green through Violet's long blond hair.

When she was done, the girl grabbed at the long-sleeved shirt Violet was wearing over another. She peeled it down over her shoulders, and Violet started shaking her head.

The girl yelled something that even I couldn't hear, and Violet relented. Shyly, she peeled the flannel-looking button-down off her body and then tied it around her waist.

All she had on beneath it was a white tank top.

My mouth ran dry.

The strange girl lifted a paint stick, and I knew she was about to draw on my girl.

"Whoa," I said, inserting myself between them. I grabbed the paint stick and smiled. "I'll take it from here."

Violet waved at her new glow buddy, and the girl smiled.

"Here!" I called and handed her a green stick. "Paint my bro!" I pointed at Nate, who was standing there dancing all by himself.

She nodded and went over to him, not shy at all, running her hands over his chest and arms.

Nate froze. The surprise on his face made me laugh. He glanced at me, and I gyrated my hips like he should be getting some of that.

Violet smacked me.

I grabbed her up and kissed her.

Pulling back, I fingered the colored streaks in her hair. "I like it!" I told her.

Vi snatched the pink paint tube out of my hand and started putting it on her mouth like it was lipstick. I had a single WTF moment, but then I got distracted by that mouth and what I knew it felt like against mine.

When she was done, she crooked her finger at me to come close. I obliged, of course. Her small hand grasped my chin and turned it so she could plant a kiss right on my cheek. Pulling back, she studied what she'd done and grinned widely.

Then she turned my face to the other side and kissed me again. Then she kissed the underside of my jaw.

With a small sound, I watched as she swiped on some more paint, then leaned close, this time going painfully slow, her target the side of my neck.

My body trembled, and I knew it was more than the beat of the song.

Anticipation coiled in my center, and beside my hips, my hands balled into fists.

"What are you doing?" I growled.

She didn't answer. Instead, her lips latched onto my neck and sucked.

My body jolted because, holy fuck, I liked it. The way her lips increased in pressure and her tongue stroked over my skin was sweet torture. She pulled back way too fast for my liking, and I went to grab her back. She laughed and kissed the other side of my neck.

Violet wound her arms around my neck, rising onto her tiptoes and brushing along the front of my body. I clutched her against me as she rose up to my mouth.

Instead of kissing me full on, she pressed another one of her hot little teasing kisses right on the edge of my lips.

When she pulled back, satisfaction shone in her eyes.

"I have kiss marks all over me, don't I?" I mused.

She smiled. "You look taken," she called.

Well. Didn't she look mighty proud of herself?

No one had ever been possessive over me before.

I kinda liked it.

"You missed a spot," I told her. Before she could ask where, I covered her lips with mine, mashing them together until I wasn't sure where I ended and she began.

When I felt her body start to slip down mine, I lifted my head. There was only a trace of glow-in-the-dark paint left on her lips now. I knew if I looked in the mirror, it would be all over mine instead.

I kinda liked that, too.

I painted a few abstract lines and designs down her arms, over her collarbone, and across the exposed part of her chest. Tiny splatters of paint dotted her face, making it look like she had multi-colored freckles. The entire time I worked, her skin rippled beneath my touch, and I made sure to work slow—you know, give her some of that sweet torture she'd just given me.

When I was done, she pulled at my shirt. "You're overdressed!" she yelled.

I glanced around. Most of the guys in here weren't wearing a shirt. Instead, their upper bodies were covered in paint.

Even Nate had lost his shirt, and the glowy girl was lighting him up.

I handed Vi my hat and glasses so I could pull off the T-shirt, then quickly replaced the props to help hide my face. It was dark, and everyone was partying and drinking, but still. I had to be cautious.

A new vibe wafted off Violet, which made me forget all about being spotted. She didn't notice what I was doing, though.

She was too busy staring.

At my chest.

I wasn't a huge guy, but I danced a lot. My job required some kind of physical stamina, so my body was lean, but it was cut.

"See something you like?" I drawled.

Her eyes flashed up to mine, then right back to my body.

I felt used.

Violet could use me anytime.

BUTTERFLY

Without a word, she stepped forward. My heart stopped when she leaned forward and kissed my chest. When she pulled back, her eyes shyly lifted.

Swallowing past the rising emotion in my chest, I swiped at her lower lip. "There's no paint left on your mouth," I told her.

"That one was just for me."

Well, didn't that hit me right in the feels? It hit me in feels I didn't even know I had.

"Paint!" she said, coming out of the moment far faster than me. Her hand shot out between us, demanding. I slapped a few tubes into her palm, and she made herself busy covering me color.

As she worked, my feet and hips moved to the music. Nate appeared with drinks in his hand. Beers and neon Jell-O shots. I took two of the shots and tossed them both back.

"Dude!" Nate scolded. "One was Violet's!"

Over the music, I yelled. "She doesn't drink, butt munch!"

Nate grinned, and I knew he was remembering all the years we weren't allowed to cuss and butt munch had been our favorite term.

Glow-in-the-dark silly string shot through the air, and people cheered. It hit me in the side of the head and hung off my hat. Violet laughed and picked it off, dropping it to the floor.

A song I fucking loved started pumping through the crowd, and I gave a shout. After taking a swig of the beer, I grabbed Violet's hand. "No more paint. Let's dance."

"I'm going to the beer pong," Nate yelled and pointed to a corner of the room where a pretty impressive game of glowing beer pong was set up. Pong was Nate's game.

He disappeared, and I towed a hesitant Violet into the dancing crowd. "I don't dance," she tried to tell me again.

I latched onto her hips, fitting my body against hers, and proved her wrong.

Oh, she danced. Her body followed mine like thunder after a lightning strike. I lost myself in the music, in how good it felt to freaking move and dance.

I don't know how long we'd been dancing, but after a while, I missed her body. Noting it was no longer pressed close, I lifted my head.

She was still there, off to the side, watching me move with awe and attraction in her eyes. She wasn't the only one watching, though. Apparently, during my dancing blackout, I'd drawn an audience. Everyone had created a small circle around me, and in the center, I was performing without even knowing it.

I stopped abruptly, my gaze flying around, looking for anyone with recognition in their eyes. Instead, they all started clapping and woo-hooing at my mini show. A few glasses were raised in my honor, and though I was flattered, it was attention I did not want.

I went to Violet, wrapped my arms around her waist, and pulled her in. Her arms came up instantly, and we started slow dancing in the middle of an upbeat pop song. Lights flashed overhead, making me feel disoriented and tilted.

"Where the hell did you learn to move like that?" she yelled in my ear.

I shrugged. "Nowhere."

BUTTERFLY

Her eyes called me a liar, so I dipped my head and kissed her. It was effective at distracting her, so I continued kissing as we moved our bodies in a rhythm only the pair of us seemed to hear.

The sound of an ear-piercing alarm drowned out everything. Violet jerked back, her eyes wide with fear. I pulled her back into my body, wrapping her tight and shielding her head with my arm as I glanced around, wondering what the fuck was going on.

No one else seemed worried, though. In fact, everyone started to scream and cheer.

The next thing I knew, tons and tons of confetti started raining from the ceiling.

"You've. Been. Bombed!" the DJ yelled into his mic.

People cheered, and the music continued as more and more of the confetti rained down from the sky.

Violet lifted her head out of my chest, gazing up. The multicolored paper covered her hair, sat on her shoulders, and even clung to her eyelashes.

She grinned and held out her palm, catching some in her hand.

Her joy was infectious, and my own chin lifted, letting it rain onto the glasses and into my face. She laughed and poured what was in her palm over my hat, and I shook my head like a dog, making it rain off the brim.

She looked beautiful standing there, glowing in the dark, covered in confetti and laughing.

My heart stuttered, and another limit of mine was met.

It wasn't enough. Not anymore. Kissing her. Touching her. Dancing. I loved it all.

But it wasn't enough.

I wanted more. Desperately.

She must have felt the change come over me because her smile faded and her stare became heavy with desire.

Cupping her face, I leaned close. "You wanna get out of here?"

She nodded.

twenty-three

Violet

Maybe it was the dark. The neon colors. The flashing lights, music, or the glow-in-the-dark paint.

Perhaps it was the way Stark danced.

Whatever it was, something came over me.

Something very real and raw. Something so strong it was irresistible.

One moment we were walking into a rave, and the next, I was brazenly leaving glow-in-the-dark kisses all over his skin. His dancing was like foreplay. The best damn foreplay I'd ever experienced.

He made me want him by the promise in which he moved. Inciting desire and leaving a trail of heat every time we touched. *And, oh.* His hands were everywhere. In my hair, caressing my bare arms, brushing over my collarbone.

Just watching his muscle move and work beneath the smooth skin I'd just covered in paint made me long for more. So when he asked me if I wanted to leave, it really wasn't a question.

It was more like a must.

After we dropped Nate off, the sexual tension in the Jeep rose to about level twenty. He didn't touch me, though, except with his eyes. They would drift away from the road occasionally to stroke over my face or my chest before returning.

By the time he parked and came around to open the door for me, my nipples were so hard you could see them through my bra and tank top.

His eyes went right to my chest when he helped me out. My body slid down his on the way, and once I was on my feet, he lifted his thumbs and brushed them across the hard pebbles.

I shuddered, quaking visibly in front of him. He made a sound of pure desire, put an arm around my shoulders, and guided me into the building.

I was nervous, probably more than I ever had been before. I wasn't a virgin. I wasn't new to attraction... but this.

This wasn't attraction.

This was something else entirely.

I couldn't explain it. I could only feel it. It was sort of a cross between awkwardness and shameless desire. A combination that didn't really go, yet here it was churning me up inside.

"Give me the key, Vi," Stark murmured, breaking me out of the trance I was under.

I glanced up, blinked. His mouth lifted in an echo of a smile. "What?" I asked.

"I need to key to get us in the building." His voice was patient.

It was his patience that also made me slightly mad. How could be so level headed? I was over here ready to explode.

"Right," I said, forgoing my usual snarky replies. I had to pull out from beneath him to reach for my back pocket.

Stark caught my hand, stopping me. "It's in there?" I felt him gesture.

I nodded.

Gently, my hand was pushed away, and his long, thick fingers delved into the back pocket of my jeans for the keycard.

I turned my face so he couldn't see the way my eyes melted closed. Or the way my tongue jutted out to wet my lips.

He found the key quickly, of course. Yet somehow, the act of retrieving it wasn't a quick thing. His nimble fingers brushed over the rounded curve of my ass, gave it a light squeeze, and then wrapped around the plastic key. He dragged it upward, as if using it to stroke my cheek, and I had to admit it freaking turned me on.

Once the card was free, my muscles relaxed, having been so tense anticipating every single second he touched me. Even though his hand was done, Stark was not.

Standing just behind me, he leaned close, pressing his chest against my back and leaning over my shoulder. Both his arms came out, caging me in, surrounding me.

He smelled like beer and paint. And slightly of sweat. My body tensed again even as it swayed backward, farther into the circle of his body. He laughed low, a rumble that vibrated his chest and my back.

The beep of the card reader on the door barely registered in my brain. Stark pulled the door open, but neither of us moved. Instead, his face dipped into the side of my neck and left a circle of wetness where he kissed.

The cold night air brushed over it when he pulled back. I shivered. Stark gave me a gentle push. "Inside, baby," he murmured. His words were a stroke to my already swollen libido.

We walked down the quiet hallway, and he swiped the keycard again, pushing open the door to my dark room.

The door closed with an audible latch, and I felt, rather than saw, him move toward the light switch.

"Wait," I said. Offering no other explanation, I moved around the room I knew even in the darkness. It took a minute of rummaging, but I found what I was in search of. After unwrapping the cord, I flipped a small stand on the back and set it on the center of my coffee table. On top of my closed sketch book.

It took a minute, but I found the outlet in the wall and matched up the prongs. Seconds later, the small floodlight flickered on.

The room immediately glowed with a purple cast. The glow-in-the-dark paint covering our bodies suddenly lit up, nearly as bright and bold as it had back at the warehouse.

Stark was leaning against the door, his hat and face paint suddenly standing out. His teeth glowed when he laughed.

"You have a black light in your room?"

"I went through a phase with glow paint."

He shoved off the door, prowling toward me. "I don't like that."

My toes curled into my sneakers, anticipation making it hard to stand still. "It was on canvas… not on a man."

"So I'm your first?"

"First human painting?" I tilted my head, and he drew up in front of me. "Yes."

Stark lifted a strand of pink-painted hair between us and smoothed it between his fingers. "There's something about you," he murmured. "Something I've never recognized in anyone else."

"What is it?" I asked, unable to hide the tremble in my voice.

His teeth glowed again. "I was hoping you'd tell me."

I returned his smile. "I don't know what it is either."

"I sure as hell feel it," we both said at exactly the same moment.

Our eyes snapped up, bouncing between each other, knowing we understood exactly what we didn't know.

Still holding his gaze, I tugged the hem of his shirt. "I can't see all your paint."

Stark dropped the hat and glasses on the table, palmed the back of his shirt, and pulled it off in one smooth movement. God, that was fucking sexy. Have you ever noticed that before? The way a man takes off his shirt, the way it basically just obeys and jumps off his body the second he gives it a tug.

His chest lit with color. I lifted my palms to rub over his pecs. Beneath my hands, the muscles bunched and the pounding of his heart smacked against my palm.

Stark reached for the shirt tied around my waist and shoved it free, fingers delving beneath the hem of my tank and caressing the skin of my stomach.

I jolted from the contact, not used to being touched there. He paused and glanced down. Feeling his eyes, I met them.

"I want you." His voice dropped to a deep rumble. "Tell me you want me just as much."

"I put glow-in-the-dark kiss prints all over you... I'm pretty sure that was me staking my claim."

The whites of his eyes glowed when they flared. "Say. It."

"I want you."

Sliding his hand around the back of my neck, Stark pulled me in. Our lips met softly at first, throwing me off balance. I thought, based on the aggression and heat in his words, he would come at me hard and fast.

Instead, his lips brushed over mine in a tender caress, then did it once more.

I made an indulgent sound, trying to curl my fingers into his shirt and pull him closer. There was no shirt, and I ended up cupping his pecs.

He smiled, as if he knew exactly what kind of game he was playing, as if he'd written the rules. His breath was warm, just like his body, when he lowered again, kissing the tip of my nose.

That one-second kiss on a spot that wasn't really considered sexual turned me into putty.

Just before my knees buckled and I slid quite shamefully to the floor, his arms wrapped around my waist, holding me firm.

This was the kiss I'd been waiting for. The one that took. The one that gave. The one that promised I would never, ever forget his lips on my skin.

Goose bumps quite literally raced over my body, heightening the sensation of just about everything. My hands fell from his chest, clutched at his belt loops, and held on. His hand cradled the back of my head when it fell back, lips parted, inviting him deeper. His tongue stroked out, reaching into me, touching far more than just the inside of my mouth.

Abruptly, he yanked away and spun me so my back was to his front. My chest was heaving as he pushed my hair over one shoulder, leaned down, and latched on. He kissed his way across the top of my shoulder and burrowed into my neck. With a groan, I tilted my head to give him better access, reached behind me, and fisted my hand in his hair.

He sucked my flesh deep, at the same time pulling my ass into his groin. His hard erection rubbed brazenly against my butt, and I wished there was a hell of a lot less fabric between us.

Stark's mouth released my neck, kissing around to the back of my shoulder and then nibbling on that spot... the sweet spot on the back of my neck.

I shuddered, and he drew away. My shirt was ripped over my head, and then slowly, torturously, he peeled the bra straps down one at a time over my shoulders. Still feeling his steely cock at my ass and his firm chest along my back, his arm came around my middle from behind and his other reached for my breast.

The fabric of the bra still covered me, but his fingers didn't care. They delved, quite skillfully, beneath the cups, baring my flesh to the air and his palm.

He covered it completely, as if testing the weight and fullness.

He grunted, satisfied. I felt his hot breath at my ear. "I always knew you had enough to fill my hands."

I arched into him, pushing the swollen, aching mound closer.

His cock jerked against me as he moved back just enough to undo the clasp at my back. The bra fell away, and both his hands came up, covering both breasts.

The attention made me squirm. It made my panties damp and the desire I'd already felt turn to desperation. As he played, his lips kissed my back, my neck, and over my shoulders.

Just when I was about to beg, he latched onto my nipples, giving them a pinch that shot a bolt of pain/need all the way down into my panties.

With a great gasp, I spun, reaching for his jeans. I felt the heat of his eyes as I unbuttoned the fabric and slid the zipper down. I didn't hesitate. Whatever nerves I felt were overruled by hard need.

The second I was able, I shoved my hand deep into the jeans, rubbed along his stiff rod, and then wrapped my hand around it. Stark hissed. His hips jutted forward, and I gave him a firm stroke, reveling in the control I had over him in the moment.

Keeping my hand wrapped around his dick, I reached up, grabbed a handful of the long strands on top of his head, and went for his lips.

If he could torment me, then I could return the favor.

My body might not be magazine ready like his, but the passion that flowed through my veins? Let's just say I could argue it was the reason I was so damn curvy.

I'd always been passionate. I felt deeply. Almost to the point it was a flaw.

But never. Not ever had I felt passion this great for anything but art.

Until now.

Until Stark.

The realization made me gasp so hard it pulled me away from him. I wobbled on my heels, using his cock like an anchor so I didn't fall on my ass.

"Where do you think you're going?" he half growled, towing me back.

"Nowhere," I replied, breathless. "I'm not going anywhere."

My hand was still wrapped around his dick. He was so hard it practically vibrated in my hand. I wished I'd delved beneath his boxers, that there was no fabric between our skin. I'd been impatient, though.

Even in the dark, I saw his eyes flicker. Or maybe it was just the emotion he carried that shifted. Either way, I felt and saw it. His body angled closer, sort of like he was realigning with me.

The next thing I knew, my face was cupped in his palms. I had a moment of marveling at just how large they were, surrounding my head.

"Vi," he spoke, his voice not cutting into the sex-hazed room. Instead, it added to it.

How had I never noticed just how intoxicating his voice was?

"Stark."

"This is me right now. I want you to know that. Me." The pad of his thumb stroked over my cheekbone. "I've never been so present with anyone as I am with you right now."

My hands circled his wrists as I pushed up onto tiptoes. I tried to reach the spot I wanted. When I couldn't quite make it, I made a sound and tried to tug his head down.

Instead, he crouched and picked me up. Automatically, my legs went around his waist. His arms locked under my ass. "Better?" he asked, tilting his face up.

There were paint smears all over his face, across his chest, and even a little in his hair. I felt his heart beating every time his chest rose. His arms didn't shake while he held me. He stared as though I were indeed all he saw.

My heart turned over. Right there in the middle of this impassioned moment when we were about to have some earth-shattering sex. He went from tender to fierce then gazing at me with vulnerability in his eyes.

Stark was gorgeous. Commanding. Had a rhythm all his own.

Know what else he was?

Something that seemed to foreshadow everything else and stir up that passion inside me unlike anything else.

Human.

He was human. Just like me.

Taking his face in my hands, he watched as I dipped my head. I kissed the tip of his nose tenderly, just as he'd done to me.

His throat bobbed as it worked. I leaned my forehead against his and let the butterflies in my stomach take over. Stark whirled around toward the bed that was glowing brightly in the black light. My back hit the mattress. Cool, soft sheets rose up to mold around my body, but I barely noticed. Stark loomed over me, his wide shoulders blocking out everything. The kisses on his face glowed like a road map, highlighting destinations I'd already been but would definitely revisit.

My legs were still locked around his hips. He settled over me, between my legs. We began kissing again, my body straining up against him. The more skin I could get on his, the happier I would be.

His hands explored my upper body; mine explored his. We moved together as if we were already having sex, yet his body had yet to penetrate mine.

Stark rose onto his knees. My legs fell to either side. His fingers hooked in the waistband of my pants, and I lifted my hips, inviting him to strip me bare.

The second I was, insecurity creeped into the edge of my mind, threatening to overshadow the way I wanted him. He tried to push me back, but I resisted, instead tugging on his already open jeans.

He fell to the side, bouncing the mattress a little, and shoved the boxers and pants over his hips. Rising onto my knees, I pulled the clothing free and tossed it all onto the floor. My gaze ate up his entire body, the way he looked sprawled out on my bed, glowing with smeared pant, his cock standing up.

His chest was smooth and hairless. His entire body was silky smooth. The lines and sinew of his body were utterly graceful, his rigid dick promising strength.

Without even thinking about it, I leaned down. The strands of my hair brushed over his abs before my lips got to his skin. His stomach jolted the second they made contact, and I smiled, but didn't lift my head.

I kissed over his abs, swirled my tongue around his belly button, and then licked down the inside of this thigh. Stark made a sound, his hand tangling in my hair.

Instead of pulling his cock up off his body, I licked up it, starting at the base and gliding up to the tip. He pulsed, and I licked him again before boldly taking him into my mouth, sheathing him with all the heat there.

His legs spasmed, then settled back on the blankets. The hand in my hair went limp, and a small sound echoed through the glowing dark.

Confession: I'd never been all that impressed with the male anatomy. I usually much preferred a pair of wide, strong shoulders, an ornery smile, and a sexy head of hair. All the cocks I'd seen had been about the same, able to give some modicum of pleasure, but nothing that had the distinct ability to really hold my attention.

I knew now, though. I knew they weren't all the same. As I stroked and sucked and felt him thrust up into my mouth, I became addicted.

I could have stayed with my head in his lap and played for hours. Every new angle, new stroke, the feel of him gliding past my lips… it was new every time.

"Vi," he murmured, sounding drunk.

I looked up his body and smiled. His eyes flared and he moved, pushing me down onto the bed and coming over me. Without a word, his lips latched onto my breast, and my mind was wiped clean.

I opened my legs when his hand slid between them, gliding his fingers up my soaked slit. He growled when he felt just how much he affected me. Lifting his head from my breast, his mouth took mine, piercing me with his tongue at the same time his finger slid inside.

I moaned softly as we kissed and his hand became bolder.

When I started to pant, he pulled back, gazing down at me with an unreadable expression. I thought he might say something, but he didn't. Instead, he slid off the bed and dug around in the pocket of his jeans.

Positioning himself between my legs, he ripped the foil packet open with his teeth, and I stared as he rolled the latex over his unyielding length. Our chests collided, and one of his arms dipped under me, pulling me closer. I titled my hips up, expecting him to plunge right in.

He didn't, though. He gazed down at me, brushing his knuckles over the side of my face. My heart was beating rapidly. Hormones screamed beneath my skin. I was desperate to feel him inside me, yet he had the power to silence all of that with just a single look.

"You're so beautiful," he murmured, dipping his head and taking my lips.

Our tongues swirled together at the same moment he joined our bodies. The hand not under me slammed down on the mattress beside my body, and my face fell to the side. Stark pulled out and thrust into me again. Pleasure sparked over my entire body.

He moved in bed the same way he danced. Like he heard music no one else did, fucking me with a rhythm no one else knew.

It crushed me. I literally felt my interior crumble to pieces as he held me with one arm and used his body to blow mine apart.

"Stark." I gasped as he penetrated me again and again.

He lowered, brushing a kiss over my cheek. My fingers dug into his back as feelings and pleasure assaulted me. I knew when he was getting close to the edge because his head tilted back, affording me a view of his long, graceful neck.

Still gripping him, I surged up and licked up his neck, my teeth latching on his jaw. His body surged deep, so deep I fell back onto the pillows.

Instead of pulling out, he held himself there, deeper than any man had ever been before. I felt his tip twitching, as if it were an act of will he hadn't already burst.

"I have to let go," he rasped, pulling his arm out from under me, bracing his body above me.

My legs wrapped around his hips, pushing him even deeper into my core. He groaned and looked down, his eyes shuttered and hazy.

"Take me with you," I intoned.

One thrust. That's all it took. He moved just once, rubbing against the sweetest spot inside my body. I arched off the mattress as his dick practically ripped me in two. Stark's shout broke into my bliss, bringing me back just enough so could feel him pour into my body. The way he pulsed made me sigh.

His arms were shaking when reality came slowly back, his body still deeply joined with mine. I reached for him, slipped my hand around his damp back, and tugged. He came, surrendering his weight, settling over me for long blissful moments.

Then, without a sound, he rolled, keeping himself anchored inside me so I was lying on top of him.

Cool air brushed over my heated skin, my cheek pillowed on his shoulder. I felt satiated, completely boneless. Strands of my hair stuck to my cheeks, but I didn't bother to move them. I was too content.

Stark's arms wrapped around me. His fingertips danced over my back, dragging up and down along my spine.

"Don't move just yet, okay?" he whispered, tightening his arms around me.

"Wasn't going to," I whispered back.

twenty-four

Ten

Wasn't it dudes who were supposed to be the ones who fell asleep after sex?

Stupid stereotypes.

I couldn't sleep. I was too fucking hyped up by what just exploded between us. And by explode, I didn't mean my dick. Though that happened, too.

Vi, though. She didn't seem to have that problem. I might be offended, actually, if she wasn't so damn adorable. I was almost one hundred percent positive Vi was the first woman to ever fall asleep after sex with me. Most women would roll over and gush about how great I was in bed or muse about the fact they'd slept with Ten.

Usually about that time, I'd be done with it (with *her*) and get up to get dressed.

Not today.

Not with Violet.

I didn't want to move. Putting on clothes was about the furthest thought from my mind. I held her, something I very rarely did with women after sex. I left myself buried in her body and enclosed her in my arms. Within just a few minutes, Vi was asleep, her breathing deep, the rise and fall of her chest steady.

Oddly, it endeared her to me more.

This girl... she was totally wrong. For so many reasons. She had no clue who I was, fell asleep instead of being awed at my cock, didn't like to party or dance, wasn't famous or a model, and didn't even drink. Or eat bread (which still blew my mind).

I had no idea how so wrong could equal so very right.

She was a strong shot of reality in my unrealistic world. I didn't know how, but somewhere along the way, everything around me and about me became totally unreal. I was seriously beginning to think becoming public enemy number one was the best thing that could have happened to me.

Sort of like how the ghost of Christmas past came and visited Scrooge to show him all the errors of his ways. Came to shine light on shit the man was too boneheaded to see.

I felt grateful right now.

Grateful to be holed up in the tiny dorm room with an unlikely woman sprawled across my chest, sleeping contently. Grateful I had to go into hiding, even if it started out as something I was bitter about, something that had just been a means to an end.

I didn't want to go back there. To the place where being grateful was a new emotion.

What the hell happened to me?

Who the fuck had I become?

I forgot about Tennison, becoming instead The Perfect Ten.

Violet made me Stark. This entire town. Being back with Nate and Derek served me a nice hot slice of humble pie.

I liked this better.

I missed music, though. Even as I lay here, totally satisfied, words of the song I'd been writing with Nate crowded my head. All the feelings swirling inside me seemed to inspire them, and more words came, adding to what we already had.

Tangled up in drama, nowhere to go but down,
Hitting rock bottom has a definite sound.
Standing among the shadows, when I'm usually blinded by the light.
Realizing how eye opening the darkness is,
Feeling imprisoned all these years by sight.
Actions speak louder than words,
But what if no one listens?

As much as I loved this new sort of existence, I still wanted my career back. I wasn't sure there was an option for both.

Fear came over me like a black cloud on a sunny day. I was living a lie, something I hated to admit but was the truth just the same. Violet didn't know me.

Wait.

I *hated* that thought. Despised. Resented.

She did know me, goddammit. She knew the guy I wanted to be. The one I never even realized was deep down inside me.

She wouldn't see it that way. I'd been lying all this time. For a couple weeks now. I'd slept with her… I couldn't stop myself. I had to tell her, but I didn't know how.

I didn't want to.

What if I lost her?

I wanted to keep her.

I wanted her to be mine. Entirely.

The truth, though, the truth might tear us apart.

Violet made a sound and shifted against me. Her foot, which had been dangling off my leg, flexed, and she made a sound.

I caressed her back lightly. "What's wrong, sweetheart?"

"My ankle hurts," she murmured, her voice thick with sleep.

There was a heartbeat after she spoke. Then her body went still. Violet lifted her head off my chest and peeked up at me with only one open eye. "I said that out loud?"

Brushing away the strands of blond hair stuck to her cheek, I answered. "Is that a bad thing?"

She shrugged against me. "Complaining after sex isn't too sexy."

"You already fell asleep. I think we're past that." I teased.

Her cheeks turned pink, and I laughed as she ducked her face against me. I poked her in the ribs, and she jolted a little. "So what can I do about this ankle problem?"

She made a sound. "Nothing. It's just the way I'm lying. It's overextended."

It was easy to not think about her illness because, like she said before, she didn't look sick. And I never had to think about the way I lay or how my joints felt. It was clear, though, it was always there for her.

I started to slide her off me so we could adjust her position. She made a sound of protest and dug her nails into my skin.

"Ow!" I hollered. "I'm trying to help you, woman!"

"I don't want to move," she retorted. Then, in a softer voice, she said, "I like where I am."

"I think we might actually be stuck together," I said, my voice turning rueful. Inside, though, beneath the humor, my heart grew with her words. "This paint is sticky as shit."

She laughed. "It's smeared everywhere." She lifted her head and glanced at the bed and groaned. "Now I'm going to have to wash the sheets." Her voice was so forlorn I laughed.

"It's still all over your hair." I brushed it back once more.

Her fingers shot out to brush lightly over my cheek. "My kisses are just messy blobs now."

I lifted my head off the pillow and captured her lips. Her body melted into mine as our tongues swirled together. She tasted so damn good. I rolled, pinning her beneath me as we continued to kiss. When our lips unlocked, I stayed close and rubbed my stubble along her cheek.

"You have stubble burn on your face," I rumbled, kissing the side of her jaw.

"My skin turns red easily." She grimaced. "I really hope this paint doesn't irritate it."

After dropping another fast kiss fully on her mouth, I pushed off her and sat up. Glancing over my shoulder, I gazed at her still spread out on the bed, blankets around her legs, and paint literally everywhere.

"You're going to need help scrubbing that paint off."

Her eyes met mine. "You wanna help me?"

A slow smile curled my lips. "Is that even a question?"

Her teeth sank into her lower lip, emotions playing quickly on her face.

"I've already seen you naked, Vi." I pointed out.

"I'm not as—" She paused as if she didn't know what to say. Instead, she gestured to my body and wagged her eyebrows.

I chuckled. "What the fuck does"—I repeated her action—"mean?"

She rolled her eyes. "You know what it means."

I dove back on her, caging her in with my body. "I know you're being stupid right now," I intoned. I hated that she seemed insecure about the way she looked. I didn't want her to be. There was no reason for it.

She pulled my hair.

"Ow!" I yelled for the second time. Then a glint came into my eye. "You into rough sex?"

She burst out laughing. "No!"

Even though we were joking, emotion rushed into my chest. "Good, because I don't think I could do it. Not with you. I don't want to hurt you, Vi."

Violet's eyes softened and her hand cupped my face. "How about that shower?"

I turned my head to kiss her palm.

The shower was small, so we had to stand extra close. Her body wash smelled like peppermint, which made me think of candy canes.

"This makes me think of the holidays," I said as I slid the white puffy thing over her shoulder and down her arm.

"That's why I like it."

"You like Christmas?" I asked.

"Doesn't everybody?"

I was silent a moment, continuing my perusal of her body and pretending it was for the sake of getting her clean. I guess it was partly, but really, it was just an excuse to touch her more.

"Stark?" She glanced at me.

I lifted my head. "Sure," I said. Then after a moment, I went on. "Actually, the holidays have been more about work for me the past few years. I haven't gotten much downtime."

Translate that to *no* downtime. It was about appearances, parades, and promo. Last Christmas, I was in a hotel room by myself because I'd done a giant parade the morning of.

"Work?" She wrinkled her nose. "You have a job?"

I stopped washing. *Fuck.* I was afraid this was going to happen. My guard was crumbling, and I was going to start slipping up, talking about the life she didn't know about. Ten and Stark were blending together. "Um, yeah." I scrambled. "You know, seasonal jobs. I usually get one over the holidays. Spending money."

"Gotta keep stocked on the duct tape." She teased and poked me in the stomach.

I tickled her, and she dissolved into laughter.

I ignored the lump in my throat and how fucking shitty it felt to lie to her.

"Maybe this year you can take a little time off," she said after I went back to washing her. "Maybe we could, uh, hang out." Her voice was shy. It was sweet. The notion of spending time with her over the holidays made my chest tight. "You know, before I go home for the break."

"Home?" I asked, nearly dropping the pouf. I hadn't even thought about that. "Where is that?"

"Pennsylvania, a few hours from here."

I realized then I didn't know much about her life, just like she didn't know anything about mine. It was as though we were two perfect strangers, except we weren't. We knew each other far too well, just not on a superficial level.

I didn't want to talk anymore. Not about anything that could come between us. I moved my hand down to her chest, leaving a trail of white bubbles across her breast. She made a sound, and I did it again.

Our bodies slid along each other's, the soap making it far too easy to glide together. We used too much of that peppermint stuff. The scent clouded the small bathroom. Suds clung to the walls, our skin, and her chin.

We made out until the water went cold and Violet was shrieking under the spray, trying to rinse the conditioner out of her hair. I wasn't cold, though. Need kept my blood near boiling.

Vi's teeth were chattering when I reached around her to turn off the spray.

"Hey!" she scolded, scowling at me from beneath dripping, long hair. "What if there's conditioner left in there." She pointed at her head.

"You're freezing." I pointed out, reaching for a towel.

"Well, if I look like crap, you're the one who will have to look at me," she quipped as I wrapped her in the fabric.

"You couldn't look like crap if you tried," I said, rubbing my hands along her arms as she shivered.

Her eyes drifted up. Drops of water clung to her lashes and her lips were wet. "Aren't you cold?" she asked.

I smirked and kept rubbing warmth into her. "You're just delicate."

She gazed at me for long moments, sucking a bead of water off her lower lip. "I kinda am. You better be careful with me."

Her whispered confession pierced me. Like a tiny needle capable of creating an immeasurable amount of pain. The air around us thickened, not from the humidity of the long shower, but from the intensity of the way our energy collided. I'd never felt anything so intense with another person.

I didn't know what to say. Even if I thought of something, I wouldn't have known how to say it, so I let the thick silence speak for itself. I focused instead on drying her completely. The towel was thick and soft, making the job much quicker than I would have liked. When her body was dry, I squeezed the water out of the ends of her long hair, then pushed them back over her shoulders.

"C'mere," I murmured, pulling her into my chest. I was still wet, but the towel around her soaked up some of the water. Violet's arms wound around my waist, and I held her close, resting my chin atop her head.

While I dried off, I watched her run a comb through her wet hair and put a bunch of shit in it before tugging an oversized black T-shirt over her head. I liked the way it brushed against the backs of her bare thighs.

While I was yanking my boxers out of my jeans, she retrieved a couple bottled waters out of her tiny fridge and carried them over to me. Without thinking, I grabbed them both, untwisted the cap on one, and handed it to her. She seemed a little surprised but took it, tilting it to her lips.

"What's the deal with your knuckle?" I said, watching her as I drank down some of my own water.

A self-conscious glint came into her eyes, and Violet ducked her head. I cursed inwardly because that was a dick thing to say. I mean, I wanted to know. But shit, I could have asked nicer.

"Hey," I said, soft, lifting her face with my fingers. "I didn't mean to sound like that. Sometimes I'm a dipshit and just blurt things out. I've, ah, never been good at…"

"Not being a dipshit?" she asked, grinning.

"Yeah." I agreed, dry. I shifted closer, angling my body into hers. "It just bothers me to see it, not because it's ugly to look at, but because it reminds me that you hurt."

She drank some more water, then set aside the bottle. Holding her hand out between us, she gazed down at the knuckle of her right hand pointer finger. "That's what RA does. It can basically deform your joints. This is the only one I have like this. It probably doesn't help I use this finger as a shading tool for my art." She shrugged.

I lifted her hand and kissed the area.

"You're the first person, outside of family, who actually kinda gets it… It's like you actually care."

"Oh, baby. I care," I whispered, threading our fingers together. "And I know what it's like to have parts of you invisible to the rest of the world."

Her forehead wrinkled, and that panicked feeling of having her find out about me seized my chest. I stepped even closer, bringing our bodies so close they touched. The air was back to being thick again. I took a deep breath, reveling in the pull between us.

I kissed her, slow and deep. I reached for something inside her, that same thing that generated the palpable feelings and tension around us. It was an overwhelming feeling to experience. To succumb to. That didn't stop me from reaching for more, though.

Violet's hands slid up my bare chest, clasped around my neck. I loved the way she always rose on tiptoe, as if she were reaching, too.

The desire that built up inside me in the shower came back like a freight train, creating a slight tremble in my fingers.

Her body started shivering again, which concerned me, and I pulled back enough so I could look into her eyes. "Are you still cold?"

Her eyes were brilliant blue fire, the pupils dilated, which only fueled the need pooling in my balls. "No, I'm not," she whispered.

Stomach muscles contracting, I pulled her into my body again, allowing her to feel the rocking boner stiffening between us. I moved, walking us toward the bed to gently push her down. She resisted, and I drew back instantly, a question in my eyes.

"There's paint all over the sheets," she said, a little sheepish. "I do not want to wash my hair again."

I chuckled and moved around her to pull all the blankets up, covering up the sheets. "Better?"

She nodded.

Before pushing her back down again, I stripped the shirt over her head, loving the fact she'd yet to put on panties. My hands caressed the outline of her body, following the dips and curves, finally settling at her waist.

The first time had been a mix of emotion. Of glow-in-the-dark paint and raw need hammering inside my veins. This time was similar... but it was also more. The paint was washed away, leaving only her and me. Now there was one emotion battling back some of the others, even at the impatience in my body.

"I want you so much," I whispered, avoiding even saying the word inside my mind.

Beneath me once more, Violet gazed up. Her eyes held that feeling I'd been reaching for when I kissed her before.

"Stark." My name slipped right off her tongue as though it were the only word she knew. Like it was the only word she would ever need.

I didn't say anything else because, honestly, words failed me. I dipped my head and kissed her, though it went deeper than her lips.

I made love to her. It was really the only way to describe it. I wanted to show her all the things I couldn't say. Hopefully, if I could make her feel the same way I did, she might forgive me when the truth about who I really was came out.

twenty-five

Violet

You know what kind of influence Stark was?

A bad one.

So bad it was good.

I didn't know what happened between us last night exactly. All I knew was it somehow bound us together. Maybe that was the artist in me, thinking or feeling a little too deep. But I couldn't help it. When he kissed me last night, something inside me surrendered to him, tangled in him... sort of like our souls were somehow now tethered. Even after he left my body, I still felt him, as if he lingered deep inside me.

Which is why I skipped classes.

I never did that. Even when I felt like crap, I forced myself to go. Not today... Today, the warm embrace of Stark's arms won out and the absolute refusal to be separated from him kept me firmly at his side.

"This is the first time I've skipped classes this year," I told him.

We were rolled up like a human burrito with our bare feet sticking out the end of the comforter. It was the only blanket on my bed that survived the paint-filled sex we'd had. Not that I was uncomfortable, though. How could I be with him rolled up with me?

Stark lifted his head and looked at me, his hair wild, and he groaned. "I'm corrupting you."

"So skipping class is something you often do?" I teased.

The muscles in his body tensed, but he smiled. "I definitely don't have a perfect attendance record like you."

"Had," I corrected, laying my cheek against him once more.

"This is where I tell you to go to class, that I don't want to be responsible for marring your perfection."

"But?" I grinned to myself.

"But I'm not letting go of you." The feel of his lips in my hair made my heart tremble.

"I can miss one day. It won't hurt anything. I'm ahead in most classes anyway. Besides, I need a break from my drawing professor. That guy gives the word eccentric a run for its money."

Stark made an amused sound. "What's so weird about him?"

"Aside from his unfortunate dressing habits, his penchant for criticism and yelling... He's decided it will be some kind of great artistic experience for us to sketch a model. Naked."

Stark paused, then burst out laughing. "A naked model?"

I shuddered. "How awkward is that? Like I want to go sit in a circle for ninety minutes two times next week with some naked person standing there. Gross."

He was still chuckling. Then suddenly he went quiet. "Wait a minute. Is it a woman or a man?"

"Who cares?" I wondered. Naked was naked.

"You aren't going to class and staring at some other dude's dick!" he exclaimed.

Ah. He didn't like that, did he? "You can't suppress the art of a fine male form," I told him, secretly enjoying the horror on his face. Served him right!

He made a strangled sound and sat up, forcing me with him. We were barely able because the comforter was so tight around us. "What the hell kind of pervert is this guy? How does the school allow this?" he demanded.

I giggled.

His eyes zeroed in on my face. "Are you laughing? You think this is funny?"

My giggles turned into full-on laughter. "You're jealous."

"Damn right I am!" He blanched. "I mean, hell no, I'm not."

I laughed even harder.

We fell back on the bed. Stark pinned me beneath him. "Like it's so unbelievable I don't want my girl staring at some other man's cock and balls for ninety minutes." He seemed bewildered I thought this was so hysterical.

He said cock and balls.

"Stop laughing," he growled. Then a second later, he kissed me.

That shut me up. Really fast. I melted into him with a soft sigh. When he lifted his head, I smiled up at him. "You called me your girl."

"Baby, haven't you been listening?" He stroked my cheek. His face was so close to mine I could make out all the different tones of blue in his gaze. "I've been calling you that from almost the minute we met."

"Feels real now," I whispered.

His head cocked to the side. "It is real. You are mine. Right?"

I nodded.

A smug look pulled his features, and I rolled my eyes.

"Now," he said. "About this business of naked men parading around in front of you."

"Oh my gosh!" I groaned. "It's not a strip club. It's art class. And trust me; I do not want to be there."

I saw an argument forming on his tongue, so I hurried to add, "It's not a male model. It's a female."

His eyes widened. "A naked chick?"

"The professor is a man. Big surprise he'd get a female model," I muttered. Add sexist to the list of complaints I had about this man.

Stark grinned as though all his problems were solved. "You drawing another naked woman?" He mused. "Can I come watch?"

I smacked him.

He rolled off me with a groan. "I had to ask."

"You know what's even worse?" I said, ignoring his lesbian fantasy that was not going to happen.

He glanced at me with overly wide eyes. "That there's going to be *two* naked girls instead?"

"Get your mind out of the gutter, man!" I yelled.

He grinned.

"I'm serious!" I said, squirming a little. This assignment seriously made me uncomfortable.

Stark tossed his arm over my waist and towed me into his side. "Tell me."

"The model has to wear a bag over her head."

Her drew back, a funny look on his features. "What the actual fuck?"

"Exactly." I agreed. "I'm telling you this professor is using class for his own deranged fantasies. He probably has a freezer full of bodies at home."

"What is the purpose of a bag?" Stark wondered.

"So class can see the body objectively and not with the humanity that comes with it by looking at the person's face," I said in the same haughty and, frankly, stupid tone as my professor.

"Vi, that shit is just weird," Stark muttered.

"I know," I replied, forlorn.

"I'm still glad it's a woman, though."

I sighed. Of course he was.

"You're not missing anything important today by skipping, are you?" I asked.

"Spending time with you is more important than anything else today," he replied, his voice oddly sincere. It was almost sad.

An unwelcome sense of foreboding worked its way down my spine. "Stark?" I asked, brushing a hand over his chest.

He caught it and pressed a kiss against my fingers. "How about I take you to get some breakfast?"

I nodded. Any excuse to not make the green shake.

Stark unrolled us from the comforter, which made me laugh because I was pretty sure he used it as an excuse to grope me. I kinda liked it.

When we were both finally on our feet, I stared down at the sheets in all their paint-covered glory. I groaned. "I have to do laundry."

I hated doing laundry. The facility was on the other side of the building, and the washers and dryers were huge. I had to practically climb into them to get my clothes out.

Stark grabbed a handful of the blankets and yanked, which practically pulled everything off in one try. I made a disgusted sound. "That usually takes me five minutes!"

He flashed me a smile and pulled the rest of the stuff off. "I'll carry it to the laundry for you. We can throw it in and then get it when we get back from getting food."

I gave him a funny look.

"What?" he asked.

Then I remembered he didn't live in a dorm, but with his uncle and cousin. "I can't just leave it there. That's a good way to get your stuff stolen."

He made a strangled sound. "People steal laundry?"

I nodded.

"And I thought I was fucked up," he muttered.

I wrinkled my nose. "What?"

With a pile of sheets and blankets at his feet, he glanced up. "We'll hit up a drive-thru, then take all this to my place. You can use the machines there, and we'll just hang out."

"To your house?" I asked, surprised.

He nodded. "There's a washer and dryer."

"What about Nate and your uncle?"

He shrugged. "Class and work."

He must have seen the hesitation in my eyes because he stepped over the laundry and grasped me around the waist. "We can make out while we're waiting." He wagged his eyebrows.

I smiled. "How's a girl supposed to say no to that?"

Somewhere in the room, his phone began to ring. He went over to his jeans and pulled the cell from the pocket. His face darkened when he looked down at the screen. Then he silenced the call and dropped it onto the table.

He saw me watching and shrugged. "Didn't know the number."

I nodded and began flexing my fingers and toes, trying to get some movement in them.

"You feeling okay?" he asked, his gaze sharpening.

I nodded and began pulling clothes out of my dresser.

Behind me, he made a sound. "My T-shirt is covered in paint."

"I have a BU hoodie, like the one you let me borrow the other night. You can wear that to your place," I said, yanking it out and tossing it to him. "I bought it big."

I watched him tug it on over his very enticing bare chest. When his head poked out the top, he announced, "This smells like a girl."

"I am a girl." I pointed out.

He held up his arm and sniffed the sleeve. "I kinda like it."

I rolled my eyes and went back to finding myself some clothes. On the coffee table, his phone went off again.

He picked it up, glanced at it, then shut it off completely.

"If you need to answer that…" I said a little puzzled.

"I don't," he replied, firm. Stepping around to where I was, he wrapped me in his arms from behind. "The only person getting my attention today is you," he whispered against my ear.

Little shivers raced up my spine. His teeth nipped at my earlobe. Snatching my phone off my dresser in front of me, I powered it down just as he had.

Stark made a sound and spun me to face him. "You giving me all your attention today, Vi?" Against my lips, he spoke. "I think it's going to be a damn good day."

It was.

At least for a little while.

twenty-six

Ten

I was not in the mood for Becca. Not today, the day I woke up with Violet in my arms. She'd called continuously—while we'd been in the shower and then several times when we weren't. It was fucking annoying.

I was seriously considering firing her ass. I was just about done with the fact she thought she ruled my entire life. I told her I wasn't ready to come back to LA, and I freaking meant it.

She was going to have to get another meal ticket.

Or, hey, here's a thought. Work her ass off for another one of her clients and make him just as famous as I'd been.

I thought I would miss the fame. The recognition. The success.

I didn't.

Not at all. The only thing I missed was the music. The studio. Don't get me wrong. Having a shit ton of money, a hella nice pad, and cars was definitely good times, but I was happier here, now… and none of that stuff was around.

Currently, I was lying in a twin-sized bed in a room I shared with my cousin. Violet was on top of me. Half her clothes were gone, and our tongues were intertwined. Her breath tasted like coffee, and the only thoughts going through my head were of her.

The sound of the dryer buzzing made her lift her head. I grabbed her back, trying to pull her back in.

"Sounds like it's done."

"I'm not," I murmured, taking her lips again.

I couldn't get enough of her. Never enough.

She kissed me back and laughed.

A little while later, we were getting dressed when she sighed and flopped down on the edge of the bed. I looked around at her, instantly noting the way exhaustion clung to her skin. Immediately, I crouched in front of her, folding her hands in mine. "You're tired."

She smiled and gave my hand a light squeeze. "A little."

It was my fault. I'd kept her up half the night, making love, went at her again this morning, then again right now. I was a horny bastard.

"How about we go back to your room? I'll make the bed for you, and then we can lie in it the rest of the day and finish that series we started on Netflix?"

Her eyes lifted to mine. "Really?"

I held up my hands like I was making a vow. "I won't even grope you."

She pouted. "Not even a little?"

I laughed. "Nah. Probably a lot."

"'Kay." She agreed, dipping her head and smiling.

"You like popcorn?" I asked. That was gluten free, right? Shit, I needed to do some more reading.

"It's my favorite," she said, perking up.

I nodded as if it were a done deal and picked up the hoodie she'd lent me and tossed it on. I noted her watching, and I shrugged. "What?"

"You have a drawer full of clothes..."

I was missing her point. "So?"

"So you're wearing my hoodie and you said it smells like a girl."

"It's unisex." I defended. "I have the same one."

"Wear yours." She pointed out.

"But when I wear this one, I take a deep breath and smell you."

Her entire face softened; the expression in her eyes turned misty. I grabbed up my Blaylock hoodie and tossed it to her. "Here, you can have mine."

"You wanna trade?" she asked.

"They're the same size."

She put the fabric up to her nose. "This one smells like you."

"You like it, right?" I said knowingly.

In reply, she tugged it on over her head.

I grunted in satisfaction and held out my hand for her. "'C'mon, let's go."

I shoved the clean bedding in the backseat of the time machine and we made a quick stop to pick up some snacks and shit before heading back to her dorm.

It was cold today. The air carried the scent of snow. The back pocket of my jeans was weighed down with my shutdown cell, and as we walked, I wondered how many more times Becca tried to call and just how pissed she was she couldn't get through.

It had been nice being shut off completely, just being with Vi. I actually looked forward to holing up in her room the rest of the day... and hopefully night.

Since my arms were loaded down with everything, she let us into the room and held open the door. I dropped all the blankets on her bed, then set the bag of food on the coffee table.

The door had barely shut behind us when there was an insistent knock. Violet glanced at me, and I arched a brow. "Expecting someone?"

"No," she replied, dubious, a hint of wariness in her eyes.

I thought of Ross, the freaking dickface, and frowned. "You haven't had any trouble with that douche from the frat, have you?"

She shook her head adamantly. "He hasn't spoken to me at all."

"Good," I growled, then walked toward the door to answer it. She was already near it, so I had to step around her.

"What are you doing?" she wondered out loud.

I glanced over my shoulder. "You think I'm the kind of guy to let you answer the door when we don't know who's on the other side?"

"What do you think I do when you aren't here?" She pointed out.

I didn't care for her logic. In fact, suddenly, I didn't care for the fact that she lived here alone at all. I knew it was a dorm building, but I'd seen the kind of riffraff running around this campus. She'd already had trouble with one.

"You need more protection than a whistle." I decided.

The knock came again, louder this time. I pulled it open, just enough so I could see who was on the other side.

It was some guy. Jesus! How many guys came around here looking for her?

"Who the hell are you?" I said when he just stared and didn't say anything. In fact, he seemed pretty shocked that he was staring at me and not Violet.

Good.

Fucker didn't need to come back.

"Holy shit," the guy said, still staring at me. I opened my mouth to tell him to get lost, when he spoke again. "Ten."

I froze, feeling like a deer caught in some bright-ass headlights. "What?" I said, trying to feign indifference.

The guy gave me a *don't even try* look and then tried to glance past me.

"V!" he called.

I bristled, moving the slam the door in his face. My stomach was twisting... He freaking knew me instantly. What if Violet heard him?

"Vance?" She gasped, and suddenly she was at my back, peering around me. "Oh my God! Vance!" she said when she saw the guy standing there.

Vance, as in... her brother, her gay brother who was in love with me? That Vance?

Oh shit.

"Surprise!" he said, holding out his arms, sliding me an eye and making it feel as though I'd taken a knife straight to my heart.

Violet squealed and ducked under my arm to launch at him. He folded his arms around her, and she laughed, hugging him back.

Our eyes connected over her head.

Yep, she was shorter than him, too.

I couldn't read his expression, other than the full recognition in his depths.

Violet pulled back. "What are you doing here?" she demanded. "You should have told me you were coming!"

"Girl. Have you even looked at your phone today?" He arched a brow and crossed his arms over his chest.

He had dark-brown hair, not blond like Vi's. His eyes were blue like hers, though. We were close to the same size, but I was slightly bigger, so at least there was that. 'Course, I was older. If he grew any more, he'd surpass me.

Violet glanced at me over her shoulder, a sheepish look in her eye. My heart cracked just looking at her.

It was over.

All of this was over now.

I might never see her look at me like that again.

The knife previously buried in my heart twisted.

"Actually, no," she told her brother, a small twinkle in her eye.

I couldn't help it. I smiled at her. I had to. I couldn't not smile when she was looking at me this way.

"We, uh, turned our phones off today."

"How convenient," Vance remarked.

"What?" she asked, not understanding the undertones in his voice.

"You gonna invite me in, or are we going to stand in the hall so everyone can hear our business?"

I pushed the door wide and held it. Violet walked by, and then Vance followed. As he entered, he stopped beside me, giving me a once-over. Then he made a tsking sound.

I shut the door and then turned, feeling totally caught in my own web of lies. I thought about running, about just getting the hell out. Ten might have done that, actually. In fact, it wouldn't be the first time I'd run. Wasn't that how I met Violet?

Ten might run... but Stark sure as hell didn't.

I wasn't going anywhere. Not until Vi told me to go.

A few lines of the ever-lengthening song I was writing floated through my head.

Trapped,
Caught,
Ensnared by a web.

"Before we get into this, I just have two things I need to say," Vance announced, spinning around to look at me.

"Before we get into what?" Violet asked, finally picking up on the weird undercurrents going on.

I gave her an apologetic stare.

"One..." Vance held up his finger. "Holy *shit*, you are just as fine in person as you are on TV. And two, whatever game you are playing with my sister, it's over."

"I can explain," I said, hoping she would at least listen.

"Wait." Violet stepped between us. "What in the hell is going on?" she said, frustrated. She turned to her brother. "This is Stark, Vance. You know, the guy I told you about?"

"You told him about me?" I asked. Knowing that made this even worse. She'd liked me enough to mention me to her brother.

Vance shook his head sadly and sighed. "He definitely is sex on a stick."

"Vance!" Violet hissed, embarrassed.

He waved it off. "Honey, that is the least of your problems."

"Vi, can I talk to you a minute?" I said. "Alone."

Vance gave me a look. "I might be gay, but I'm not a dumbass. I think you've had enough alone time with my sister."

"If someone doesn't explain to me right now what is going on, you're both out of here." Violet insisted.

"If you only listened to me when I talked, this would not have happened," Vance said as he fished his phone out of the pocket of his bomber jacket.

Violet made an impatient sound.

After he tapped the screen a few times, he glanced up. "You told me you didn't go see Ten."

Violet sighed loudly. "OMG, Vance! How many times do I have to apologize. I'm sorry I didn't get you an autograph."

He glanced at me. "Clever, using your last name since no one ever uses it. It's like lying without actually telling a lie."

"What's a lie?" Violet turned and looked at me, confusion in her beautiful blue eyes.

Vance held up his phone. A picture of me onstage with a guitar filled the screen. "You're not dating some college student named Stark, V. There is no Stark. He's Ten."

Violet made sound and snatched the phone out of his hand, staring hard at the photo and then up at me. Her face went white. "No way." She denied.

"You think I wouldn't know him?" Vance scoffed. Then he glanced at me. "I have like four posters of you hanging on my bedroom walls." He shook his head. "Now I'm going to have to take them down."

"Stark," Violet said, holding the phone down at her side. Her eyes searched my face, looking for recognition. A denial. A confirmation. All I could do was stand there and stare at her. Take in her face and feel sick.

I didn't want to lose her.

"The hat you always wear, the dark party, the drive-thrus, the vague answers about school…" Her voice drifted away. "You… You're…"

Swallowing, I pushed away from the door, taking one step closer to her. "I'm sorry."

"It's true?" she asked, her voice lowering. She glanced back at the phone, then to me. "You're Ten… the guy with a number for a name?"

I wished in that moment I could say no. I wished I could forget who I really was and be just exactly who she thought.

I couldn't lie. Not anymore.

I stared her straight in the eye and finally told her the truth. "Yes, I'm Ten."

twenty-seven

Violet

You know, I had a pretty good imagination. I came up with all kinds of scenarios and horrible sequences of events that could befall me or any random person on a daily basis.

But this?

Not even my morbid and over-busy mind could come up with something this insane.

I laughed. It was forced and kind of made me sound like a horse, but it was the best I could do. I gestured between the two men. "Who thought of this?" I asked. "This is quite the joke."

"I'm always down to cut class, but would I drive all this way for a joke?" Vance asked.

Oh no. No.

I glanced at Stark... Ten... whoever the hell the man standing in front of me was.

"That night at the gallery," he said, his voice low and deep. "The night we met…"

I nodded.

"I'd just come from that lecture at the music hall. I'd been trying to get some air, walk down one of the empty side streets. But some people saw me, and I took off. I came in the gallery to hide from them."

I remembered how he looked as if he'd been hiding. My heart was beating slow and heavy. Trepidation filled me. I didn't want to hear this, yet he kept talking.

"You didn't recognize me," he said, a note of wonder in his voice.

"Seriously, though, sis. I know you don't always listen when I talk, but to not recognize Ten, of all people… I'm insulted," Vance put in.

"It's not like I expected some huge star to walk into the gallery!" I burst out. Geez!

"I'm not a star," Stark said instantly. "I'm a celebrity, but my reputation is too shitty for me to be considered a star."

"It's true." Vance agreed.

"You lied," I said, suddenly feeling deflated, like a boat whose sails were out of wind. I couldn't even wrap my head around this, around the truth.

No wonder I believed the lie. It was so much more believable.

Oh my God, he'd made a complete fool out me! My eyes flashed up, anger suddenly giving me some energy. "Did you laugh when you went home at night? Did you and Nate have a good old time making fun of Violet, the poor, stupid girl who fell for every word you said?"

"It's not like that." He took a step toward me, pleading in his expression.

"Don't even think about it!" I snapped and backed up. "Oh my God, I slept with you!" I shook my hands out as if it would somehow get him off of me.

It wouldn't work.

He wasn't on me. He was *in* me.

"You had sex with Ten!" Vance burst out.

Stark and I both turned to glare at him. Vance pressed his lips together. I turned back to Stark.

Vance leaned close. "I'm gonna need some details later."

"Can I talk to you alone?" Stark implored. "Just for a few minutes."

"Anything you have to say can be said in front of me." Vance sniffed.

"Please," Stark said, ignoring my brother's remarks.

I wanted to give in, but how could I? Did his reasons/excuses even matter? A lie was a lie. I totally turned away from him, not wanting to see the look in his eyes. Focusing on my brother, I asked, "How did you even find out about this?"

Vance tossed his hands up in the air. "I seriously don't know how you survive."

He continued to mutter about my deficient survival skills and took his cell out of my hands. "It's all over the internet, V. I was uber intrigued when I saw the headlines filling my notifications this morning when I got out of bed." After a few seconds, he read some of the lines out loud. "*Ten and new mystery woman. Ten turning his life around for new love? Ten quitting the spotlight for a commoner?* Then there's my favorite." He concluded. *"The bad boy of pop and the good girl."*

I glanced at Stark. His face was confused, as if even he didn't know what Vance was talking about.

"Can I see that?" he asked my brother.

Vance handed him the phone. "Imagine my shock when I pulled up the articles and the leaked photos were of my sister… with my biggest, uh…" His words faltered.

"He already knows you're in love with him," I told Vance, dry.

"Your loyalty is terrible," he admonished like I'd broken some sisterly code by confessing his deepest secret.

Um, please. If his love for Ten was a secret, it was the worst kept one in the history of the universe.

"Not in love. Just his biggest fan." My brother corrected, embarrassed.

I rolled my eyes. "My loyalty is fine. I told *Stark* that. I didn't know he wasn't actually who he said he was." I slid a hard look over to him.

He didn't react to my words, though. He was still flipping through the phone, a dark look looming over his face. "What the fuck is this?" he ground out.

"It's all over the internet. There's pictures of you two at some rave," Vance said, looking between the two of us. "You really haven't seen it?"

Stark growled, and I felt the blood drain from my face. "You're seriously Ten. The famous popstar turned bad?"

The disbelief in my tone took his attention from whatever was online. He looked up, eyes softening apologetically. "Yes, baby."

"Baby!" Vance gasped at the same time as I said, "Don't call me that."

BUTTERFLY

Stark sighed, wearily. "Please, Vi."

My shoulders slumped. I turned to my brother. "Can we just have a minute? Please?"

"I skipped school, drove hours because you're all over the news. You won't answer your phone... And you want me to wait outside?"

"I'll give you sex details," I told him mildly. I wasn't actually going to give my brother sex details.

"The hell you will!" Stark barked out.

His anger made me a little happy. Served him right.

"Fine. I'll wait in the hall." Vance agreed.

He brushed past Stark on his way, giving him a look. "Such a shame," he said sadly before reaching for the door.

Stark caught his arm, not rough, but enough to make my brother glance at him.

"You haven't told anyone where I am, have you?" he asked low. The anxiety in his voice was real. It made me feel a modicum of worry for him. I told myself to squash it.

"Like I would rat out my sister like that," Vance retorted.

Stark nodded, relief evident in the set of his jaw. "Thank you."

Vance gave me a look before going out in the hall and closing the door behind him. I always thought if being a designer didn't work out for Vance, he could be an actor. The boy loved drama.

"I really thought I'd get more time with you," Stark said, his voice low and regretful.

I made a rude sound. "Yeah, I bet it was a real trip seeing how long I would believe your lie."

He scrubbed a hand over his face. "I didn't like lying."

I laughed. "Yet you did it anyway."

281

"Yeah. I did." He agreed, coming farther into the room.

I moved away, sinking down on the couch. My mind was spinning. I could barely keep up with my own thoughts and questions. "Is Nate even your cousin, or just some guy you got to go along with your plan?"

"Yes, Nate is my cousin. Derek is my uncle. I used to spend every summer here as a kid. I didn't lie about any of that. It's all true. And there was no plan. I didn't set out to… hurt you."

"Yeah, well, you failed miserably," I told him. There was no use in even pretending this wasn't hurting me.

Moving around the coffee table, he sat down on it, directly in front of me. I thought about moving. The closeness to him beckoned me, something I didn't want, but couldn't deny. "Let me explain."

I held out my hand. "Let me see the phone."

His knuckles went white around my brother's phone. I knew he didn't want to show me. He wanted to be able to spin this with his pretty words coming out of his pretty mouth.

I'd been under his spell long enough, a spell so good I hadn't even known I was enchanted. I made an impatient sound and shook my hand at him. He pressed the phone into my palm.

I looked down, and everything became that much more real. I couldn't deny what was right in front of my face. It was a headline and a "leaked" image. I wasn't really sure what leaked meant, but clearly, it wasn't good.

The picture was of Ten and me standing in the center of the rave, kissing. Our faces couldn't be made out, but it didn't matter. The next pic I flipped to was of us leaving the warehouse. We were holding hands. Stark wore the neon-orange hat and sunglasses in both pictures. And my outfit was the same. The kiss prints all over his face were hard to ignore. The pictures made an airtight case that we were indeed more than friends.

I flipped through a few other photos the next site called "exclusive." It was more of the same. More of me and who I'd thought was an ordinary college student. There were plenty of articles to pick from, lots of juicy details divulged from an "anonymous source" and an "insider close to the couple."

Our sources have confirmed that while in hiding, Ten has fallen hard for an art student at Blaylock University in Upstate New York, who not only has won several scholarships, carries a near 4.0 average, but is also the artist behind a local famous comic strip. This comes after his fall from grace, a stint in rehab, and a number of failed relationships with models and actresses. We've been hearing around the pop world Ten has definitely been trying to clean up his act, but people have remained unconvinced. We wonder, though, if this promising student believes in Ten, then perhaps the rest of us should, too.

I made an incredulous sound and set aside the phone. "How do they know so much about me?" I felt violated in a way.

"That's what the media does," he answered, weary. "They dig and dig until they've made a headlining story out of almost nothing."

"They have pictures of us," I whispered. Then I thought of something and sat up rigidly. "Did you do this?" I pointed at the phone. "Did you call someone and tell them where we'd be? Did you set this whole thing up for some publicity?"

"No!" he shot out, denial swift and clear.

How was I supposed to believe him, though, when he already got caught in a pretty big lie?

"I didn't know I'd been spotted or that someone was taking pics of us. I was too focused on you."

I gave him a withering look. "Don't you try and sweet talk me, you dickface."

"Did you just call me a dickface?" he said, incredulous and slightly amused.

Do not let him affect you.

"If the shoe fits," I sang and sat back against the cushions.

"I was going to tell you."

I made a sound. "When? After you were finished with me? Was all this just a game to you?" Agitated, I got up and moved away from the couch and him.

He surged to his feet, frustration written on his face. "You can't honestly think that. Not after last night."

"I don't know what to think," I yelled. "One minute, you're Stark, this really amazing guy with a crap Jeep who shares a bedroom with his cousin. And the next, my brother is at the door, waiving around pictures and headlines, telling me how stupid I've been because I didn't realize who you actually are."

His voice was hoarse. "I'm still that guy."

"Are you?" I doubted. "Because the headlines say different. Your *lies* say different. Every article on that phone spins me out as some unfortunate nobody who caught the attention of a celebrity. Now my life is so much better because I have Ten's interest. Now, suddenly, you look like a saint because you're in love with a no one, and isn't that just precious?" I spat.

"I had nothing to do with any of that crap in the media," Stark argued. Then his voice softened, took on a more meaningful tone. "You aren't a no one."

But in a way, I was. I wasn't a celebrity. Or a model. I didn't fit in his world.

"I like to stay home and draw, I listen to classical music, and my best friend is my brother. I need to lose fifteen pounds, and I probably always will. My skin isn't perfect, and I won't wear makeup every day just to make it look better. I like sneakers and leggings. I shop at Target, not Fifth Avenue."

Stark's lips thinned as if what I was saying pissed him off. Well, too bad, buddy. I didn't want to hear it. I was hurt and betrayed. I listened to him drone on about how he never meant for this to happen. He could listen to me now, because it *did* happen.

"I'm not some project or some amusing challenge. This isn't a movie from the nineties where the frumpy, wallflower of a girl gets a makeover and suddenly everyone loves her. This is me." I spread out my arms so he could get a good look. "If you thought you could somehow make me into a media show and make yourself look good for loving and then "fixing" the poor, pathetic college student, let me make something clear to you right now. You picked the wrong girl."

His eyes glittered when he surged close. Stark's hands closed around my upper arms, but even though the look on his face was fierce and angry, his touch wasn't. His fingers were gentle. His hands only gave enough pressure to keep me in place. "What did I tell you about saying negative shit about yourself?" he intoned.

"It's not negative. It's the truth, and you know it. I know who I am. I like myself. Do I wish I could lose weight? Hell yes. Have I tried? Countless, exhausting times. I fight with my skin, and some days I look in the mirror and wonder why my body hates me so much."

"Vi." His voice was soft, almost pleading.

I pulled away, stepped back so he couldn't touch me. Not like it mattered. I felt him even when he wasn't.

"Even still, I like who I am. I like myself enough that I can stand here and look you in the eye and tell you with one hundred percent clarity that I won't change. Not for you. Not for anyone. I won't let you use me to fix the career you trashed." I paused, tilting my head. "And for the record, you peed on people. Like, what the fuck, man?"

His lips twitched, but then the amusement faded and he groaned. He looked as tired as I felt in that moment. His dark hair fell over his forehead and shadows darkened his eyes.

"I don't like myself." He dropped the words quietly into the room. They were heavy words, so much fewer than the ones I'd just hurled at him, yet they seemed to decimate everything. "I haven't, not for a long time."

I swallowed and resisted the urge to go to him. I so badly wanted to. The sadness and truth in those words made me ache.

"I was so shocked when you didn't know me that night in the gallery. At first, I thought you were playing me, but then I saw the drawing and heard you say you didn't like me." His mouth tilted up. "I liked the fact that you didn't like me."

"I don't understand," I said, finally calming down enough to listen to what he wanted to say. Plus, I wouldn't admit it out loud, but his obvious pain lay thickly over my anger and dulled some of my own hurt.

"You were a clean slate, Vi. A chance for me to be someone and no one at the same time. I wasn't public enemy number one to you. I wasn't someone with mad money, a famous face, or connections in the business. You didn't look at me with calculation in your eyes and wonder what you could get out of me. Hell, you thought I was a criminal."

"You were being shady," I commented.

"You were nice to me anyway."

"I didn't call the police." I corrected.

"You treated me normal. Made me *feel* normal. Like an actual person. You didn't care I was broke and drove a ghetto Jeep. You didn't want anything at all." Then he mused. "Except for me not to murder you."

I tried not to smile. Why did he have to be so utterly charming? I totally saw why he skyrocketed to fame when he did. The same thing that drew me to him was the exact same thing that drew everyone else.

Well. Wasn't that a kick in the teeth? I wasn't special. I was just one of the masses who had fallen for Ten.

"I asked Nate if he knew you. He said he didn't, but he could ask around. I just wanted to be around you. With you, I could be whoever I wanted. There were no expectations."

"Nate being outside my dorm wasn't a coincidence. He'd been looking for me." I realized.

Stark nodded. "He saw Ross hassling you, so he stepped in. I did *not* tell him to ask you out. But I'm kinda glad he did."

"You are?" There I went again, getting drawn in.

He nodded. "It gave me an excuse to see you again."

"You lied to me." I reminded him. I reminded me.

"Yeah, I did. I was afraid to tell you who I was. Afraid what was happening between us would change. It was selfish and a bastard thing to do, but you were the first thing I took just for me in a long, long time."

The words he's spoken just last night—which seemed like forever ago now—replayed through my head.

This is me right now. I want you to know that. Me. I've never been so present with anyone as I am with you right now.

He'd basically been admitting all this without actually saying a word. My stomach clenched, and I pressed a hand to it.

Stark saw and came forward. His hands shot out, hovering close, but not touching me. "You feeling sick?"

"Worrying about me isn't your job," I said, straightening.

"I want it to be." He spoke softly.

My hand went back to my stomach.

"I lied about who I really was, but that's all. I never lied about the way I feel about you. The connection I know you feel between us is real. I couldn't make up something like that if I tried."

I turned away.

"Tell me you feel it," he implored. "After last night, after this morning... tell me, Vi."

"You should go." My voice was thick. I was close to tears, but I refused to let them spill over.

The tentative touch of his fingers at my elbow made me stiffen. When I didn't pull away, he went a step further and curled them around, gently tugging so I would turn to look at him.

"I know you feel it," he whispered.

In a moment of weakness, I went forward, leaning into him, resting my forehead against his chest. Stark's arms wound around me instantly, and a deep sigh moved through him. "I'm sorry, Violet. So fucking sorry. I just didn't know how to tell you. I didn't want to be him to you. I just wanted to be Stark."

Everything he said brought it back, made me realize I couldn't find solace in the man who caused the storm. I pulled away, wiped at my damp eyes, and straightened.

"Go."

He shook his head. "We can work this out. Just talk to me."

"There's nothing left to say."

His eyes narrowed. The jawline that made me swoon hardened. He was prepared to fight, but me? I wasn't.

I dropped down on the corner of the unmade bed. "Please. I'm so tired. Just go."

He deflated. The stubborn set to his face went slack and so did his shoulders. "Call me if you need anything. Or if you want to talk."

"I won't."

I didn't look at him again. I was afraid to. He went to the door but stood there for long minutes. I felt his eyes. I felt the pull of whatever it was still tethering us together. The way it tugged and stretched when he finally let himself out made a few of the tears I tried so gallantly to hold back finally slip free.

twenty-eight

Ten

Vance was leaning against the wall when I let myself out of the room. I didn't want to go. It was the last thing on this planet I wanted. Surprisingly, I wanted to fight... something I hadn't been inclined to do for anything recently.

Anything but her.

The fight would have to wait for another day, though, because Violet was tired. The whole point in coming back to her place was so we could chill and take it easy. So much for easy.

Her brother pushed off the wall, staring at me. I wanted to be mad at him for coming here and ratting me out. Hell, in the past I would have gone off, threatening with lawyers and any kind of retribution I could. I'd have gone and grabbed the first bottle of vodka I saw to numb some of the shit whirling around inside me.

BUTTERFLY

I wasn't mad at Vance. I didn't want to retaliate or drink myself stupid.

It was an odd realization, knowing deep down something in me changed immeasurably.

I glanced back at the door, knowing the catalyst for that change was inside.

Stuck as a caterpillar, but I want to be a butterfly. Butterfly.

"She okay?" Vance asked.

I blinked, tucking that line away for later. "I don't know."

"I've always given you the benefit of the doubt, always one of those fans who knows that behind the scenes, everything is a lot harder than it looks." He shook his head. "But this? Lying to my sister, using her for press. I think that's the shittiest thing you've ever done."

I stiffened. "I am *not* using her."

"Then why'd you lie?"

Because if I told the truth, she wouldn't have let me near her at all.

I turned and started down the hall. "Take care of her, okay? She needs some rest."

Vance seemed mildly surprised by my response. The second I stepped out on the sidewalk, a familiar feeling came over me, one that pissed me off. Immediately, I started glancing around, searching among the people walking and the cars nearby for reporters and press.

Someone knew I was here. Someone was likely following me, taking pictures, and selling them to the press.

Whoever it was deserved my fist in their teeth because they just totally fucked up everything.

No, Ten. You fucked up everything. You always do.

Even though I searched as I went to the Jeep, I didn't see anyone. Inside, I leaned my head back against the seat and let out some cuss words.

How the hell did people find out where I was? How did they know there was a girl? The only thing that made sense was that I was ratted out. Someone had to have tipped off the press to my whereabouts.

But who?

It didn't take long for the name to pop into my head. For all the calls I ignored this morning to come flooding back. Fishing the cell out of my jeans, I powered it on and waited impatiently for it to start up.

The second the screen blinked to life, the device started buzzing with missed calls, notifications, and texts.

Most of them were from Becca. A couple were from Nate.

Dude, answer your phone. Shit hit the fan, Nate texted.

Then an hour later, *I hope you're with Violet because she's gonna be pissed.*

I didn't bother listening to the voicemails or reading all the other texts. Instead, I punched in a familiar number and waited as it rang.

"I take it you're done ignoring me?" Becca said the instant she answered.

"What the fuck did you do?" I growled.

She paused. "Brilliant, wasn't it? Nothing the world loves more than a tale of star-crossed lovers."

"You had me followed." Rage, the likes of which I hadn't felt in a while, began to consume me. "You had pictures taken of me. Of Violet. You leaked them to press."

"That's my job, Ten. To make you look good. Human. People are already frothing at the mouth to forgive you for all you've done because you went and—I quote—*'fell in love with someone beneath you.'"*

"Violet is not beneath me," I ground out. "She's better than you and I will ever be."

"I hope so," Becca said, unrepentant. "Her spotless reputation will make you look even better."

"I'm not using her!" I yelled, my fist pounding against the dash.

Becca paused, surprised. "You like her."

I laughed. "Like it fucking matters now. You went too far this time, Becca. You never should have crossed me."

Sensing my deadly and serious mood, it finally seemed to dawn on her that I was not okay with this, and her smooth talk wouldn't get her out of it. "I'm trying to help you," she said.

"No. You're trying to help *you*. You don't give two shits about me. I ought to fire you right the fuck now."

"You can't fire me!" She gasped. "We have a contract."

"And I have lots of money and lawyers."

I felt her panic reach through the phone. The shock that she'd finally pushed me way too far. "It would just be more bad press. You can't afford that."

She was right, and I knew it. But I wasn't giving her an inch. I wasn't even sure I cared about my career anymore.

Stop being fucking hasty, I told myself. *Don't do anything until you know what you want.*

Kneejerk reactions had gotten my career into the place it was. Going forward, I needed to be smarter than that.

"Call off your dogs," I told her. "If I see one more leaked photo of me or Violet, you're out, and I don't give a flying fuck if it takes me out, too."

She was silent.

"Becca," I intoned. "I mean it."

"Yeah," she responded. "I can tell."

"Call them off," I repeated.

"Consider it done. But you know they know where you are. It won't matter how many calls I make."

I knew it. It only pissed me off more.

"Ten…" She began.

"I'll be in touch." The finality in my voice was nearly chilling as I disconnected the call and tossed the phone in the empty passenger seat. The seat Violet had been riding in earlier.

The seat she might not ever sit in again.

twenty-nine

Violet

Remember how I told you the universe hates me?

You believe me now, don't you?

The weekend dragged by, despite the fact Vance stayed in town to keep me company. I loved seeing my brother, something I didn't get to do enough. Unfortunately, the visit wasn't as awesome as it could have been because of Stark.

Or Ten.

What the hell was I supposed to call him now?

Nothing. If I was smart, I'd run far, far away and never speak to him again. My heart was proving to be particularly dumb. And that tether I'd mentioned a million times since his body joined with mine?

Still there. Still tugging at me every single time I moved. It wouldn't matter how far I ran; he would always be there.

Vance would probably live off this for years. I'm serious. Years. The fact that his sister was involved with his greatest crush didn't make him angry or jealous. Vance said, "If he wasn't going to turn gay, there was only one other person on this planet good enough for Ten, and that's you, V."

I reminded him that Ten lied to me. Repeatedly.

My brother grudgingly decided perhaps I was too good for Ten after all.

Obviously, the picture I just painted was an accurate description of the entire weekend. We stayed in, Vance ate pizza, and I had smoothies. I did break down and eat some Sour Patch Kids. If a girl couldn't eat her feelings once in a while when a famous rich guy broke her heart, then why even make candy?

I rest my case.

Besides, what was it going to do? Make me gain weight? I laughed in the universe's face as I shoveled in those little kid-shaped sour suckers. *Pause* I just realized how wrong it is to eat candy shaped like children… *Unpause* Meh. They're gluten free.

In between watching movies, we basically talked about what happened. Vance knew all about Ten, something that saved me from having to stalk him all over the internet to find out everything I could.

I guess I really should have paid attention all those times Vance went on about him. Probably should have actually looked at the posters on his walls, too.

Ten was quite the prince of pop. Some of his songs held records all over the world. Vance tried to play me one, and I started crying the minute he started singing. Just the sound of his voice…

I rubbed a hand over my chest.

Well, he was the prince of pop. Until he made headlines again and again for wild behavior, and then the coup d'état of using his audience as a bathroom.

It just didn't fit. The guy I'd been spending time with and all the information Vance told me... it was like two different people. Which naturally confused me more. I refused to look online, afraid of what I might see. Knowing there were pictures of me on *KMZ*, one of the biggest celeb gossip sites on the internet, made me queasy.

I could only imagine what the comment section was like.

Vance read them all; I was sure of it. Every time I looked over, his nose was stuck in his phone. I asked him once, in a moment of weakness. All he would say was how curious everyone was about me, the girl who got Ten's attention.

I was miserable. More miserable than I'd ever been. Vance wanted to stay longer, but on Sunday afternoon, our parents called and demanded he get himself back home so he didn't miss any more school.

I wasn't sure if they knew what was going on. I doubted it. When I spoke to my mother, she didn't let on she'd seen anything on TV. Of course, the only thing my parents watched was cooking shows. I highly doubted they gave a flying fig about Ten.

I didn't say anything. I was going to let Vance handle it. He was good at it anyway.

My mom did pick up on how tired I sounded. I knew she worried, and then we had a ten-minute conversation about making sure I was taking my medications, blah, blah,

blah. After promising I would call her after my doctor's appointment, she let me go.

My doctor's appointment—something that came every three months, something I was dreading this time.

There was too much going on right now. Everything with Ten, school... the fact I didn't feel well. I'd been pretty good at staying positive, keeping it all under control, and then everything crumbled. It was hard to stay positive when everything was falling apart.

And now it was Monday. Joy.

After Vance left yesterday, I'd gone to bed early. Yes, if you must know, I cried myself to sleep. In the sheets *he* washed for me. In the bed we'd slept in *together.*

And if you must, *must* know... yes, I wore his hoodie to bed. When I'd asked him to go, he'd walked out with mine on. I was still wearing his.

It was just a stupid sweatshirt. I mean, geez, I had the exact same one. Except they were totally different. It had been his.

As I was lying there all weepy in the dark, I reminded myself it was the hoodie he'd bought so he could carry on the charade of being an actual BU student. That only made me cry harder.

If all that wasn't enough in the shit circus that was my life, I was on my way to class to draw a naked woman's cooter. I was seriously considering finding a seat behind her. I think I'd rather draw her naked butt than the other side. Ew.

I sincerely hoped she'd shaved for this.

A giggle erupted out of me. The person walking a few feet ahead of me glanced over his shoulder. I ducked my head so all they could see was the top of the yellow knit beanie I was wearing. It was cold today, colder than I was prepared to deal with. My joints felt creaky and hesitant to bend; my overall body was worn down and wanted to go back to bed.

Instead, I'd gotten up and thrown on thick navy leggings, tall Ugg boots, a long-sleeved white T-shirt, and a super-soft poncho-looking tunic in a beautiful blue. It had a cowl neck so I didn't have to pile a scarf over the outfit. I left my hair down. Vance had braided it before he left, so when I got up this morning and took it out, my hair fell over my shoulders in big waves. All I did was add the knit beanie just to keep my ears warm.

I wondered what he was doing, as I did twenty million times a day. He tried to call me over the weekend. I didn't answer. He tried to text, too.

Vance suggested maybe I give him a chance, that maybe he really did just want me to like him for him and not everything on the internet. Maybe. But at the same time, how was I supposed to like him for him if I didn't know him?

I think my brother still had a crush on him.

I pushed thoughts of him out of my mind as the art building came into view. Gripping the strap of my messenger bag, I told myself to take it one thing at a time. First up, drawing a naked lady with a bag on her head while some ill-dressed, possibly deranged teacher marched around, telling us all we sucked.

Next, my doctor's appointment this afternoon. I wasn't looking forward to this either. I'd almost whined to my mother and pleaded to let Vance stay to come with, but at the last minute, I decided against it. I hated making a big deal of my RA. My parents worried enough about me. I didn't want to add to it. Of course, now that Vance wasn't here to give me a ride, I was mentally kicking myself. Since I didn't have a car, I had to take an Uber.

Here's to hoping I don't die during the forty-five-minute ride.

Seriously. I read this book once. It's called *Taxi*. It's about a woman who gets kidnapped by her taxi driver because he wants her kidney... *Shudder.*

Clearly, I wasn't the only person on this planet with an overactive imagination.

Anyway, after I got through all of that, I could go home and pout about Ten.

The professor's office was right beside the classroom, and when I went in, I noted his office door was closed. Ew. That naked girl was probably in there waiting to come flash her goods for all our ready pencils.

I was one of the last ones to walk in, so I had to take one of the only seats left. My back was to the door, facing inward to the center of the circle where there was a platform already set up for the model.

Large wooden easels were all set up with chairs in front of them. I sank down and pulled off my bag, dropping it at my feet. Everyone busied themselves getting out their drawing supplies. Once I had everything out, I went across the room to get my large sketchpad out of the stack. We usually kept them here because they were too big to carry around campus all the time.

The pile was near the door, and as I was digging around for mine, I heard the professor's door open.

"I guess it will have to do," he muttered, grumpy.

My teeth sank into my lips. Was this guy ever in a good mood?

"Totally unprofessional," he bellowed. "But the art must go on!"

I practically jumped out of my skin when he appeared, striding into the room, wearing his ugly red pants. "Ms. Meier," he called. I held back a wince. "Hurry up now. You're going to need all the time the class is allotted today, knowing how slow you draw."

How rude!

I gasped before I could stop myself and pull the pad into my chest. He heard, stopped, rotated to look at me. "Did you say something, dear?"

"No, sir," I said, wishing I had the guts to just blast him right there.

He motioned for me to get away, so I went back to my station and opened the book up to a fresh page.

"The model I hired to be here today decided not to show up," he announced.

Inwardly, I had a mini dance party. No model? No nakey drawing! This day was looking up!

"Something I find to be rather unprofessional. I will be putting her on my blacklist. She will not be invited back."

If I were her, I'd be thrilled.

"But, as I often say, the art must go on!"

The girl beside me groaned. I glanced at her with a commiserating look.

"I was able to find a new model at the last minute." He went on. "Not exactly as I wanted, but desperate times…" His voice faded, and he went to dim the lights overhead.

Oh, ew. What was this? Mood lighting for nude drawing?

Gag.

"In keeping with the theme of not knowing the subject personally and remaining absolutely objective, the model's name will not be given. Nor will his face be seen."

"His?" someone called out.

"Yes. We'll be drawing the male form this week."

I had a vivid memory of Stark's face when we were in bed, tangled up together, and he'd been absolutely adamant I not be looking at some other man's "cock and balls" for class.

Unable to help it, I smiled.

"If I could have the model," the professor bellowed.

I heard someone come into the room and close the door behind him. I stiffened, but didn't look. I was going to get an eyeful soon enough.

"Over this way, please."

The man stepped into the circle, I peeked over at him and sighed. He was in a pair of black boxers, so not totally naked. There was a bag over his head. It was light colored and didn't look entirely opaque. Something that was proved by the way he was able to move into the circle to the platform. It wasn't see-through enough for any of us to be able to make out any of his features, though.

My stomach started doing funny tricks; my nerves grew jittery. I could barely look toward the platform. How was I supposed to stare enough to draw?

A few instructions were given to the class, and then the professor told the model to disrobe. I stayed safely hidden behind the easel and sketchpad, not daring to look.

There were a few murmurs and giggles from the girls nearby, but the professor hushed them instantly.

"Draw!" he announced, as though this were some great tournament or something.

Gripping my pencil, I took a deep breath and leaned around the easel. *Please let it be just his butt,* I prayed.

It wasn't.

In fact, the model was pretty much posed so he was facing me... and *everything* was on full display.

My stomach dropped to my feet, my eyes went wide, and recognition slammed into me so hard I actually leaned back in the chair.

Oh. My. God.

I blinked. Blinked again. It couldn't be.

It was.

That wasn't just some new model the professor managed to find at the last minute.

It was Stark.

I didn't have to see his face, his blue eyes, or the scruffy jaw. I'd recognize his body anywhere. My hands had been all over it just days ago. I'd spent the night wrapped up in his arms.

My fingers started aching horribly, and I glanced down, realizing I'd been gripping the pencil tight. I released it immediately, and the stupid thing fell out of my hand.

It didn't just stop, though.

No. That damn pencil never did.

It rolled. Right across the uneven wooden floor, right into the circle, directly in front of the platform.

I swallowed, brushing a gaze over Stark again. My heart squeezed. A homesick feeling came over me, so strong I sighed.

"Meier!" the professor yelled from right behind me.

I jumped so forcefully in my chair I almost fell out of it. "Sir?" I said, turning.

"Get your pencil and get to work!"

Standing from the chair, I felt a strong tug inside me as if I were being towed into the center of the room. My foot hit the pencil, and it skidded a little closer to the platform.

Holy shit balls. I could not believe Stark was in this room, naked! How dare he walk in here flaunting his... his.... *items* for everyone to see? He did this on purpose! He wanted to affect me... and dammit, he was doing a good job.

"I cannot believe you," I hissed, bending down to pick up the pencil.

His warm, familiar chuckle brushed over me. My hand trembled, and the urge to reach out and stroke his stomach was damn near irresistible.

When I stood, I was practically eye level with his package. I made a choked sound, and Stark's shoulder's shook with his effort not to laugh.

"You are so paying for this," I said under my breath before rushing away.

When I took my seat again, I stared at the paper, not seeing it really, instead reliving all the moments we had together that night and the way his body felt against mine.

"I have to admit," the girl sitting beside me leaned over to say, "I'd been dreading this assignment for days, but now? I'm not minding the view."

I gasped. "Get your mind out of the gutter!" I snapped. "Don't even look at him!"

"Meier!" the professor yelled again. "What is it with you today? Get the hell to work!"

The girl I yelled at was staring at me as though I had five heads. I thought about poking her in the eye with this misbehaving pencil of mine. Then she wouldn't be able to see Stark and all his naked glory.

The rich, low laughter stopped all my vindictive, jealous thoughts in their tracks. I peeked around the easel again to where Stark still posed, his laughter muffled by the bag.

Oh. He was going to pay for this.

thirty

Ten

Ah, sweet satisfaction.

She knew me the second her eyes really looked. I felt her reaction even from across the room. Violet didn't have to look at my face or even hear my voice to know me. We spent one night together, and her body recognized mine instantly.

Knowing that, *seeing* it with my own eyes, was totally worth getting naked in a room full of strangers.

And hearing her snap at the girl beside her? Jealous much? Good thing I had this bag on my head to hide the giant shit-eating grim plastered on my face.

She still cared about me. Whether she wanted to or not.

It nearly gave me a hard-on. I kept it under wraps, though. I mean, if the girls in here were impressed by me without one, I might send them all over the edge if I started rocking some serious wood. Violet might get into a brawl.

The ninety-minute class felt like an eternity. I'd done this so I could see her, but I hadn't thought about the fact that I'd actually have to stand here and model for the full ninety. It was hard knowing she was right there, but I couldn't touch or speak to her.

And shit, she hadn't been lying about the professor. Dude liked to yell. Loud. And what the hell was up with his pants?

When the class finally came to an end, I grabbed my drawers and pulled them on, then went back into his office next door so I could get dressed.

I banged my shin on the desk and nearly fell over in my haste, but I wanted to be sure Vi didn't leave without me seeing her.

Thankfully, she was still in the classroom, packing up, when I peeked in. On the other side of the classroom, there was another room a few feet down.

I slipped into the doorway and waited.

When her familiar form appeared, I reached out and snatched her out of the hallway, half dragging her into the empty room.

She gasped and tried to fight, until I leaned down and spoke into her ear. "It's just me."

She jerked away from me, her blue eyes wide. The yellow knit on her head made them even bluer. She smacked me in the chest. "What the hell do you think you're doing!"

I grinned. God, it was fucking good to see her. I missed her so freaking much, but not even I realized just how much.

"Don't you grin at me like that!" she hissed. "Naked! You were naked!"

I crossed my arms over my chest and decided to have a little fun. "I told you the only cock and balls you were going to look at were mine."

"Everyone else looked at them, too!" she burst out. Her cheeks were pink, and so was the tip of her nose.

Shit she looked adorable in that hat, shaking her finger at me, all angry.

"Aww, baby," I crooned. "Are you jealous?"

She smacked me in the stomach again. "Of course I'm not."

"Liar."

"You are unbelievable," she muttered and shifted the bag on her shoulder.

I reached out and took it, pulling it over my head and across my body. This damn thing was heavy. What the fuck was she hauling around? This couldn't be good for her joints.

"How the hell did you manage that? Why did you?" she said, not acknowledging the fact I was carrying her bag.

She missed me, too. I could feel it. I saw it in the depths of her eyes and the way they never once left me.

"You wouldn't return my calls," I said, mild.

She made a sound. "So you come to my class, naked!"

A slow smile spread over my face. "Got your attention, didn't it?"

A laugh erupted out of her. Hearing it, she slapped her hand over her mouth, trying to hide it.

Moving slow, I reached out and pulled the hand away, wrapping mine around it. "I've missed you so fucking much, Vi."

"Stark." Her voice was shaking as she pulled back her hand.

"Talk to me. Please."

"I can't. Not right now."

I shook my head. Determination settled inside me. "I'm not taking no for an answer."

"Walk with me." She motioned toward the door.

I pulled the baseball hat out of my back pocket and tugged it low over my face. A shuttered look filled her eyes, and I hated it. I reminded myself I would hate it more if the press got more pics of us together.

We didn't say anything as we went through the building and outside. The air was cold, and Vi ducked her head against it. I wanted to put my arm around her to block some of the wind, but I wasn't sure she'd let me.

"It was my manager," I told her, keeping my voice low. "She's the one who had us followed, leaked the pictures and info online."

She glanced up at me, surprised. "Your own manager?"

I grunted. "She was pissed I refused to come home."

"You wouldn't?"

"No."

I felt her curious gaze. "Where is home?"

"LA. She wants me back there. I need to start working on my next album."

"So why are you here, then?"

"Because you are."

Violet stopped walking and turned. "You can't say that stuff to me."

"Why?"

"Because I don't know if it's the truth or a lie."

"Oh, baby," I murmured, stepping close. Taking a chance, I grabbed the ends of her hair and rubbed them between my fingers. "It's the truest thing I've ever said."

She turned away and started walking again. My chest felt hollow. I wanted to touch her again.

"She doesn't seem like a very nice person." Violet observed.

"She's a bitch," I said truthfully. "She doesn't care about anything but success. I'm thinking about firing her."

Violet seemed surprised. "Can you do that?"

"I can do whatever I want," I said, a hint of my old cocky attitude coming out. "Honestly, though?" I asked.

"I do prefer the truth," she said, bland.

So sarcastic.

"I'm afraid if I fire her, no one else will work with me."

She digested that for a few moments. A few autumn leaves blew in front of us across the sidewalk. I gazed up at all the buildings, all of them were old and large, all of them had beautiful architecture. I could definitely see why this campus made a good backdrop for an arts school. It was definitely inspiring.

"You've done a lot of bad things."

"Yeah, I have."

"Do you feel bad about them?"

I considered the question. Weighed the answer. Violet wanted truth, so I decided to give it to her. "I regret the distance it's put between me and music. I love music. The way you love art."

She nodded, understanding.

"And I regret taking my anger toward the business and my own personal demons out on my fans. They deserve better. After all, it was them who made me famous."

Her voice was quiet. I loved the fact she was actually listening to me. Trying to understand. "Being famous is hard, huh?"

I laughed low. "A lot harder than it fucking looks. It's not all just money and traveling the world."

"Traveling is exhausting," she said. "I get tired just driving a few hours home to see my parents."

I reached out and laced our fingers. She let me hold them for a few minutes before stiffening and pulling away.

"I don't really understand being famous, but I can see your point, I guess. I know how I felt when I saw my face all over the internet with all those crazy headlines."

"I'm so sorry about that, Vi. That's what I regret most. Hurting you."

She pulled her phone from the pocket in her loose sweater and lit it up. "I've listened to one of your songs," she said, still looking down at her screen.

I felt my eyebrows shoot up. "You have?"

She nodded. "You have a beautiful voice. It's very smooth. I can tell you love singing."

"I thought you only listened to classic." I teased, elbowing her softly.

She didn't reply, instead staring down at her phone and tapping the screen a few times. It annoyed me I wasn't getting all her attention. I wanted it.

"Hey," I said, tugging her arm so I could see her phone. "What are you doing there?"

"Ordering an Uber."

I drew back. "An Uber. What the fuck for?"

She hesitated, then sighed. "I have a doctor's appointment."

I made a sound and snatched the phone out of her hand.

"Hey!" she protested, trying to grab it back. I held it up out of her reach and glowered down at her. "Give me my phone!"

"No," I said, then stuck it in my pocket. I was wearing her hoodie. It didn't smell much like her anymore. But it still reminded me of her. Of that morning. Of our night together.

"Stark," Violet growled.

"I'm driving you."

She crossed her arms over her chest. "No, you aren't."

"You aren't going alone, Vi. I don't care how pissed with me you are. Besides, it will give us a chance to talk in the car."

"I'm done talking," she said, looking away.

"Fine. I'll talk. You can listen."

The stubborn set to her chin made me want to grab her up and kiss her.

"You could get kidnapped by the driver, baby. Do you want to get kidnapped?"

Her gaze swung around to collide with mine. "Did you read *Taxi*, too?"

I suppressed a laugh. "What? No." *I just know how your mind works.* How quickly I had learned her. It frankly amazed me.

"Do we need to leave now?" I asked.

She glanced at me. "It's a forty-five-minute drive."

As if that would deter me. If anything, it made me more intent on going. The idea of her riding that distance with a stranger made me sick. "I don't care how long the drive is."

"Okay, then." She nodded once, cautiously.

I felt like I did when I won Song of the Year at last year's music awards. Placing my hand at the small of her back, I steered her in the direction of the Jeep.

It was another small victory when she didn't pull away.

A small spark of hope ignited inside me.

I pulled up to the curb after what was a way more silent ride than I intended.

I'd wanted to talk. To make her see reason.

She really wasn't having any of it.

It was beyond frustrating.

I pushed, but not enough. I didn't want to force her, something that was also extremely frustrating. The only way I'd get through to Violet was by pressing the subject, by making her see reason. I just wanted her to understand.

Forcing her to do anything, though, it felt wrong. My instinct was to shield her. Protect her. I wanted to make sure she was okay and not stressed the fuck out. We were on the way to her doctor, for fuck's sake. It was a piss-poor time to push her, to fill her mind with anything more than her own health.

I would rather Violet be healthy and in the proper state of mind for this appointment than understand me.

That's how I knew.

How I knew I was really in love.

I cared more about her than I did myself.

I cared more about making sure she was okay than making sure she was with me.

Fine time to grow up and give a damn, Ten. My subconscious scolded me. I told it to shut the fuck up.

It was Violet. She helped me see. Helped me change. Actually, not really change, just *transform* into the man I already was deep inside.

She transformed me.

And I loved her.

The Jeep jolted to a stop, but neither of us braced or was even shaken by the way this car moved anymore. We both expected it, were ready for it. We'd spent enough time in here to know.

"I'll just park and be right in," I said.

Her head swung around. "What?"

"I'll meet you inside," I repeated patiently.

"No."

"No?" My eyebrow lifted.

"This is my doctor appointment. It's private."

"I care about your health, Vi."

"You're not my boyfriend." She reminded me.

"I would be if you let me," I retorted softly.

Emotion passed behind her eyes. Want. Pain. Then it was gone, and the blue hardened. "And who would I be dating? Stark or Ten?"

"It's the same man, baby."

"Don't call me that," she said wearily.

The small spark of hope I'd won by driving her here was slowly starting to dim. Maybe I gave her too much time to think during the drive.

"I'm going to be here for your appointment, Violet," I intoned. I wasn't prepared to push her, but this? This I was dead set against. Jesus, if I hadn't pulled that stupid stunt earlier today in her class, I wouldn't have even known about the fucking appointment.

It was unacceptable. This was just totally unacceptable.

"You can sit in the waiting room." She compromised, her voice softening just a little.

It felt like a freaking hard-won victory.

"It's past the check-in desk, around the corner, and on the left."

I nodded once. "I'll be there."

She hesitated before opening the door. I thought she might say something, but whatever it was, she decided against it. I sat at the curb and watched her until she disappeared behind a pair of sliding doors and into the medical center.

She was still sitting in the waiting room, a clipboard in her lap and a pen with a giant flower taped to the end in her hand.

There was someone sitting right beside her, and her chair was on the end.

I wondered bitterly if she'd chosen that chair on purpose so I wouldn't be able to sit beside her.

Like that would stop me.

I stalked across the room. A few nurses at the desk whispered, and I was pretty sure I heard my name.

Fuck me. Could I get no goddamn privacy? My girl was at the doctor, being treated for her incurable fucking autoimmune disorder. This was not the time to be all a twitter about Ten.

With bold derision, I ripped the hat off my head and shoved my hand through my hair, giving everyone a better look at my face.

Violet must have sensed my presence or maybe my mood. She looked up and then away, as if she could dismiss me.

Finally coming to where she sat, I reached out, sliding my arms beneath her legs and behind her back. I picked her up as she gasped and sat down, plopping her right in my lap.

The older woman sitting right beside her stared at us openly. I glanced her way and smiled. "How are you today, ma'am?"

She chuckled. "Would you like my seat?"

"Not necessary. I've already got one."

"So sweet," she murmured.

Violet was giving me a look that probably should have killed me. Good thing I was a resilient asshole. "What do you think you're doing?" she growled.

"Sitting with my girl," I replied mildly.

"Find another seat," she hissed and started to get up. My hands wrapped around her waist, clamping down and holding her where she was.

"You wanna be on the news tonight for being seen at the doctor's office with Ten?"

"I hate you," she said and went slack in my lap.

"Oh, baby," I murmured. "No, you don't."

"Who's Ten?" the woman beside us asked. She was totally eavesdropping.

"No one worth knowing, ma'am," I replied.

Violet made a rude sound.

"Fill out your paperwork," I instructed and tapped the papers on the clipboard.

She turned her head away from me to face the papers. A few strands of blond wavy hair wacked me in the face.

I guess I deserved it.

Violet began to fill out the top of the sheet, and I glanced around at the people sitting in the room. Across from us was the door with the word Rheumatology on it. Then off to my right was another door with only a curtain dividing it from the large waiting room. I watched as a woman in scrubs came out and called someone in.

"What's that?" I asked, keeping my voice low.

Violet glanced up. "It's the lab. It's where patients get bloodwork done."

My stomach turned. "Do you have to get bloodwork today?"

"I don't think so. I had it done a few days ago so they could have my results for today's appointment."

I let out a breath I'd been holding. "But you might have to?"

She turned to glance at me for a second before turning back. "Maybe."

"I want to hold your hand if you have to."

The woman beside us sighed. "You two are just precious. Did you just get married?"

"No, but I'm working on it," I replied smoothly.

Violet turned and looked at me again, her eyes unreadable. I patted her hip. "I'll hold your hand."

"I have to fill this out." She pointed at the form.

I nodded.

She went back to the form, and I watched her over her shoulder.

The questions were all relating to her symptoms and level of pain. All of them made me feel sick in some form or another. I didn't like this. I didn't like knowing she dealt with this shit on a daily basis and she would for the rest of her life.

How difficult is it to get dressed? Wash yourself? Lift a cup to your mouth? That was the kind of shit she was being asked. This was shit I never even thought about. I just did it. I just took the ability for granted.

It broke my heart because at one spot she checked "with some difficulty."

The bottom had a scale from one to ten, wanting to know what her pain level was today. She put a six. My body stiffened. She paused and glanced back.

"Are you reading my answers?" she hissed.

"Yes," I said, unashamed. A six? That was too fucking high.

"Don't!"

"Wouldn't have to if you talked to me."

"I'd talk to you if every word out of your mouth wasn't a lie."

Now would not be the appropriate time to tell her I loved her. I had to tell myself that three times to keep from blurting it out.

"Miss Meier," a nurse called, coming out of the door.

Violet leapt out of my lap, and this time I had to let her go. She turned back to me. "Stay."

"If you need me, come get me," I said.

She sighed and retreated back into the office.

The woman beside me turned her head. "She's lucky to have someone who cares so much. It's not always easy to find. Especially when you are sick a lot."

"You have RA, too?" I asked.

She nodded and held up her hand. It was bent and crooked. My stomach sank, and I thought of Violet's one crooked knuckle. "Had it half my life."

"I'm sorry," I said sincerely.

The nurse at the lab called for someone, and the woman got up and limped away.

A dark cloud settled over my mood. This place was fucking depressing as hell. Most everyone in here was over the age of seventy. And then there was Vi. Bright. Young. Talented.

Saddled with this forever.

I knew she hated me right now, but I had to fix what was between us.

She was in the back for a while. I was starting to get antsy, and the nurses started finding reasons to walk by where I was sitting. I let them look. I didn't smile or acknowledge them. This wasn't the time or the place. I just hoped we were gone by the time the fucking press showed up.

Antsy and unable to sit still another minute, I stood and stretched, turning in a circle and checking the place out. Nearby the lab, there was a large counter with a woman behind a computer. I heard her telling the lady who sat beside us earlier the balance of her bill for the day.

The woman counted out her change, her disfigured hands and fingers moving slower than most.

I didn't pity her.

But shit. It wasn't easy to see. I heard her words, how she said Vi was lucky because not everyone had someone to stick by them in poor health. She was here alone. Without anyone.

My stomach hurt, and the feelings working up the back of my throat made me hella uncomfortable.

This was all Violet's fault. It was her fault I had all these *feelings*. That my eyes were open to those around me.

On impulse, I strode away from the row of chairs to the counter.

"Excuse me," I said, sliding up to the old lady.

"Just one moment, sir," the nurse behind the counter said. Then she did a double take. Recognition filled her eyes.

"I'd like to pay this fine lady's balance, please. In full."

The woman gasped, and the nurse's eyes went wide.

"Young man, that is not necessary."

"I know that. Sometimes it's nice to have someone," I said.

Her eyes grew watery, and she brushed at the corner of one with her finger.

The nurse's fingers hit the keys on the computer a few times. "The copay left for the rest of this is over one thousand dollars."

I pulled out a wad of cash and handed the woman twelve hundred in cash. "This cover it?"

"You had that in your pocket?" The older woman gasped and pointed at the money.

"It's how I roll," I quipped and winked at her.

Since I'd been "outed" being here in New York, I went back to carrying around my normal amount of change.

"I can't let you do this," the woman said.

"It's already done," I replied and glanced at the nurse. She nodded and printed out some paper.

"Here is your receipt showing everything is paid in full."

"Oh heavens," she said and pressed the paper to her chest.

The next thing I knew, she was hugging me, and I was surrounded by the smell of old lady perfume. She kinda smelled like my grandma.

I hugged her back.

"God bless you," she said, pulling back.

"Have a nice day, ma'am."

"If that girl doesn't marry you, she's not right in the head," she announced, shaking her crooked finger at me.

"I'll marry you," the nurse informed me.

"He's taken." The woman scolded her, then patted me on the cheek.

As she was walking away, Violet came out of the back. Her eyes went to the chair I was supposed to be in, and she frowned.

I lifted a hand and waved. When she saw me, her eyes actually looked relieved. The muscles between my shoulder blades tightened.

Something was wrong.

"It's going to be the same thing for this one," I told the nurse before pushing away from the counter and going to Violet's side.

I folded my hand around hers, and she didn't flinch away. "I have to pay," she said.

Keeping her hand in mine, we went to the desk. The nurse took the form in her hand, and her fingers flew over the keyboard. She glanced up at me. "Twelve hundred."

I pulled a gold card out of my pocket and handed it over. "All out of cash."

She nodded and took it to swipe.

"What are you doing?" Violet asked, alarmed.

"Taking care of you," I said, cupping a hand around her neck and leaning in to kiss the top of her head.

"That's not your resp—" Her words cut off. "Oh, never mind."

I would have taken some joy in the victory of her finally giving in, except I knew it was because she was tired.

That wasn't a win.

The nurse handed me the card and a paper to sign. I had to let go of Vi's hand to sign the receipt, and then she tucked the remaining paperwork into her bag and slung it over her shoulder.

"We can go now," Violet told me, her voice low.

"Wait," the nurse called. We both glanced back. "Can I have your autograph?"

Annoyance slapped me so hard it nearly made me dizzy. Beside me, Violet bristled. I grabbed her hand again, ignoring the fact it was rigid.

"Sure," I said, smiling. She slid a paper and pen across the counter, and I scrawled my name across it.

"My name is Hannah," she said.

I paused, then wrote her name at the top with a general "thanks for listening" beneath it.

She beamed when I slid it back, and I forced myself to smile again.

"Let's go," I said, tucking Violet into my side and ushering her through the building.

"Everyone is staring," she murmured.

"Keep walking," I instructed.

Outside, the sun was bright, and Violet recoiled against it. I was a dirty bastard because I used it to my advantage, pulling her tighter into my arms and bringing my arm up to shield her eyes.

On the sidewalk, I turned so her back was to the sun and stopped walked.

Violet lifted her head and looked up at me.

"What's wrong?"

She burst into tears.

I was *not* prepared for tears. For crying of any kind. Especially not from her.

"Okay, easy." I soothed and pulled her into my chest.

"No," she said, stiffening.

"I'm going to hold you, Vi." There was no room for argument in my voice.

She cried some more, her shoulders shaking. "M-maybe for just a minute."

Enclosing her against my chest, she burrowed against me, pressing her face into my neck and straining on her tiptoes to get even closer. I hunched in, palmed the back of her head, and rocked her back and forth gently, and she sniffled into my shirt. I wanted to savor the moment, the feel of her against me. But I couldn't. I needed to know what happened in there.

"Vi, what's wrong, baby?" I knew I should have gone in there with her. She shouldn't have to deal with this on her own.

Her arms tightened around me, and I didn't ask again. She just wanted comfort right now, and she wanted it from me. Thank God.

"Ugh," she said after a few minutes of being in my arms. Lifting her head, she brushed at her eyes. "This is so stupid. I never cry at these appointments."

"So why now?" I asked.

"I knew it was coming." She went on, almost to herself. "It's not like it was a surprise. It's just this and…" She pulled back and threw out her arms. "And you!"

"Me?"

Her shoulders slumped. "I'm tired, Stark. So tired."

I made a sound and moved toward her. Another tear tracked down her cheek.

A car screeched to a stop at the curb, several doors opened and slammed, and the sound of pounding footsteps approached.

"Ten!" a man with a camera yelled. "Over here, Ten."

"What are you doing here, Ten?" another person with a camera yelled out.

"There she is," the third photographer called. "Are you dating Ten? What are you doing at a hospital?"

"Is she crying?"

That little observation served to turn all three photographers onto Violet. They rushed closer, snapping their lenses and trying to get in her face. She shrank back, and I reached for her, but one of the jackasses shoved between us.

"Are you sick? Do you need Ten's money and connections to cure you?"

I saw red. Her tears. This entire situation… These peckerheads with cameras.

I tapped the guy between me and Violet on the shoulder, and he turned. I nailed him right in the face with a hard fist. He shouted and fell. While he was down, I grabbed the camera he was holding and threw it out onto the road, satisfaction filling me when it broke into pieces.

"That cost me a lot of money!" the man yelled, jumping to his feet.

I punched him again.

"Stark!" Violet's voice broke into the angry haze. Her hand curled around my forearm; the other clutched at the fist I was making. "Stop," she said quietly.

"Vi," I murmured, flexing my hand and letting it go slack.

The remaining photographers circled us.

Hell, the guy I decked was pulling out his phone. "I'm calling the cops," he announced.

Violet gasped. "No!"

"Go ahead," I spat. "See if I give a flying fuck."

"C'mon," I said, pulling her into my side and leading her away. "Jeep's right over here."

We went quickly, but of course were followed. They shouted more questions at us. At Violet. A crowd formed.

At the Wrangler, I ushered her into her seat and closed her in before jogging around and jumping in. "Don't fail me today," I prayed as I started her up.

She purred to life, and I pulled out of the lot as quickly as I could.

"Are they going to follow us?" Violet worried, glancing out the back window.

"I sure as hell hope not," I muttered. "Right about now, I wish I was driving my Lamborghini."

Violet's eyes swung to me. "You have a Lamborghini?"

"I have a lot of shit that doesn't matter."

"Are you going to get in trouble for punching that man back there?"

I shrugged. "Probably."

She gasped.

I reached across the seat and covered her thigh with my hand. "Don't worry about it, sweetheart. The last time, I just paid a fine."

"The *last* time?" she admonished.

I shrugged. "They piss me off."

"I can see why," she muttered and leaned into the seat.

Concern overruled the agitation I felt. "You okay?" I asked, letting my gaze skim over her. "They touch you?"

She shook her head. "I'm fine."

"What did the doctor say? Why were you crying?"

"The upped my dose. That's all."

My lips thinned. "Which one?"

The answer was quiet. "The methotrexate."

My knuckles turned white on the steering wheel. I tried not to react, to show any kind of emotion that might make it harder for her. But *fuck!*

Now I knew why she was so upset. They basically increased her dose of chemotherapy. I knew from all the reading I'd been doing that just meant her immune system would be even more at risk. The side effects would be worse... Shit.

I reached across the seat again, offering my hand, palm up. After a moment's hesitation, she put hers in mine. Just that simple touch made my heart skip a beat. And then another.

"Why'd they up it?" I asked.

"It's working, just not well enough. I've been having a lot of symptoms lately. More swelling, more aching."

"It's my fault," I spat, angry with myself. "I've put you under too much stress."

"It's not your fault, Stark," she murmured, giving my hand a reassuring squeeze. "I definitely have been more stressed the last few days, but I was having these things before."

"Why didn't you say anything?" I asked.

"Because I was happy."

That reply was like a swift kick right in the gut. If I hadn't been driving, I might have doubled over from the pain.

She *was* happy. Past tense. Before I blew up her world with my identity. Correction: before Becca blew up her world by leaking a story to make me look good.

"I can make you happy again, Vi." My words shattered the silence pressing in on us both.

"It's not that easy anymore." Her voice was sad.

"The only thing that's not easy is being away from you."

Her hand tightened around mine. I took pleasure in knowing I still affected her. I still felt the chemistry we always had wrap around us.

I could fix this.

I could.

I just had to figure out how.

thirty-one

Violet

He walked me to my door. I wanted him to stay.

I wanted him to stay so badly.

I told him to go.

He argued, as he always did. He was so stubbornly charming. I almost buckled because, damn, I wanted his comfort. His arms. The way he smelled.

I told him to go.

Letting him in my room would only make it harder. Harder to think. To make an actual choice. Because when Stark was around, it was only him.

My guard was down. I was tired and weak. Not only was I mentally drained, but I was physically drained as well. Upping my meds wasn't really a big deal, but it sure felt like one.

It took a lot just to get me to put that first dose in my mouth. Then I waited around for weeks for nasty side

328

effects to show. Waiting for a bad reaction… or worse, a reaction that made me sick but was considered tolerable.

I only took the methotrexate once a week. But once was enough that it cast a shadow over all the other days. Take it at night, they said. Make sure the day after is an easier day for you because you might be sick. You might have a headache. You might be nauseous. You might lose some hair. So I took it on a Friday, because if one or two days had to be trashed, the weekend was better, when I didn't have class.

It sucked because the weekend was my free time, and who in the world wanted to be sick during their free time? Luckily, I didn't have many side effects. Just a headache and sometimes more fatigue than even I was used to.

But now I had to take more.

And the process of being brave enough to swallow it down, then wait around, almost anticipating some kind of sick feeling or bad side effect, would start all over again.

I knew I had to do this, though. I had to get all the inflammation and symptoms under control. I had been getting better, so it gave me hope. But it just hadn't been good enough. Not yet.

It all seemed pretty impossible right now, most of it being Stark.

Or Ten. Whatever I was supposed to call him.

He said he would be my boyfriend if I let him. He said he wanted to be around. How could I trust him after that lie? How stupid was I for not even knowing who he was?

Even if I could get past all that ('cause deep down I knew I could), what about his lifestyle? The fact that he wasn't a student here at Blaylock, but a worldwide sensation who lived on the other side of the country? The press was all over him, which I'd already had not-so-great experiences with. If I was with him, they would be all over me, too.

I just didn't fit in his world.

I asked him for time.

He gave it to me. Stark left me at my door that day with a broken look in his eyes and walked away.

Now I just wanted him back. Time away from him wasn't all it was cracked up to be.

Even with all my doubts and fears, I missed him.

I should have called him. But I didn't know what to say.

As I walked across campus, the cold air blowing, I barely paid attention to anything happening around me.

Someone called my name, and I glanced up. Nate was jogging toward me, his bag banging against his back as he moved. He had a black knit cap pulled over his head, hiding all the dark-red hair. It made his green eyes stand out, though. It was the first place I looked when he stopped in front of me.

"Hey," I said, unable to stop my eyes from searching the space around him, hoping Stark might be with.

"He's not here," he replied knowingly.

I nodded, and he fell into step beside me. "He asked me to come see how you were."

I glanced at him out of the corner of my eye. "Is that why you're here?"

"I like you, too," he quipped and poked me in the side.

I smiled. "How are you doing, Nate?"

I hadn't seen him since the night of the rave. My belly tipped just thinking about that night. About how good it had been. About the time I spent with Stark when we got back. About all the time we had... leading up to my brother knocking on my door.

"I'd be doing better if you'd talk to my cousin."

I sighed. "He lied."

"He kinda had a good reason."

I stopped walking and looked at him. "Maybe. But he could have told me who he was. I wouldn't have told the world."

Nate's eyes softened. "Yeah, I think he knows that."

"How is he?" I said, walking again. I couldn't stop myself from asking. I was hungry for information about him.

"He went back to Cali."

I jolted in surprise. He left? "What?"

"He left day before yesterday. Said he had some business to take care of that couldn't wait."

"He didn't tell me," I murmured.

"You told him you needed time." He pointed out.

"He told you?"

He held up his hand, crossing two fingers over each other. "We're close."

I smiled.

"So how have you been?" Nate asked, dropping his hand. "Any more naked drawing?"

I made a choked sound. "No! Thank God."

After Stark didn't show up for the second modeling session, the professor had a hissy fit and cancelled the whole thing.

"How you been feeling? How's the meds treating you?"

I glanced up at Nate. "Did Stark ask you to give me a deposition?"

His face went blank. "A depo-whatta?"

"Ask me a million questions." I clarified.

"He's worried about you."

My chest tightened. "I'm fine. I don't start the updated meds 'til Friday."

"You should call him. He's freaking out," he replied.

"He left." I reminded Nate.

"He's coming back."

I glanced over. "He is?"

He rolled his eyes. "You thought he left for good? Ten doesn't give up that easily."

"When?" I asked, suddenly feeling a little less depressed.

He shrugged one shoulder. "Soon."

"Tell him I'm fine, okay?"

"You could call him yourself."

"Maybe," I murmured, noncommittal.

"The truth is in a name, you know," Nate said as I started to walk away.

I turned back "What?"

"You still call him Stark."

"So?" It was hard not to call him what I'd been calling him all this time.

"So deep down, you know who he is. He's not Ten, the giant popstar about to make a huge comeback. He's Stark, the guy with a shit Jeep and a good heart." Nate stepped forward and tapped on my head, then down over my heart. "You know, so just admit it already."

He turned and left me standing there as a few fat snowflakes fell from the sky and floated dizzily toward the ground.

Maybe he was right.

thirty-two

Ten

The only way a caterpillar can become a butterfly is to let his world end so his new one can be reborn.

Strangely, I identified with the caterpillar, ugly and lost. But I was ready. Ready to perhaps become a butterfly.

I wasn't sure, however, I wanted my entire world to end. Some of it I really wanted to keep. Maybe that's where the real struggle lay for me all along.

In reconciling who I wanted to be with who I already was.

I never thought I could be both a man and a pop star. The very thought nearly ate me alive and killed both. I still wasn't sure how it would all work together, but I did know something.

It would.

BUTTERFLY

By sheer will, I would transform the life I had to the life I wanted. Some of it I would bring from the past... to be transformed into something new and more beautiful.

Like a butterfly.

Stuck as a caterpillar, but I want to be a butterfly. Butterfly.

The song in my head had become a reflection of me. Of the life I was living. And I was beginning to believe Nate. Beginning to think it might be the best song I'd ever done.

Time was the last thing I wanted to give Violet, but now I realized she was right. I needed it, too. Taking time didn't mean I loved her any less.

It meant I loved her more.

In order to go back to her and promise we could make it work, to prove to her that I was no shit for real about wanting to be with her, I had to get my life in order. I had to be the man she brought out in me. A man who deserved her.

So that's what I did. It was a lot easier than I thought it would be. Instead of walking into the label as a drunk, angry kid with too much talent to be ignored, I went in there sober, with a level head and a list of shit I wanted.

I still had way too much talent to be ignored, which obviously worked in my favor.

My newfound confidence (actually, I always had confidence; I just chose to channel it in a different— shittier—way) earned me some approving nods, and I got pretty much everything I wanted.

Before the meeting with the label, I sat down with Becca. I told her exactly how it was going to be from here on out, and I set up serious boundaries. She wasn't my mother, my boss, or fuck, even my friend. She was my manager. I employed her. Yes, she had say in my career. That was her job, but I had the power to veto everything. She learned real fast that I was going to start exercising that right.

She put up some resistance. I knew she would. In the end, she caved because I already had another manager frothing at the mouth to work with me, and I made sure she damn well knew it.

Guess that time Becca told me there were still people in the industry who liked me, who remembered who I was before fame turned me into a monster, was true. Soon as I came in humbled and apologetic, with that passion back in my eyes and rules in my hand, people were willing to take a chance on me.

I wasn't going to let them down, not this time.

I wasn't going to let myself down either.

I finally understood something they kept saying in rehab. *You can't help someone who doesn't want to be helped. You can't find a solution if you won't admit there's a problem.*

I don't know why it took me so long to admit there was a problem. I was grateful, though. I finally got there.

A lot of the credit went to Violet for showing me what it was like to be real again. To be grateful for what I had, even if it wasn't perfect.

Ha. Imagine that. The Perfect Ten wasn't actually perfect.

She didn't even know she was teaching me those things. Maybe that's why the lesson stuck this time.

Or maybe it's because my heart got involved. Because I fell in love.

The entire flight back to New York, I stared out the window at the white, fluffy clouds that stretched across an endless sky, and I thought.

A few new team members were with me. I'd already promised them I wouldn't be a dickface. Everything was set up. Everything was put in place.

There were just a few more things I needed to handle.

I picked up the phone and punched in a familiar number, a number I had no intention of forgetting again.

"I'm eating all the Fruity Pebbles," Nate said, chewing obnoxiously when he answered the phone.

I laughed. "Your ass better go get some more."

"You coming back?" he asked, smacking his lips.

"Will be landing within the hour."

His voice was more serious when he replied, "You get everything straight?"

"Almost," I said, then glanced back out at the clouds.

"Anything I can help you with?"

I smiled to myself. "Actually, I need your help with all of it. You game?"

"I like games," he said, crunching loud again. "Hit me."

I told him. Then I told him more.

I had to hold the phone away from my ear when he replied. The guys on the other side of the plane laughed.

After I hung up the phone, I was full of excitement, the kind I hadn't felt in a long time. With Nate onboard, everything was finalized.

Now I just needed to get the girl.

To spread my wings and fly.

thirty-three

Violet

I finally decided to call him.

He didn't answer.

Another sign the universe hated me?

Or perhaps a sign Stark had no intention of actually coming back.

I mean, really. He could have had anyone, literally anyone. I broke down and spent some time on Google. It was not a good use of my time. In fact, I was pretty sure it was what lead to these self-deprecating thoughts.

Stark had dated some of the most desirable women in Hollywood. All of them were gorgeous and perfect—nothing like me.

Maybe it was for the best he didn't answer. After all, this probably would've ended badly. Better to let him go now before it hurt even worse.

Could it really hurt worse? It's already excruciating.

I was already totally in love with him.

That's what hurt the worst. Him lying. Me loving him anyway.

I glanced back down at the phone still clutched in my hand. I hadn't bothered to leave a message. As I was sitting it down, it rang.

My fingers tightened and small jolt of adrenaline burst inside me. Maybe it was him. Maybe he'd seen the missed call and was returning it.

I accepted the call without even looking to see who it was. My heart was fluttering as I mashed it to my ear. "Stark?"

Someone cleared their throat. "Nate."

I deflated like a balloon with a giant hole in it. "Hey, Nate."

"Meet me outside."

I perked up. "What?"

"I'm out in the parking lot. Meet me out here. We have somewhere to be."

"I don't feel like going anywhere," I told him. I just wanted to sit in my room and pout.

Pouting was totally therapeutic.

"Get your ass out here, Violet." I think it was the bossiest I'd ever heard him. Who knew there was some steel underneath all that goofy sarcasm?

"Fine." I sniffed and disconnected the call. I had to admit I was curious about where he thought we had to be.

I was dressed in a pair of navy leggings and a long, loose wheat-colored sweater with a thick cowl neck. The sleeves were long, and I liked to wear them over my hands, so I'd cut some thumb holes in the sides just because I wanted to.

I was tired and feeling lazy this morning, so I'd pulled my hair up into a messy bun on top of my head and hadn't touched it since. Strands fell out around my face and against my neck, but I ignored them.

Since it was cold outside, I had on a pair of knee-high socks the same color as my sweater, so I stuffed my feet down into a pair of tall brown boots, letting the top of them peek out. I grabbed the mini backpack I carried instead of a purse (it was less pressure on my shoulder because it distributed the weight evenly) and shoved my phone and room key in as I left.

Nate was parked at the curb, the white Wrangler stuttering behind him. My heart squeezed seeing him lean against it because it wasn't him I associated that hunk of junk with. It was Stark. Stark, who actually drove cars that cost more than my entire college education.

"I was afraid to shut her off," Nate called, pushing away from it. "Damn thing didn't want to start."

Maybe it misses Stark as much as I do.

"Is this really your Jeep?" I asked, pushing past the ache in my heart.

He made a face and crossed his arms over his hoodie-covered torso. "Do I look like the kind of guy that would drive this bucket of bolts?"

As if offended, the Jeep shuddered.

"They keys are in your hand." I reminded him, suppressing a smile.

He blanched. "It's Stark's. He bought it from my dad."

I blinked, caught off guard. Stark bought the Jeep from Derek? Why would he do that? Especially when I knew he had better.

Nate didn't say anything else, instead gesturing for me to get in, so I did.

When I was beside him, I said, "Do you call him Stark or Ten?"

"No one's ever called him Stark until you."

I already knew that. I still asked anyway. "Is it weird when you call him that, then?"

Nate shrugged. "It was at first. Now it fits him."

It did fit him. So much. "Where are we going?" I asked.

"You'll see."

I sighed. Loudly. Hoping to convey how annoyed I was. "I'm really not in the mood for cryptic, Nate."

He paused in backing the Jeep out of the lot, glancing at me. "He wants you there."

I felt my eyes widen. Hope blossomed in my chest. "Who?"

He gave me a withering look. "You know who."

I crossed my arms over my chest. The action made my elbows ache and my wrist burn. "I just tried to call him. He didn't answer."

Nate made a sound. "He's busy."

I made a sound in return. "Not too busy to get you to come and collect me."

Nate gave me a stony look, and I glanced away.

We rode the rest of the short distance in silence. When we pulled up to the main building of the music department, I noted how packed the parking lot was and how there was a bunch of cars lining the curb and street.

An excited, jittery feeling bloomed in my stomach.

"Is he here?" I whispered, partly mad at myself because I desperately wanted him to be.

"He called a press conference. He's officially announcing his comeback."

My body went rigid against the seat. "I guess all that good press lately really helped," I said, sour.

What the hell was I thinking being here? Wanting him. Hoping.

He might have said he wanted me, but that was before he went back to LA. Before he basically got his life and career back. Sure, he came back like Nate said he would, but it was to make an announcement about his comeback. It wasn't for me.

"There's nowhere to park." Nate observed, slowing to turn down another crammed row. "Guess that's what happens when you're late."

"Why are we late?" I gasped and swung around to stare at him accusingly.

"Thought you didn't want to be here," Nate countered slyly. I noted the way he watched me out of the corners of his eyes as he continued to drive.

I thought about giving him the finger. I mean, really.

After about the third pass through the parking lot and down the street in front of the building, Nate sighed dramatically. The Jeep jolted suddenly as he drove over the small curb and onto the concrete walkway leading to the building.

"What the hell are you doing?" I gasped and gripped the handle. "This is not a parking spot!"

He drove forward, then stopped and cut the engine right there in the middle of the sidewalk, the Jeep facing the double-door entrance.

"We're going to jail," I announced and slid down in the seat so when the police came, they might not see me.

"Good thing Ten has a shit ton of money for bail."

I made a choked sound. "You need to move, find an actual parking spot. *Hell!* Even just an actual road!"

He chuckled as if he thought our impending arrest was adorable and shoved a phone in front of my face. "Here, watch."

I would have argued, but the words died on my tongue. Stark filled my sight, and speaking was no longer an option. My eyes drank in the sight of him.

How long had it been? Not even a week, but too long. Much, much too long. My chest felt as though someone just sent their fist through it, and I could barely breathe. Still slouched low in the seat, I grabbed the phone out of Nate's hands, clutching it. I brought my knees in, balancing my heels on the edge of the seat, and stared intently at his image.

"He cut his hair," I murmured. "And shaved." My finger reached out and brushed over his face, as if I could reach through the screen and touch him.

The action minimized the window, and I made a distressed sound.

Nate reached over and hit the corner, expanding the picture so it was edge to edge. I smacked his hand away because it was blocking my view.

"What the hell, woman? I'm trying to help you!"

"Shh!" I said, pulling the screen closer.

"Why, no, Violet. I didn't want to watch the press conference, too. On *my* phone," he muttered.

"Shh!" I demanded again.

He leaned across the center to try and watch, but I ignored him. My attention solely focused on Stark. He was standing behind a small podium. Flashbulbs and the clicking of cameras created a lot of background noise.

He was dressed simply in a plain white T-shirt and probably a pair of jeans and designer sneakers (though I couldn't see his lower half). His hair was shorter now, cut closer at the sides and around his neck. The top was still long, but not so long it looked unkempt and outgrown. Instead, it was cut so the long pieces in the front stuck up, slightly angling to the side. His face was free of the stubble I'd grown accustomed to; his skin was smooth and blemish free. He almost had a baby face, though his jawline was a little too sharp and his eyes a little too wise to give him the look of complete innocence.

A sudden image flashed into my mind of a poster Vance had on his wall several years go. It was of Ten. He looked clean cut the way he did right now. Except he was missing something, a leather jacket.

Even though he was standing there in front of the press, looking every bit a popstar—even though the scruff was gone, the hair cleaned up, and a hat was no longer pulled low—there was something still the same.

The way I felt when I looked at him. The way he made me feel.

I didn't care about any of it. Not really.

Not his money or cars. His job or fame. All that really mattered was how every time I saw him, the urge to press a hand to my chest, to somehow calm the ache or still the flutters inside me, was all I felt.

This was the man who sat with me when I was sick, who drove me to the doctor even though I yelled at him. He held me when I cried even when I told him not to. He was the one I drew comics about. He snuck into my art class, naked, just so he could see me.

He lied about his name... but deep down, I knew exactly who he was.

"Thank you all for being here today. I know it's an unorthodox place to call a press conference," he said.

The sound of his smooth voice halted all thought inside my head. Without thinking about it, I pressed my palm against my heart as it slowly pounded.

"I'm well aware that I've been branded public enemy number one and that my behavior for the past year and a half has pretty much tanked my career." He paused, clearing his throat. "You all should be aware that a lot of the shit I'm about to say is probably going to give my manager a heart attack."

People laughed in the background. But not me. My fingers tightened on the phone.

"You see, she didn't want me to come out here and say any of this. She wanted me to put on my designer clothes, the leather jacket I always wear, and come out here as the star you all know and love to hate." He reached out, palming the sides of the podium, and my attention was momentarily stolen by his hands. I knew exactly what they felt like when he grabbed my face and kissed me.

"As you can see, I didn't listen to what she said. I'm done being controlled by management. By other people who don't know what it's like to be me. I don't expect anyone to feel sympathy for me. I mean, after all, anyone who whines about being famous is pretty much a douche. Am I right?"

People laughed. Some yelled out agreements.

I stiffened. He was not a douche! How dare anyone say he was?

"Thing is I didn't handle my rocket to fame as good as I should have. The more famous I became, the angrier it seemed to make me. The more backed into a corner I felt. I realize now it's because I lost myself. Who I am beyond The Perfect Ten. So I acted like a jerk. Like a nineteen- and twenty-year-old kid. I think everyone makes mistakes and does shithead stuff. Just not everyone has a camera following them around. I'm not making excuses. I own everything I did."

When he paused, people started yelling out questions, but he held up his hand and went on.

"I came here, to Blaylock, to give a lecture on how not to act like an asshole, 'cause you know, they needed an expert, and I was the biggest asshole they could find."

I felt myself smile.

"But I never went back to LA. I went into hiding, hoping you all would forget about all the bad shit I'd done while my manager worked overtime trying to make me look good again.

"I reconnected with some people here that used to mean a lot to me. One in particular reminded me I basically walked out on my life. Of all the people who loved me before I became Ten."

"He's talking about me!" Nate yelled in my ear. "I did that!"

"I realized he was right."

Nate smacked me excitedly on the shoulder. "I was right!"

"And then I met someone else... someone you've all seen in the press with me lately."

"The girl!" someone yelled. "Tell us about the girl!"

I sucked in a breath and pressed my lips together.

"You're totally the girl," Nate said, as if I didn't know.

I tore my eyes off the screen long enough to give him what I hoped was a withering glance.

He made a face and drew back.

"Truth is she had no idea who I was. She was the first person in what felt like forever that didn't have any kind of expectations of me. In fact, the night I met her, she'd actually insulted Ten, not realizing he was standing in front of her." Stark smiled and glanced away from the people, from the camera.

Look back up. Look back at me.

When he did, there was a new light in his eyes. A softer one.

"The more I got to know her, the more I realized how small my world had gotten… and how big the real one was. To her, I was just some poor college student who didn't even have a job. When, really, here I was, this guy who drank himself into rehab, flushed his career down the toilet, and had everyone on his staff quit. I was literally hiding… I thought my life was over." He paused, and everyone hung on every word he said. Including me. "But she liked me."

More silence.

He glanced up. I felt he was staring right into me.

"I love her."

I gasped. My feet fell off the seat, and I skyrocketed forward. I reached out and grabbed Nate, not tearing my eyes off Stark's face. "Did you hear that?" I asked him.

"Shh!" Nate retorted.

"My life wasn't over, it was just changing. Transforming. A caterpillar to a butterfly."

A tear rolled down my cheek. He was exactly that. A beautiful butterfly.

"My manager had me followed. Released those pictures of us without my consent or knowledge. All for the sake of my career. I don't want a career like that, at the cost of the only woman I've ever loved."

Everything erupted, drowning out what he was about to say next. Even though the camera remained focused on him, the voices from the crowd came through crystal clear.

"Are you retiring from pop?"

"Are you quitting your career for love?"

"He can't do that!" I gasped.

"It's a grand gesture," Nate announced.

I flung open the door and leapt out of the Jeep. The second my feet hit the ground, I started to run, ignoring the protest in just about every joint in my entire body.

Stark just told the world he was in love with me. But when he said it, I swear it felt it was only me he was talking to.

I flung the door open and rushed through the lobby of the building. I heard Stark talking again, but didn't bother to lift the phone to listen. I had to get to him.

I had to tell him.

I burst through the auditorium doors as if everything behind me were on fire. I stumbled in with the force of my hit, my sneakers slapping over the carpet, making me sound like an elephant instead of a woman on a mission.

Stark stopped talking midsentence.

I ran farther into the room, down the center aisle, and stopped.

I felt the stares of a million eyes, but it was only his I saw.

The room fell silent, as if everyone waited with bated breath for what would happen next. My heart was thundering beneath my ribs, my breath coming in short gasps.

"I love you, too," I yelled.

All eyes shifted back to Stark, waiting for his reply.

He didn't say anything, though. He reacted.

Instantly, gracefully, Stark maneuvered around the podium and leapt off the stage. I gasped, thinking he was going to fall on his ass (how embarrassing; I totally would.), but of course he didn't. He landed like a cat, with all nine of his lives still firmly intact. I stood, frozen in place, watching him run toward me as if this were a field of flowers and I was in a really bad perfume commercial.

Except this was no commercial. If it were, it wouldn't be for perfume. Those commercials are weird.

Just before we collided, Stark stopped, teetering on his feet so close to me I could smell his familiar scent.

I took a deep breath, letting his presence fill me.

"Vi," he said, reaching for my hand.

"That isn't what I meant to yell," I told him, suddenly totally and completely nervous.

"Did you mean it?" His blue eyes implored.

I nodded. "I meant it."

He lunged, grabbing me around the waist and lifting me off my feet. Sound erupted around us, noise taking over the entire auditorium. I didn't hear, though.

He was kissing me. Finally, I was back in his arms, beneath his lips. A place that had never felt so right. When the kiss broke, I thought maybe he would pull away. We were, after all, being watched.

He didn't.

His forehead leaned against mine as he slowly lowered me back to the floor. "I love you," he whispered.

I smiled. Then I frowned. "You're not giving up your career, are you?"

"How 'bout you come up there with me and find out?" He held out his hand.

I glanced between his offered hand and him, then surrendered mine.

The doors I'd just come through banged open again. Everyone in the place turned to see who it was now. Nate didn't seem to notice. He pinned me and Stark with a dark look and stomped down the aisle. When he reached us, he gave me a sour look and held out his hand.

"I was watching that, too, you know!"

I grimaced and handed him his phone. "Sorry, Nate."

"What did I miss?" he asked.

"She loves him!" someone nearby called out.

Nate rolled his eyes. "That's old news."

Stark laughed. "C'mon. This announcement involves you, too."

Nate forgot all about me running off with his phone and followed us up to the stage. A woman was standing near the podium when we arrived. She was tall and thin; her entire look screamed Hollywood.

"I hope you know what the hell you're doing," she warned Stark in low tones.

Stark regarded her coolly with an unrelenting look in his eyes. "I told you, Becca," he ground out. "I'm the one in charge now. Now stand back and collect your paycheck before I fire you."

Shock rippled over her features, and I suppressed a smile. She must have sensed my amusement because her eyes shifted to me.

"Don't even think about it." Stark warned, the veiled threat so clear.

Becca's eyes left me instantly.

For someone who'd just stood up here and talked about how everyone ruled his life, he sure was good at taking charge.

It must be those new wings of his.

Speaking of...

"Your neck," I said. "It's..."

He glanced over his shoulder and winked at me. My belly flipped over.

Stark kept hold of my hand when he stepped in front of the mic again. "As I was saying..." He went on as though we hadn't just confessed our love and made out in front of everyone. "I have no plans of leaving music. I might have gotten lost, but music has always been my passion. I'm here today to announce my return to pop. I'm still Ten... just not so perfect anymore. And I think my new album will reflect that."

The crowd went crazy again. All the flashbulbs and cameras made me dizzy.

"What can you tell us about the album?"

"When does it release?"

"The release is to be announced. I'm just here to let you know it's in the works. Also, I will be taking a more hands-on approach to the writing, along with my new songwriter, Nate Roth."

Nate's face lit up as if someone just announced he'd won the Powerball. He glanced over at Stark and held out his fist.

Stark smashed his into it. "So glad you said yes, man. I couldn't do this without you."

"Next stop for the Nate train is LA!" Nate announced.

What the hell was a Nate train?

Someone in the crowd stood up. "Can you explain the new tattoo on the back of your neck?"

Stark's lips pulled into a smile, and he glanced at me. "It's for the title and first single of my upcoming album. *Butterfly*."

He turned and showed everyone the design I'd already noticed.

It was a butterfly. *My* butterfly. The one on display when he came to my room that day. The orange-and-black wings stretched across his neck, and the black body wasn't really a body, but the word *butterfly*.

"How did you get it to look so much like the one I drew?" I asked while his back was still turned to the crowd.

He smiled. "I took a picture of it that day in your room."

"You know, technically, that drawing is copyrighted." I teased.

"Good thing the artist loves me." He winked.

I totally loved him.

The reporters were shouting questions. Flashbulbs were going off. The entire room pretty much erupted into chaos. Stark glanced between me and the crowd, a note of concern creeping into his eyes. Taking my hand, he walked over to where Becca stood. "You can take it from here."

She nodded once.

Becca stepped up to the podium like some kind of queen about to wield unbending power. Have I mentioned she wasn't going to be on my Christmas card list this year?

Or ever.

Stark and I disappeared behind the thick, velvet burgundy drapes, Nate on our heels. People were yelling for Ten, and my muscles tensed. Stark wrapped an arm around my waist, tucking me into his side.

Two men in suits stepped up beside us almost the second we appeared. They were both tall, wide men who wore serious expressions.

"Tarte and Craft," Stark addressed them, "this is Violet, the girl I told you about. When she's around, I'm second. Got it?"

My gaze whipped up to his. "What?"

"These are my new bodyguards. *Our* new bodyguards." He corrected himself.

"I don't need a bodyguard," I protested, my stomach clenched.

"Oh, baby," he said, almost sad. "Yes, you do."

I frowned.

"What about me?" Nate interjected.

"Dudes," Stark addressed the two men. "This is Nate. No one ever bothers him."

Both bodyguards nodded.

"That was incredibly rude." Nate observed.

One of the men (I didn't know if he was Tarte or Craft) tried to hide a smile.

"Where'd you park?" Stark asked Nate.

"Just out front," he answered.

I made a sound. "On the sidewalk. We almost got arrested."

Stark raised an eyebrow to his cousin.

"Girl drama," Nate whispered as if I wouldn't be able to hear.

"There's a side door over here. It leads to the main lobby." One of the security spoke. They led us out into the main lobby and to the front doors. Both men escorted us to the Jeep, which was remarkably still there.

Stark held out his hand, and Nate slapped the keys into it. After I was in the passenger seat, I watched through the windshield as Stark spoke to both men. After a moment, he smiled and shook their hands.

When he was in the driver's seat, I had a sudden case of diarrhea of the mouth. "I tried to call you earlier. You didn't answer."

Like that even matters anymore.

"I'm here now." His voice was soft, just like the way he caressed my cheek.

"Umm, guys," Nate said, sticking his face between the seats. "Your little romance is the stuff unicorns dream of, but a tow truck just pulled up."

We jerked apart, and as a unit, all three of us turned to peer out the foggy plastic back window.

"I told you!" I told Nate.

"So you were right on time," he muttered. Then he glanced at Stark. "We should probably leave now."

Stark laughed and turned the key. The Jeep made a sound like it might not start. He tried again. It rumbled to life.

BUTTERFLY

We pulled away from the music building, escaping just as reporters flooded out the main front doors and the tow truck driver stepped up onto the sidewalk.

thirty-four

Ten

I didn't wear a hat. There was no point anymore. I didn't have to hide. From the world, Vi… myself.

Instead, I walked hand in hand with my girl across the parking lot, away from my favorite shitty Jeep, smiling a genuine smile and not giving two shits who saw.

I didn't have a reason to hide anymore. I owned everything about me, everything I'd done. Everything up to this point, even the shit, got me here.

Got me Vi.

People in her hallway stopped and stared. Some called out my name. I waved and kept walking, never once letting go of her hand.

The second she let us in the room, I shut the door firmly behind us and pushed her up against it.

"I fucking missed you so bad," I growled and went for her lips. Violet offered them up instantly, lifting on tiptoes and wrapping her arms around my neck. The feel of her body pressed against mine unleashed all the desire I'd been trying not to feel.

It was okay now. Okay to feel it, to let it consume me. For a while there, I thought I'd lost her permanently. I was unsure if I could win her back. Here she was, in my arms, beneath my lips.

I was a fucking lucky man.

Using my body to press her into the door, my hands went up to get lost in her hair, but couldn't because it was pulled up. Making a rough sound, I pulled back and yanked out the hair tie and tossed it over my shoulder. The blond waves fell down around her shoulders, and I sighed, shoving my fingers in and going back for her mouth.

This was home now. She was home.

Violet was something money couldn't buy, fame couldn't bring, being a celebrity wouldn't keep. I loved that about her. Her realness was something that would always, *always* be admired.

Her small, cool fingers delved beneath the hem of my T-shirt—the T-shirt Becca thought I was insane for wearing to the press conference. She'd brought some designer outfit and thrust it at me. I shoved it back and told her I was wearing what I had on. A plain white shirt and jeans. I wasn't going to be that guy anymore.

The guy who only wore designer. The guy who always looked like he was completely put together. It was a lie. I was done lying.

Shoes, though… that was something else entirely. I liked my designer sneakers. I was going to have to get Vi a pair. Or maybe two.

Thoughts of what I was wearing ceased the second her fingertips dragged over my sides and abs. I shifted, angling so she could have better access, inviting her hands to go wherever the hell they wanted.

Flattening her palms, she ran them over my chest and around to my back. The feel of her nails tightening against my skin made my already stiffening cock go rigid.

I wanted her.

My eyes bore into hers when I lifted the shirts over her head. The second they were free, she reached behind her and unclasped her bra. It fell away, too, revealing full, creamy breasts that rose and fell rapidly with the rhythm of her breathing.

With a groan, I went for them, filling my hands and kneading. Her head fell back against the door, and my lips latched onto the side of her neck. Violet's nails dug into my back, her hips tilted toward my body.

Impatient, I pulled her away from the door, and we walked together to the bed. My shirt joined hers, my jeans following. Vi stripped down until she stood before me in nothing but a pair of tiny shorts made of lace. The small glimpses of skin I could see through the fabric about drove me insane.

I grabbed her around the waist, my hands fitting perfectly in the dips above her hips. Her lips kissed across my chest, and she licked around a nipple before latching on and sucking.

I moaned, cupping the back of her head as my dick jumped between us. As if she heard its silent plea, she delved down and wrapped her hand around it, giving it a gentle squeeze.

Pushing her back onto the bed, I took one moment to stare down at her lying there.

"I really do think you are the most beautiful woman I've ever seen."

She smiled, pleasure lighting her eyes. "I'm a sure thing. You don't have to flatter me," she quipped.

I lunged forward, coming over her. She squealed a little, but I didn't let my weight slam into her. "Look at me," I said seriously, hovering just above her.

Blue eyes met mine, and I searched them. "I love you," I told her. "I love you more than I love myself."

She sighed my name and cupped my face. "You're the most beautiful butterfly I've ever seen."

I kissed her long and slow. Her legs wrapped around me, pulling me into her body. My bare cock rubbed against the softness of her lace panties, and my body shuddered.

We stayed like that a while, kissing and exploring, moving together with the lace between us. Eventually, it was just not enough. Eventually, I had to be inside her. Vi pulled off her panties, and I rolled on some protection, settling back between her legs.

In one gentle push, I slid inside her warmth, incoherent words slipping from my lips.

"Stark?" she asked.

I lifted my head from her neck, gazing down. "Did I hurt you, baby?"

She smiled and stroked my bicep. "No."

"What is it?" I asked, fighting the urge to move.

"Can you feel it, too?" she whispered, stroking across my shoulder, curling her hand around my back.

I pushed a little deeper inside her, enjoying the way her eyes flared. "Feel what?"

"The way we're sort of connected, like an invisible string tethers us together."

I smiled.

"Ever since the first time…"

I pulled out and thrust into her again. Her words fell away.

"It's not a string, sweetheart," I murmured, brushing a kiss to the side of her mouth.

I began moving again. It was impossible not to. The way she felt around me, how her body sheathed mine perfectly, was just too good not to explore.

"What is it, then?" she murmured, her head falling to the side.

I thrust into her again and again, unable to reply. She was perfect beneath me, hair spread out across the pillow, cheeks pink, and eyes hazy. Moving my hips, I dragged backward, sliding out so just my tip was poised at her entrance.

She glanced up at me, trying to clutch me back to her. I evaded her attempts, and she made an impatient sound.

I chuckled.

"It's our hearts." I was finally able to answer. "We share the same one now. Where you go, I go…"

"Where I go, so do you." She finished.

I plunged back into her body, burying deep. Both of us cried out, and she clutched my back, rocking against my cock.

Her breathing came in short gasps. I felt the rise of the tension in her body and also in my own. We strained against each other until bliss took over and our bodies followed, victims to pure pleasure, the best casualty a person could suffer.

When my body and mind were my own again, I rolled to the side and reached my arm out to tuck her close. We hadn't even pulled the covers back. We lay on the made bed. Under my foot, I felt the softness of a throw so I lifted it with my foot, grasped it, and then spread it out over us.

Violet sighed.

"You forgive me," I said, stroking her hair.

Beneath the blanket, she drew lazy circles over my stomach. "Yes, I do."

So simple, yet simplicity is very rarely simple to attain.

"Why?" I murmured.

"Because I glimpsed the man you are beneath the lie you told. I saw your beautiful wings even before you showed them to the world."

"Even before I saw them myself," I added.

"You found them on your own, though. You're the one who set them free."

"Because of you," I told her.

"No. Because of you. You're so much stronger than you realize."

She was right. I was. The quiet strength I found in me was a surprise but a welcome one. "I think I had to be weak before I could be strong," I said quietly.

Then I rolled onto my side, propped up on one elbow, and let my eyes explore her face. My chest felt tight, something I knew might never change. That's what happened when you shared a single heart with someone.

"You showed me what real strength looks like. You're the strongest person I've ever met, Vi."

"I'm not so strong." She ducked her head.

I lifted it back up and stared into her eyes. "Yes. You are. You fight a silent battle every day, and somehow you don't let it destroy you. You find a way to accept yourself for who you are... and who you aren't."

"You think we can make this work?" she asked, gesturing between us. "I'm so not from your world."

"Neither am I," I confided. "Not anymore."

I saw the doubt in her eyes, also the hope. I smiled. "We'll make it work. It won't always be easy, but we're connected and I'm committed to you. To us."

Her teeth sank into her lower lip. "I don't think I can call you Ten."

"You can call me whatever you want," I murmured, leaning down to kiss her. Then I pulled back. I saw the smile in her eyes, the words forming on her tongue. "Except dickface," I intoned.

She laughed. When her smile died away, she asked, "Stark?"

"I think I like it better than Ten."

Ten wasn't me. He was someone the media knew. Someone who sold records.

"The number for a name." She mused.

I tickled her. "It's actually Tennsion. After my grandfather."

"It's beautiful." Her eyes softened. "Tell me something else."

"I went to rehab not too long ago. I'm, uh..."

"An alcoholic?"

I shrugged one shoulder. I didn't like that term. I didn't want to be that. "They say I am. I don't feel like one, though. I can still drink a beer and not go off the rails."

Her hand caressed my cheek. "We'll work on it, 'kay?"

"Yeah," I said. "Okay." Then I thought to make something clear. "I'm not going to be a problem for you.

You're not going to have to babysit me. Or worry I'm going to do something crazy."

"Like pee on people or model naked with a bag over your head?" Vi deadpanned.

"You whip it out one time…" I muttered.

"Um, technically, it was twice."

I laughed.

She scowled and reached down to caress my sack. "I'm the only one allowed to see this from now on, got it?"

I grinned. "Possessive."

"That wasn't an agreement."

"You're the only one." I readily agreed.

She made a sound like she was happy and lay back. "Nate told me you bought the Jeep."

"I like that thing. More than any of my other crazy expensive cars. When I offered Derek some cash for it, he laughed. I think he was shocked I actually wanted it."

"But he sold it to you anyway."

"Of course he did. That's my Jeep. *Our* Jeep."

"I like it, too," she confessed.

I grunted. "Good. Since you're going to be driving it."

"Me!" she said, her eyes widening.

I nodded. "I know the duct tape is charming and all, but it's a fire hazard. I can't let you be driving it around like that, so I'm putting a whole new engine in it."

"Stark…"

I gave her a look. "You need a car when I'm not here to drive you around, Vi. You're not taking a fucking Uber."

"You aren't buying me a car," she insisted.

"No, I'm not. I bought that Jeep for me. But you can take care of it when I'm in LA." I really did buy it for me. It basically represented everything I'd learned the past few weeks.

Looks are deceiving. Money isn't everything. Even covered in duct tape, that Jeep still ran. It had heart and determination. The duct tape was totally going, though. It really was a hazard.

"You're going to be in LA a lot," Violet said, her voice growing a little insecure.

I gathered her close, folding both my arms around her, resting my chin on her head. "Technically, it is where I live. I have a place there, with a pool. You can swim when we're there. Swimming is good for your joints."

Right at this moment, I was having a hot tub put in, too, right beside the pool. I was doing it for her. I knew it would be good therapy.

"I can't come live in LA. I have school," she said, trying to lift her head off me.

I pushed it back down. "I know, baby. I meant during breaks and maybe over the summer. I know you have school and family on the East Coast."

"But what about you?" She pouted.

"I worked it out with my label. I'm going to be staying here while the album is being written. They gave me approval to write three of my own songs. Nate's helping co-write them. They're sending the writers here to work with me for the rest."

"Really?" she said. This time I let her lift her head to meet my eyes.

I nodded. "Derek said we could use the music department during off hours to come up with the music."

"You're staying."

"For now. I will have to go back to LA to record. And then promo. And I'll have concerts, travel…" I slid my eyes to her, suddenly worried how she would take all this. We definitely weren't going to have a traditional relationship.

"The pitfalls of dating a popstar." She sighed.

My heart skipped a beat. "So we're dating?"

"Well, we do share a heart. I think we're kinda stuck with each other."

"You aren't stuck with me," I told her, firm. "If it's too much…"

She pressed her fingers against my lips. "I'm not thrilled with the idea of sharing you. But it's your job, and I know how much you love it. And I love you."

I kissed her fingers, speaking against them. "You're only sharing Ten. Stark is all yours."

She smiled. "I can live with that."

"I want you at my side whenever you can get away, and I'll be here as much as I can." I cautioned her.

She nodded. "I'd like that."

"And you're getting bodyguards," I said, no give in my voice. "I already have some lined up for interviews. I didn't hire them yet because I wanted you to have a say."

"How generous," she muttered.

I gave her a light squeeze. "I'm serious, Vi. The press are monsters. People are going to be different to you now. They're going to try and use you. They'll want things. People who hate me… they're going to hate you."

"You come with a lot of baggage," she retorted.

"Yes," I said seriously. "I do."

Violet pushed up into a sitting position. The blanket fell down, revealing her bare chest. "I have some of my own."

"Your health is not baggage." My voice was firm.

"I was talking about my brother."

I laughed. "I'll give him backstage passes."

"That should do it," she said, a twinkle in her eyes.

"I love you, Vi. I'll do everything I can to make you happy."

"I already am. I don't care about your baggage, the press, or even the stupid bodyguards you're going to make me get. I love you. Everything else is just details."

I leaned in to kiss her. I was so goddamn happy I could burst.

Just as I was about to seal her words with my lips, she leaned back and held up a hand. "One thing, though."

"Name it."

"I don't want anything to do with Becca."

"You're off-limits to her. I made that perfectly clear. She'll do as she's told, or I'll get a new manager."

"You can kiss me now," she declared and stuck her face out, puckering up her lips.

I kissed her nose instead.

Her eyes opened, and the heart we shared reflected in their gaze.

"I love you, my butterfly," she whispered and pulled my head down to hers.

Life as I knew it definitely was over... but the one I got was so much better.

4 STAGES OF FALLING IN LOVE — AS TOLD BY A BUTTERFLY

VIOLET

epilogue

Violet

Ten's comeback was quite arguably one of the biggest in pop history. The naysayers all claimed it really wasn't a comeback at all because he really hadn't left. Even in his absence, the media still made him a headline.

The people closest to him knew, though.

We all knew what he went through and what it took for him to get to where he was today. It most definitely was a comeback… Actually, it was more.

More like a rebirth.

Like a butterfly emerging from a chrysalis.

It had been a little over a year since I'd burst into his press conference and screamed for everyone to hear that I was in love with him.

I loved him so much that day.

I loved him even more now.

BUTTERFLY

Standing backstage with a custom pair of paint-splattered headphones (I could still hear everything; it just wasn't as loud) perched over my ears, I watched him dominate the stage and the sold-out arena totally eat him up.

No one else wore headphones back here, but Stark made me. He said he needed to protect my ears.

He was ridiculous, but I loved him for it.

It was summer, and Ten was on tour. He told me it was one of the shortest tours he'd done, lasting only three months. I thought that was like an eternity, but everyone else seemed to think it was barely anything.

He'd been insistent, though, nothing longer than summer break. He didn't want to be out of the country when the new semester started back up and I had to go back to Blaylock. We struck a deal with each other back when we were first working everything out. We wouldn't go more than a week without seeing each other, and even a week sometimes felt too long.

His life was definitely a whirlwind. I could see how easy it was to get caught up in it all. It definitely was a challenge to deal with at times. Like when the press camped out in front of your dorm building, or the time Ross tried to sell a story to the press about how Stark kicked his ass. That story never made it to print because, well, Ross would have to tell the world Stark kicked his ass because he was a violent turd toward women.

Challenge or no, it was all worth it. Every time I looked at him, our tethered hearts tugged in my chest, and I knew as long as we were together, nothing else mattered.

Ten was onstage, playing one of his new songs, a collab with some DJ named Vein. It was a good song. I liked the beat, and I especially liked the way it made Stark's hips move when he danced.

I licked my lips just thinking about going back to the hotel later, where we could finally be alone.

As if he knew my thoughts, he glanced over his shoulder and tossed a smile in my direction.

Becca stood about twenty feet from me. We'd barely had a conversation since we met. I still didn't like her, and she still was banned from my Christmas card list. However, she did her job well, so Stark kept her around.

Beside me, Vance cheered, and I laughed. My brother joined us for the last couple weeks of the tour. He still fangirled pretty hard over my boyfriend, but at least he accepted he wasn't going to convince Stark to be gay with him.

Now he just reveled in the fact that his idol was basically his brother.

When Stark asked Vance to design him a jacket to wear onstage during the tour, he almost peed his pants. I swear he went into total design mode and came up with an entire line of stuff for Stark to choose from. Stark, being the amazing guy he is, chose a couple pieces to have custom made and wore them around for the press to ask about them.

The one piece was my favorite. A leather jacket (which apparently Ten was famous for) but with a twist. He had me paint a butterfly on the back, the same one that was tattooed on the back of his neck. He wore it constantly, telling me it was his favorite piece.

Vance started Blaylock basically with a built-in fan club. After all, he was a freshman design student who already scored a few jobs with a celebrity.

BUTTERFLY

The music for the upbeat song went off, and Ten stepped up to the mic. "This next one is the song that means the most to me. It's inspired by my own journey and co-written by my best friend, Nate Roth."

The crowd cheered, and Nate appeared beside me. He had a corndog in his hand. I gave him a WTF look. Where the hell had he found a corndog?

"I love this song!" he shouted. Then he cupped his hand around his mouth and yelled, "Sing it, Ten!"

Nate was such a goober. But I loved him, too. He was like a brother to me, just like Vance. He was earning quite a name for himself in the music world after having successfully co-written several number-one hits with Ten. He went on to write a few on his own, one of which sold to a huge country singer, and there was another sale in the works with another pop star.

The music for "Butterfly" started up, and all my attention went to the stage. It was my favorite song. I loved to watch him sing it. I loved the sound of his voice and knowing the meaning behind the lyrics. Sometimes I hung out in the music department when he and Nate were working. His voice combined with the piano (he was like a musical genius; he could play almost any instrument) never failed to lull me to sleep. I always woke up later, when he was carrying me to the Jeep, bummed I'd missed the rest of whatever song he'd been singing.

There's a fine line between love and hate.
People turn their back on a dime.
Sometimes it seems this is all just a waste of time.
You don't see me,
Only the mask I wear.

No one bothers to look beneath it.
I'm not the man I was anymore,
Just someone they all want me to be.
Trapped,
Caught,
Ensnared by a web.
Stuck as a caterpillar, but I want to be a butterfly. Butterfly.
Spread those colorful wings and fly.
Tangled up in drama, nowhere to go but down.
Hitting rock bottom has a definite sound.
Standing among the shadows when I'm usually blinded by the light,
Realizing how eye opening the darkness is,
Feeling imprisoned all these years by sight.
Actions speak louder than words,
But what if no one listens?
Trapped,
Caught,
Ensnared by a web.
Stuck as a caterpillar, but I want to be a butterfly. Butterfly.
Spread those colorful wings and fly.

The song went on, and I mouthed the words. I knew them all by heart. When at last the show was over, Stark beelined for me, grabbing me up despite being a sweaty, breathless mess.

I gave a squeal, but didn't pull away. I never would.

He pulled the headphones down around my neck and grinned. "How's my favorite girl?"

"Better now that you're here."

"I'm his favorite boy," Nate said from beside us.

"No," Vance argued. "I am."

We looked at each other and laughed. Nate and Vance continued to argue, but Stark and I got lost in our own little world. Standing amongst arguing brothers, a crew of people milling about, and our bodyguards standing watch over it all, we were completely alone.

Two hearts melded into one.

A butterfly and his flower.

"I love you," he told me, brushing a kiss across my mouth.

"I love you," I answered.

This time, the kiss was more consuming, and no, we didn't care who saw. I wrapped my arms around his neck, letting my fingertips caress the tattoo he would have forever.

It wasn't the only thing Stark had forever, though…

He also had me.

PS: Maybe the universe didn't hate me so much after all… since, you know, the good I got far outweighed the bad. Sorry, Universe, for, you know, all the trash talking I did about you.

AUTHOR'S NOTE

I really like this one. I probably say that about every book I write, in every author's note. It's true in all of them.

But I do like this book.

I still recall the first idea and how it all came to be. I saw a little graphic on Facebook one day, something my cover designer made. It had the saying on it that's on this cover. I made a comment on what a beautiful book cover it would make. Fast-forward a couple days, and she sent this cover to me in a message. I bought it immediately, even though I didn't have a book for it yet. It didn't matter because it inspired me.

During this time, I was actually in Maine, visiting family. It was a hella long drive. Like for-everrrrr. Seriously. Like almost a twenty-hour trip. Not sure if I ever mentioned it, but I always get ideas when I'm driving. Not really sure why, but they always seem to hit me like that.

So there I was, driving home on good ol' hellacious I-95 (You are totally riveted by this tale, aren't you? I know.) when I got this idea… What if the *guy* in the book was the butterfly? Up until that point, I was thinking it would be the girl. You know, girl comes out of her shell, yadda, yadda—but it didn't feel quite right.

Bang! It's a dude. Then I pondered if it was too girly to make the dude the butterfly… I mean, what would people say?! Did I mention this was a long car ride, and I had a lot of time to ponder? LOL Anyway, I decided I liked it. So then I thought, *Ooh, what if it looks like he has everything, but really his life is falling apart? What if he were public enemy number one?* I wanted to know more. The brainstorming continued, and the idea for Ten was born.

By the way, Ten had like four names before I finally settled on one. Actually, technically, the guy still has two… #IGiveUp.

When I turned my attention to Violet, I decided I wanted her to be a college student because I miss Alpha U (from the *Hashtag* series), I love a good college romance, and I wanted to write one. **Stomps foot** Then, to add to her character, I decided to give her some artistic ability and rheumatoid arthritis. In all honesty, Violet is probably the most like me a character has ever been. They always say write what you know, right? I started out just wanting to give her RA, but she kind of morphed into having other traits like mine, so I went with it.

RA is something I've been dealing with a long time, but only just got diagnosed about a year ago. It's been a lot of transition, a lot of adjusting… a lot of thinking. I decided to bring that into this book because I thought it fit well. I liked some of her internal struggle about accepting herself, the way she looked, and who she was. I feel that's something we all deal with in some form or another. Somehow, I felt Ten could learn from Violet and all the things she's been through and overcome. You can decide that for yourself, though.

So yeah. That's a little background on *Butterfly*. I hope above everything, it entertained you and offered a little escape from this crazy world. If you enjoyed it, please take a moment and leave a review. Reviews help!

See you next book!

XOXO,
Cambria

ABOUT CAMBRIA HEBERT

Cambria Hebert is an award-winning, bestselling novelist of more than forty books. She went to college for a bachelor's degree, couldn't pick a major, and ended up with a degree in cosmetology. So rest assured her characters will always have good hair.

Besides writing, Cambria loves a caramel latte, staying up late, sleeping in, and watching movies. She considers math human torture and has an irrational fear of birds (including chickens). You can often find her painting her toenails (because she bites her fingernails), or walking her Chihuahuas (the real rulers of the house).

Cambria has written within the young adult and new adult genres, penning many paranormal and contemporary titles. She has also written romantic suspense, science fiction, and most recently, male/male romance. Her favorite genre to read and write is contemporary romance. A few of her most recognized titles are: *The Hashtag Series, GearShark Series, Text, Torch,* and *Tattoo.*

Recent awards include: Author of the Year, Best Contemporary Series (The *Hashtag* Series), Best Contemporary Book of the Year, Best Book Trailer of the Year, Best Contemporary Lead, and Best Contemporary Book Cover of the Year. In addition, her most recognized title, *#Nerd,* was listed at Buzzfeed.com as a top-fifty summer romance read.

Cambria Hebert owns and operates Cambria Hebert Books, LLC.

Made in the USA
Columbia, SC
21 May 2018